THE KILLING TIME

A SHANNON AMES THRILLER

TJ BREARTON

D1534184

INKUBATOR
BOOKS

For my good friend Dave Press; journalist, author, and family man
— hug those little babies!

1

W ater. That was the first thing. A sense of floating.
The sound of water, as if in a sink or a tub, gently
lapping.

Then it changed. Instead of being the one suspended in
liquid, she was holding her baby in the tub. Joe, her firstborn.
An infant, with the remainder of the umbilical cord like a
purple tag stuck on his belly.

Joe.

And then there was his sister, Kyle. But they were teenagers
now. Practically grown up ...

Her weight somehow shifted. Someone was holding her – a
hand at the back of her neck, propping her up. She tried to
move her arms and legs, but her limbs failed to respond.

This was a weird dream. A tough one to wake up from. She
tried opening her eyes – but wow, they were heavy, the lids like
thick canvas.

There – she saw something. A person. As if hovering above
her. Manipulating her in the water. Something brushed against
her flesh, a rag or a sponge. The astringent stink of cleaning
chemicals hung in the air ...

The person was all in white, like some kind of doctor. A mask over his face. Thick eyebrows threaded gray over his dark eyes.

"Almost done," he said. "Almost time, Monica."

Monica tried moving again and managed to twitch the first two fingers of her right hand. Bizarre, surreal – she could practically feel the signal travel down her arm from her brain. The fingers jerked in the water, not quite hot water, but warm, just warm enough to keep her from shivering.

She fought to keep her eyes open and she stared up. Yes, it was a man. Yes, he was dressed entirely in a white jumpsuit and wearing a blue surgical mask over his nose and mouth. And he was bathing her. God, it was becoming the worst dream she'd ever had. This man was bathing her for some reason, like she used to bathe her little babies in the tub ...

A flash memory: the subway ride home. Emerging from the station. The parked car, the man standing beside it. He walked over to her, and she hadn't been afraid, no – he'd been dressed quite differently then. But those were his eyes.

This was the same man cradling her now, scrubbing her down.

He raised a gloved hand from the water – blue, same color as the face mask – holding a yellow sponge. He squeezed the sponge and the water squirted out, and he set it down out of sight. She tried to move again, to get more out of that right hand, and was just able to make a loose fist. The man was doing something beyond her field of view, and she worked on her legs, her knees. If she could bend a knee and get her feet planted ...

You've been abducted.

Not yet – don't think that yet.

This is no dream.

His face came back, looming over her, and he looked somewhere just above her eyes, and she felt his fingers in her hair. "I washed it out," he said. "Probably not your usual shampoo."

She tried to speak. What she summoned was a mumbled "Hmmpf." Her voice sounded like it was coming down a long tunnel.

Drugged. He drugged you. The effects are just wearing off.

She squeezed her right hand again. Made the fist tighter. Well, tight enough to hold a bag of potato chips, anyway. A start.

Oh God oh God oh God ...

"We're going to get you out of there now."

He moved away, and she was left staring up at ductwork suspended from a high ceiling. Where was this? *What* was this?

She tried to recall more detail from the street, more about the parked car and the man and what she felt when he stepped toward her. Nothing more came. She could only remember with confidence leaving work and taking the usual trains home. Emerging onto her Brooklyn street, and walking.

He'd called to her – "Excuse me, miss ..."

And she'd trusted him. She'd let him approach her. Then things grew murky. Between that moment to waking up in water was pitch-black nothing.

And now he was bathing her. Cleaning her – cleaning with vigor, from the smell. Was that bleach?

She saw him stand up out of the corner of her eye and walk away. She heard the squeak of a wheel a moment later, like he was rolling something over the floor. A fresh rime of terror curled around her spine: *They said Eva Diaz was spotless when they found her. Like she'd been sanitized, all evidence of her assailant removed ...*

Diaz was a reporter. *Had been* a reporter. For WNBC's Channel 2. Found dead two weeks ago. Strangled to death and dumped in Maspeth, Queens, without a speck of DNA on her, not a trace of semen nor stray hair belonging to her killer.

Her killer. This man. The one who seemed to be painstakingly preparing her for the same fate.

He was suddenly back, looming above her. He leaned down and slipped his arms beneath her and hoisted her up. She tried to scream, but managed only more garbled moans. She sought to kick, but her foot merely wiggled on its ankle. He looked at her as he carried her. His eyes were even darker. She managed to reach up with her working arm and touch his face ineffectually; her fingers flapped his lower lip, dragged down his chin, and her arm fell back onto her chest as he set her down.

He began to dry her off. The cloth worked against her flesh. She said, "Aaaaaahhhh!" in a rising voice. The sound she made terrified her further, and the hot tears rolled down her cheeks.

When he was finished, he placed a fresh towel over her and began to move her. She was on wheels now. A hospital gurney, or something like it. She watched more ductwork overhead. And pipes; plumbing. Everything echoed. The spaciousness, the stink of rust and oil – something was familiar. A story she'd done: "The Abandoned Places of Brooklyn and Queens."

Oh God. Eva Diaz.

Diaz had been a field reporter. Beautiful, trim, mocha-colored skin – she'd looked like another Eva, the actress Eva Mendes. Diaz was younger than Monica by a decade at least, but Monica was pretty, too. They'd coaxed Monica out of the back room where she'd been a media producer for ABC-7 since graduating college, and stuck her in front of the cameras. It paid better and she'd grown inured to the stage fright. She liked her cast and crew – they had a good show. Late morning, the kind where you bake cakes and talk about movies and, occasionally, substantive issues like ISIS or intelligent automation. Not too much, though – you didn't want to upset the middle-aged, Midwestern female demographic.

But she was on TV daily; that was the point. Had been for

years now. Five days a week. Just like Diaz, up there on the screen for the world to see. For a man like this to see. For a man who strangled Eva Diaz with some kind of tensile cord or belt, they said. Strangled her until she saw stars and her eyes bulged and throat burned and she blacked out forever. Washed her body down like some kind of living doll.

Monica tried to scream again, and this time produced a louder moan. She tried moving some more and realized that, while she was steadily regaining control, he'd strapped her to the gurney, or whatever it was he was pushing her on – and now stopping and tilting forward and locking in place. She was almost completely upright.

What was this? Some kind of makeshift TV studio?

The black, lifeless eye of a camera stared at her. A decent make, a Canon, the model used for both taking pictures and video. The walls in the room had been soundproofed with professional-grade eggcrate-style foam insulation. Even the light setup looked pro: a key light, a side light, and a fill light with the little umbrella attached to it for a diffused glow.

Having locked her gurney into place, the man came around in front of her. He was still wearing the white jumpsuit and large surgical mask, everything tucked in and airtight. Booties covered his shoes.

She tried to speak. "Please ..." She sounded drunk. Benumbed. *Pweesh.*

He showed her his back as he worked on something beyond the camera. A moment later he approached her with a small cord in his hands and she shrieked and tensed against her restraints.

"Relax," he said.

He held a miniature microphone, one she knew from experience was called a lavaliere. He clipped it to one of the straps, the one just above her breasts. Then he walked back to the camera and stuck his eye in the viewfinder. After making some adjustments, he put on the attached headphones and said, "Say something."

"Please …" Getting better now.

"Say 'test, test-one-two,' or something like that. Do it."

"Please …"

"Do it or I'll kill you right now."

"Test. Tesh-ting one-two."

His eyes narrowed and shined, as if with the slightest smile. He removed the headphones and hung them from the camera. He walked behind the lights and then returned holding an easel. Finally he placed a pad on the easel, and she began to read to herself what was written there, suddenly vibrant with hope.

She might get out of this yet. Oh, if she just did what she was told, he might let her live. Maybe Eva Diaz hadn't complied. Maybe that was what had happened to her. But *she* would comply. She would do whatever it took to get back to them.

Joseph, my baby boy …

Kyle, my darling daughter …

As the man explained what he wanted her to do, she listened, and she nodded, and she wondered: What time was it? Ben had to be worried by now. Both kids were gone to summer camp – Kyle was in northern Westchester County, Joe up a little farther near Poughkeepsie – and she and Ben were enjoying the alone time. Well, she was taking advantage of the summer and putting in some extra hours at the job, but it was amazing to have the alone time with Ben. Summer camp only lasted two weeks for Kyle, four weeks for Joe – like a second honeymoon for Monica and Ben.

He would've called the police by now, surely. They might already be out looking for her, especially since Eva Diaz was recent. All she had to do was hang on a little longer. Do what this nutcase was telling her to do, and have faith.

Just have faith.

You'll be okay.

Everything is going to work out.

The red recording light came on.

2

WEDNESDAY MORNING

A t first, Shannon thought it was her father waking her. The call of the rooster in the distance. On the farm, you'd get up by dawn. Here, she didn't usually need to rise that early, and in fact, she relied on a windowless bedroom, or the relentless noise of New York City would keep her awake all hours.

It wasn't her father.

She grabbed her phone off the nightstand and recognized the number. She cleared her throat and answered, "Shannon Ames."

"Special Agent Ames, need you to come in early this morning."

She sat up in the bed, swung her feet to the ground and toed into her slippers. "Yes, sir."

Mark Tyler, her boss, continued, "Get down here as soon as you can and I'll bring you up to speed."

THE OFFICE WAS the Brooklyn-Queens Resident Agency – a satellite office – for the FBI's New York City division. She lived just two and a half miles west of it, in Rego Park. On normal days, she could walk to work. Today, she took the M train four stops to Union Turnpike and caught a few of the usual looks while on the subway. Living in New York for just shy of a year, at first she thought the looks she drew were because she was an outsider, and people could sense it. Then, about eight months ago, someone asked her for an autograph. Apparently she was a dead ringer for Emma Watson, the actress. Though didn't she live in London?

The FBI occupied the seventh and eighth floors of the 80-02 Union Turnpike in Kew Gardens. The building was also home to the Queens District Attorney's Office, a fitness club, two law firms, a medical school called the Access Institute, and an orthopedic surgeon. On the eighth floor, she paused outside the double-door entrance for a laser to scan her face. Then she said her name, "Shannon Elizabeth Ames." The lock disengaged with an audible thump.

Mark Tyler was the supervisory agent in charge and saw her the moment she entered. He was walking fast – he always walked fast – and she had to double-time it to keep up. They went into his office and he closed the door. Another agent, Bufort, was already there.

Tyler took his seat. Shannon knew he was a native New Yorker, born and raised in Manhattan. Just forty years old, Tyler was the kind of guy with a high metabolism who hardly had to exercise. He did so anyway, compulsively. He wore his dark hair fashionable – tight cropped on the sides – and his suits were expensive looking.

Shannon sat in the available chair fronting Tyler's desk. She said good morning to Bufort. Bufort was more relaxed. He was heavier and thicker than Tyler, blond surfer hair, mid-thirties, and he sipped a Snapple green tea.

Tyler took a breath, then spread his hands and spoke. "We've got a missing person, Monica Jean Forbes, aged forty-two, from Williamsburg. Her husband is a general contractor, called 911 at four twelve a.m. this morning. 911 polled the call and it went to NYPD 90th, right there in Williamsburg, and they've been looking into it."

Shannon waited, anticipating the catch; the FBI didn't get involved in missing persons reports less than three hours old. Even for NYPD to have taken it on board before twenty-four hours raised questions.

Tyler said, "Monica Forbes – you recognize the name?"

She shook her head. "No."

Tyler pushed a picture across the desk. Shannon picked it up – a headshot of a pretty woman who did, yes, look vaguely familiar.

"She's on one of these late morning news shows," Tyler said. "You know, she co-hosts with a bunch of other women. They sit at a table."

"It's called *The Scene*." Bufort sipped his tea.

"They cover entertainment," Tyler said. "Among other things."

Shannon kept looking at Monica, her brown eyes, the Mona Lisa smile, and she understood. She pictured another pretty face, darker-skinned, from recent headlines. "Eva Diaz," she said.

Tyler nodded. "That's right. So Forbes is a TV personality on Channel 7, currently missing. Diaz was with Channel 2, NBC who was abducted and found two weeks ago."

"In Maspeth," Shannon recalled.

"Correct. Found in Maspeth, but lived up in Ditmars-Steinway."

"So they're not too far apart. Geographically."

Bufort set down the Snapple on the table beside him. "In

New York? Half a mile separates entire worlds. And Diaz was a field reporter. Not a – you know – not a host."

Tyler ignored Bufort and studied Shannon. "I'd like you to monitor this, Special Agent Ames. Head over to 90th and get up to speed with those guys." He glanced at a note on his desk and said, "That's a lieutenant named Whitaker and a lead detective, ah, Luis Caldoza. Be of assistance, but stay out of their way. You're monitoring. Okay? This is a good chance for you to get your feet wet."

Shannon nodded. "Yes, sir. Thank you."

On her way to the elevator, she let herself process a bit more of what had just happened, the glimmer in Tyler's eye: She was a test probe – get in there and see if this was going to shape up to be something. Tyler had ambitions to run the field office in Manhattan, to be promoted to assistant director when the current AD, Moray, retired next year.

But that wasn't for her to worry about. She didn't care about the politics of it – this was her shot, no question. The past year had been educational and exciting, but mostly had focused on white-collar crimes and healthcare fraud. When she'd applied to the FBI, it had been with the intention of working in violent crimes. But the FBI put you where they needed to, and taught you the ropes by exposing you to various sections before considering you fully formed, anywhere from eighteen months to a few years later. Shannon was in just over a year and technically still in her probationary period.

Tyler had given her a car, and she pulled out of the 80-02 parking garage still not a hundred percent confident in her New York City driving skills. It was chaos here. Her hometown featured one blinking yellow traffic light – this was like driving inside a giant pinball machine.

With the Williamsburg NYPD precinct plugged into the GPS, she got the dark blue Chevy Impala up to speed on the parkway. She was prompted to turn right onto Metropolitan Ave, which would take her most of the way.

Waves of heat rose off the asphalt. Sunlight spangled off the chrome and glass of the careening cars and trucks. Eva Diaz had been abducted, yes. And then she'd been found a day later with the life choked out of her. If the two were connected, that meant Monica Forbes might have less than twenty hours to live.

3

He unclipped the microphone from her and carefully wound the cord as he walked back behind the camera. It was over, and the fear returned:

He's done with you. Now what?

"Sir," Monica said, "please."

He kept his back to her as he packed away the tiny lavaliere mike in its own small case. Finished, he focused his attention on the camera and began to unseat the accessories: the zoom and focus control, the headset. He detached the camera from the tripod, and the shoe from the camera, ignoring her as she spoke.

Scream!

"Please. I have two children. A boy and a girl. They need their mother." Her voice trembled on the edge of a whisper. "I have a husband. I have a life. Please. I'll quit my job. I'll leave the city. We'll all just leave."

He placed the camera in a case. Pelican brand, she recognized. Top of the line.

She scrutinized him. Still in his surgical mask and white jumpsuit, booties on his feet and hairnet on his head, he was nevertheless familiar. Something in his posture, in his gait, in the very vibes coming off him.

Who are you?

She wondered, out of nowhere, if he was someone Ben knew. Maybe even one of Ben's guys. Ben had jobs in places like this. His crew would come in and do the renovations on an industrial space turned residential. It was happening all over the city, and not just in the boroughs, but across the East River in Jersey City – millennials buying condos in buildings that used to warehouse coats and shoes or make plastics. They even had a name for it – "residustrial." Hell, it was happening all over the country. All over the world.

Ben had worked some contracts, some big jobs, places in Queens and Brooklyn. Places that, until the right developer came along, just sat there, rotting, rusting, infested with rats.

"Please," she said. "I'll do what you want. I'll go on air tomorrow and–"

"Shut up," he said. He set down the cord he'd been winding and strode over to her. At first she thought he was going to hit her – there was unmistakable rage in his eyes – but then he went around behind her. A moment later, she was moving. He was wheeling her again, upright.

She let the scream rip. She screamed, and then she called for help.

Then the resonance of her high-pitched cries soaked into the walls and died.

They went through a doorway, and he banged the edge of the gurney in the doorframe and shoved her through. This room was dark, funky with mildew and something fouler – like bodies, like homeless drug addicts living in their own urine and vomit. He stopped the gurney and moved away, scuffing in the dark.

Her breathing was rapid, her pulse working in her throat. "I'm sorry I screamed. A lot of what you said, it makes sense," she said. "You're right about a lot of things. I want to help you. Please, let me help you. Think of all the good I can do out there ..."

Suddenly it was bright. He had an area light on a tripod, an orange extension cord snaking out of the room to whatever battery or generator he was drawing power from. She thought she even heard a distant engine ...

Not that it mattered. What mattered was what was right in front of her, on the wall.

Two pictures, side by side. He'd affixed them to the rust-stained, crumbling wall with duct tape.

As she absorbed the images, Monica stopped breathing.

She stopped thinking she was going to be okay.

She began to understand what this was, and she knew that these were her final moments.

"Oh God ..."

A single fresh tear carved a hot line down her cheek.

He was just behind her. She could feel his exhalations on the side of her face.

Scream again!

Something sharp and tensile bit into the flesh of her neck, cutting off her air. She struggled to free her hands, to claw at the thing across her throat, but the restraints were rigid. She heard sounds, her own sounds – gurgling noises, like the last of the water being taken down the drain.

And as she faded, she stared at the two pictures. The one on the left, such a bright and beautiful face, so full of promise and hope. The one on the right ruined and dead.

Monica thought of her children once more, pictured their own faces, remembered the smell of them, all at once, babies and teenagers and everything in between, their smiles, their tears, and she waved to them as they sat at the breakfast table – Joe, Kyle, and Ben. The three loves of her life. She smiled and waved to them as she said goodbye.

4

Williamsburg's local 90th precinct was on the corner of Montrose and Union, a gray, squat, two-story building. The law enforcement vehicles parked around the building were white with blue letters: *NYPD*. The building also housed the local Fire Department and Emergency Services Squad #8, and a large sign above an open bay door thanked the squad for its help during 9/11. Shannon circled around and found more parking in the back, near an elevated subway line.

She passed through a security checkpoint inside, and a female officer in a blue uniform took her to a small office. Lieutenant James Whitaker was under forty, according to his bio, but had that high-blood-pressure look, making him appear older, his white collar too tight against his neck. He was talking on his desk phone when the uniformed cop showed Shannon in. He held up a finger, then motioned her to sit.

Shannon thanked the uniformed cop, who left, shutting the door, and Shannon took a seat.

"All right," Whitaker said into the phone, then listened. "Look, I gotta go. The woman the FBI sent over just got here.

All right, yeah. All right ..." He hung up and fixed Shannon with a smile, the kind a scarecrow might have. "Find the place all right?"

"Yes, thank you."

"Yeah, I guess today, it's all GPS. I can't get used to it. I mean, we use it here, in our line of work, of course. But we go somewhere, and my wife is yelling at me because I never want to switch it on."

His faded blue eyes lingered on her for a moment. There was a thing people did, both men and women – this initial evaluation. They looked at her hair – she had a lot of it, but had tamed it back into a tight braid – and her small nose, light freckles; she knew she looked young. So they checked her out, asking themselves to what extent would her age and inexperience be a liability. Then they packed that question away unanswered – most of them – because they had no choice.

Whitaker lost the smile and stood. "Need a cup of coffee or anything?"

She stood, too, shaking her head. "No thank you."

"Let's get right to it. Come with me."

He moved past her, redolent of cologne and cigarettes, and she followed him out the door. Down the hall, a couple of uniformed officers going in the other direction, a man and woman, and then to a larger room, a squad room or "roll call" room, with long desks and chairs set out classroom style and a podium with whiteboards behind it. Two detectives were sitting and chatting and stopped when Whitaker came in.

"Boys, this is Special Agent Ames, FBI." Whitaker stopped in the middle of the room and faced her. "Sorry – it was Cheryl?"

"Shannon."

"Special Agent Ames, this is Detective Greg Heinz and Detective Luis Caldoza."

They nodded at her; Caldoza stood and extended his hand

and she shook with him. He wore jeans and a white T-shirt and had kind eyes. Heinz stood and offered his hand as well. Heinz was tall and blond and wore a dark Brooks Brothers suit. Both men had their badges hooked to their belts. Heinz wore a hip-holstered pistol, Caldoza a brown leather shoulder holster.

Whitaker walked toward the front of the room, saying, "Okay. All right, so this is what we've got." He pulled down a map in front of the whiteboards, and Shannon got a bird's-eye view of the five boroughs. He pointed to a spot near Central Park. "Monica Forbes works here. This is Channel 7, which is WABC-TV, the New York affiliate. We've got video of her leaving work, leaving the building, last night at ten thirteen p.m."

Heinz asked, "Why so late?"

Caldoza answered, "Husband says she was working on a project. They've got two kids, both of them upstate at summer camp, so their being away was giving her some extra time to work."

Whitaker was waiting for Caldoza to finish. "Right." Whitaker then faced the map again. "Her normal route is this – she takes the A/C/E from Columbus Circle down Eighth Avenue to Fourteenth Street, where she switches to the L. Takes the L over into Brooklyn, practically drops her right at her door – just a couple of blocks. We're going through MTA video to verify she was on her usual trains. So far, we've got her going through at Columbus Circle. Fourteenth Street had some issue, but that footage is forthcoming." He looked at Caldoza. "Lou? What's the deal on the husband?"

Caldoza picked up notes from the desk beside him. "Ah, okay, the 911 call was placed by Benjamin Forbes, Monica's husband, at 3:58 a.m. He said he'd been waiting up for his wife since midnight."

Heinz said, "Why'd he wait so long to call?"

"We'll ask him. Ah, so, she was working late on a project, he said. Maybe he was giving her space? Anyway, we sent a patrol car to their condo at 308 North Seventh Street, and our two officers talked to him, took his statement. He said there was no reason why she wouldn't have taken the usual route home." Finished, Caldoza looked up from his notes. He glanced at Shannon, then watched Whitaker.

Still at the podium, Whitaker said, "Okay, so, because of Eva Diaz over in Maspeth, this isn't the ordinary missing persons case. Heinz, you talk to them over there at 104?"

Heinz nodded, looking at a small spiral notebook in his hand. "Eva Diaz, twenty-eight years old, from Ditmars-Steinway, found on Forty-Eighth Street in Maspeth by a construction worker at four in the morning on Wednesday, July eighth. So two weeks ago. She was last seen leaving work that previous Monday, just after six in the evening. Ah, victim was strangled. Rape kit came back negative. No blood, hair, tissue samples to work with, no touch DNA. Medical examiner said she had been cleaned with astringent chemicals."

Shannon spoke up for the first time. "Posthumously?"

Heinz glanced at her. "That wasn't determined. Probably, would be my guess. She was strangled, then this guy cleaned her up to get rid of any trace evidence."

There was a pause, and they waited for Whitaker. Whitaker said, "Okay so we're pinging Monica Forbes's phone, we're checking video, and we're going to do a press conference" – he checked his watch – "in half an hour. We'll put out the hotline and see what turns up. And we got the BOLO out." He looked around the room and shrugged. "You know, we'll try some door-to-doors, but at the moment, we don't know if something might've happened between Fourteenth Street and Bedford Avenue."

Shannon asked, "Is her phone not showing up?"

Whitaker shook his head. "Nothing." A moment later he added, "I mean, you ask me, she could have had an accident, fallen onto the tracks. It happens." He straightened upright. "All right. Boys?" He watched Caldoza and Heinz and waited.

Heinz said, "I'll keep on it until we get that video from Fourteenth."

"I'll go follow up with the husband," Caldoza said.

Whitaker clapped his hands. "All right. And we've got everybody out looking, so ..." His eyes connected with Shannon, almost approval seeking.

"I'd like to go along to talk to the husband, if that's okay."

Caldoza nodded. "Let's hit it."

5

Nine a.m. It was already hot and getting hotter. "You believe this?" Caldoza walked fast toward an unmarked white car in the parking lot. He'd donned a pair of black Ray-Ban sunglasses. "Going to hit a hundred degrees today by this afternoon."

"I know." Shannon looked for her car, saw it, and glanced at Caldoza. "I'll follow you?"

"Or we could just ride together."

She thought about it. "Sure."

Caldoza was nimble with traffic and didn't drive too fast. "So where you from?"

"Upstate."

"Oh yeah? Westchester?"

She laughed a little. "Way farther. The Adirondacks."

He came to a full stop at a traffic light. "Wow, yeah, okay. Almost to Canada, eh? Hey, but not bad – you're not too far from home, though. Did you request New York? Is that how it works?"

"You can put in a request, yeah. I didn't."

"So it's by chance you're here and not Hawaii."

"They try to put people where they're going to have some experience, some background." She looked out the window at the hustle and bustle – scaffolding that surrounded a building under construction like some kind of overgrowth; a double-parked delivery van, drawing shouts and honked horns and shaken fists; a deli next to a tattoo parlor next to a Realtor next to a corner grocer teeming with fruits and vegetables. "Not that I had any real experience with New York City before getting posted. The one time I was here was on a class trip in the eighth grade."

The light changed and Caldoza hit the gas. "Where they put you up?"

"I live in Rego Park. It's just a mile away from the resident agency."

"Yeah, that's mostly Jewish over there. Nice area. It's coming along a little bit. Some of these areas, though, it's crazy. The gentrification. I mean, don't get me wrong, I see women in big sunglasses pushing double-strollers I think, 'good – less crime.'" He had a smooth, easy laugh. "Right? It's just a lot different from when I grew up."

"Where did you grow up?"

"Right here. My parents came up from Puerto Rico in the sixties. Back then, you had close to a hundred thousand manu-facturing jobs in this area. In the 1990s? That dropped to around ten thousand. So you can imagine what type of hole that left. That was the seventies and eighties. That's when I grew up. Crime, drugs. If you could move out, you moved out. But we didn't. You know that movie *Serpico*?"

"Yeah."

"That was here. Real-life Frank Serpico shot during a drug bust in 1971. That shit was right here."

"Wow," she said.

Moments later, he made a left off Meeker Street onto North Seventh and then pulled off quickly in front of an orange-brick and gray concrete building for Northside Williamsburg School. Caldoza leaned over, opened the glove box, and took out a package of gum. He offered her one and Shannon declined. "All right," he said, loading a piece of gum into his mouth. "Here we go." He opened the door.

Across the street from the school, 308 North Seventh Street looked brand new. Caldoza waved his hand, palm out, in a kind of semicircular motion. "This building used to be two stories, red brick. Graffiti all over it."

It didn't look that way anymore. Beige stucco, with the first four floors all the same dimension, but the top four done in fancy art-deco fashion, all angles and glass. They crossed the street, went in through the double glass doors, and spoke to a concierge, who buzzed Forbes on the top floor.

A few seconds passed before the concierge pointed to the elevators and said, "Go on up."

BEN FORBES OPENED the door and showed them into the sizeable seventh-floor condo. Forbes was an emotional wreck. He hadn't slept at all the night before, he said, and his eyes showed it; dark smudges beneath the bloodshot blue. He was a tall man, his blond-going-gray hair in a shaggy cut, and he stood in the living room in sweatpants and a sweatshirt that read *Forbes Contracting – we nail ya good!* Behind him, floor-to-ceiling windows yielded an expansive view of the city, from the rest of Williamsburg to the East River and the Manhattan skyline beyond.

"The kids are coming home soon," Forbes said. "They're coming home and I don't know what to tell them."

Caldoza stood beside Shannon, facing Forbes and the view. "Probably best not to say anything right now."

Forbes frowned, touched his forehead and looked into

space. "No, I know, I know. I just ... I don't understand where she would've gone." When he looked at Shannon, she saw desperation. "Monica used to travel," he said. "Through college and for years after, she'd travel abroad. She's been all over. I thought, when we got married, oh no – she's not going to like staying in one place. But she dialed right into it. She started with ABC-7 and never looked back. She was a media producer, and then they offered her the daytime spot, you know, the kind of show for the stay-at-home mom, and she took it. She's not the flashy, on-air type, but it was better pay."

Forbes started pacing. He left the living room and walked to the kitchen area dominated by a white marble island surrounded by stools. Suddenly he stopped and looked at them. "I'm sorry – please – can I get you something? Coffee? Tea?"

"We're fine," Caldoza said, chewing his gum. But he glanced at Shannon.

"No, thank you," she said. Then, "Mr. Forbes – would you mind if I have a look around?"

His eyes widened and his spine seemed to straighten. "No. Not at all. Please." His eyes flicked to Caldoza. "Have you found anything out? What's the latest?"

Shannon wandered off as Caldoza brought Ben Forbes up to speed. She peeked in the bathroom – same white marble forming the sink and tub as formed the big kitchen island – and then moved down a carpeted hallway. The first door was shut and she knocked, just a habit, then opened up. It looked like the daughter's room. Spartan, not even a poster on the wall, but the rack of hair ties gave it away. That and the faint smell of citrus soap or shampoo. The next room was the boy's room, the walls painted dark blue, baseball trophies on the dresser. In the master bedroom, a family portrait hung near the en suite bathroom. Shannon drew closer, examining their faces. Joe was tall, like his father, but had his mother's eyes. Kyle resembled her father through her smile. A handsome family. A pretty mother, looking fit, looking as though she was right where she wanted to be, here in the heart of her life.

Ben had a different look, though. A different feel. Like someone not quite comfortable in his own skin.

Or maybe she was reading into it too much.

Shannon noticed her own reflection in the glass, and she moved away. They'd need to have a close look at everything here. They were already into Monica's phone, but would need her laptop, too, statements from co-workers, her bosses. Shannon browsed Monica's things on the woman's dresser, took a look around in the walk-in closet at the shoes, noticed a couple of boxes on a high shelf, and had just a quick peek at them – photos in one, old bills and paperwork in another. Ben's side of the closet was messier, with piles of boots and work gloves and a couple of hard hats.

When she returned to the kitchen, Caldoza was sitting on a stool, his hands folded, and he watched her as she approached. Ben Forbes was holding a cup of water in both hands, gazing down at nothing. Then he looked up and seemed to remember she was there.

Shannon said, "You said Monica was late, working on something – do you know what it was?"

Forbes pushed away from the sink and set the water glass down on the island. He rubbed his hands together and shook his head. "Ah, you know, she never really told me when she was cooking something up."

Shannon nodded, look around, then said, "Did she do that a lot? Look for stories?"

"Well, it was in her. I mean, that's what she did for years as a media producer. She would find stories. She'd do the research and pull the resources to cover them. So when she took the position on *The Scene*, it was with the caveat she'd want to keep pursuing stories, and they went for it."

"So," Shannon said, "eventually she'd tell you what she was working on. Or maybe you'd see it on air."

"Right. Yeah. I mean, they didn't always go for it. She had maybe ten, maybe twenty percent of her ideas taken up by management." A light came into his eyes and he snapped his fingers. "You know, she was looking into something about a month ago ..."

Shannon glanced at Caldoza, who raised his eyebrows at her and turned back to Forbes.

Forbes continued, "She had this thing where she was looking at some land-use issue, something that they deal with at city hall. From up in the Bronx. We talked about it a little because I'm a contractor."

"What came of the story?" Shannon asked.

"I don't know. I think she was hitting a wall with it. Monica liked to push journalism, but the edgiest the producers of *The Scene* wanted to get was to talk about football concussions, too much high-fructose corn syrup in soft drinks, things like that."

"You work as a contractor," Shannon said.

He nodded and twirled his finger in the air to indicate his surroundings. "This building, this was my project. But I'm all over the place. All the boroughs, both sides of the river, and a lot of restorations and renovations ..." He trailed off, looking at Caldoza.

Caldoza's phone was buzzing. "Excuse me." He stepped off the stool and took the call.

Forbes watched him walk away, desperation filling his features again.

Shannon asked, "Mr. Forbes? What do you think happened?"

His haunted eyes found her. "I was up all night ... I just ..." He sobbed then, a noise that sounded like he was choking, then regained his composure. "I kept thinking about the thing with the other reporter."

"Eva Diaz."

"Monica and I talked about her. It was just an *oh my God, can you believe that* kind of thing, but we thought, you know, her being a reporter was arbitrary. But when it was going on two o'clock this morning, and Monica wasn't here, all I could think about were those pictures of Eva Diaz on the side of the road ..."

Caldoza came back, walking fast, before Forbes could fully sob. Caldoza's eyes darted between Shannon and Forbes. "Mr. Forbes, thank you so much for talking to us. We've got to run, but we'll be in touch."

Shannon got the vibe: something happened – someone found something or learned something new.

She followed Caldoza to the door, with Forbes on her heels. "What do you want me to do?" Forbes asked.

Over his shoulder, Caldoza said, "Just sit tight, Mr. Forbes. We'll be in touch." He opened the door and stepped out into the anteroom and pressed the button to summon the elevator.

Forbes lingered in the doorway. "Did something happen?"

"Everything's fine. We'll be in touch." Caldoza pressed the button again.

Shannon looked between Caldoza and Forbes and then stepped toward Monica Forbes's addled husband. Her voice soft, she said, "A couple things you can do. One, try to get some rest. Eat something. We could find Monica today, and she might need you to be in your best possible shape. The other thing, start a list. Everyone Monica knows in the area–"

"I gave that all to the police already. At four this morning."

"I know. I know ..."

He dropped his gaze and nodded thoughtfully. "But yeah, maybe there's more. Maybe there's something I missed."

She touched his arm. "Hang in there."

The elevator chimed as the doors opened.

6

They ran.

"Call came in through the hotline," Caldoza had explained in the elevator. "A witness says she saw a man approach a woman last night, put her in the back of his car, drive off."

Abduction.

The location given by the witness was two blocks west of Monica's home address – they were practically right there. Whitaker had already sent uniformed officers to the location and Shannon saw them up ahead as she jogged along beside Caldoza. Just a couple of blocks in the humidity and she could feel the sweat breaking her skin, even though the sun was still low, the street in flat light.

One block closer – and one just east from the Bedford Avenue subway station – an African-American woman in a bright, colorful head scarf was talking to two uniformed NYPD cops. Two more officers cordoned off the area with yellow crime scene tape.

"Nobody touch anything!" Caldoza called, hustling. A few bystanders were gathering – two shaggy-haired teenagers on skateboards, a middle-aged man in jogging shorts and a beard, a pair of mothers pushing matching strollers, an elderly woman pulling a shopping cart. Caldoza spoke to one of the uniformed officers first. He stepped off the curb with the officer, a scrubbed-faced kid all of twenty-four or twenty-five, and they talked in low voices. The officer did a lot of nodding.

Finished, Caldoza moved closer to Shannon again. "All right. I'm calling crime scene." He meant a forensics unit to look for trace evidence. Shannon and Caldoza approached the witness and introduced themselves.

"Olivia Jackson," the witness said, with a soft handshake. "You got here fast."

Caldoza smiled, showing a row of even white teeth. "I know what you're thinking – missing-white-woman syndrome."

Jackson cocked her head back. "I didn't say that."

Still smiling, Caldoza nodded. "I know. No, we were right down on the corner. The missing person we're investigating, she lives right there."

"Well, there you go," Jackson said. She relayed looks between Caldoza and Shannon and then, for some reason, stayed focused on Shannon. "I live right up there. Right over there – see that jade plant in the window? That's me, third floor. I can't sleep most nights. I try to go to bed, nine, ten o'clock. I can't stay up for those TV shows. So late. But I heard some folks talking out here …"

"What time was that?" Shannon asked.

One of the two uniformed cops, a woman, also young looking, answered: "11:34."

Jackson shot the female cop a sidelong look, then refocused on Shannon. "Mmhmm. That's what I said, yes. I know because I had gotten up to … nature called, and I checked the clock on the stove as I was coming back to the bed. Now, my AC unit is busted. So I'm up there on the third floor – you know what happened last week? It got so hot, a candle melted on my nightstand."

Caldoza sounded impatient. "You said you heard voices ..."

"I heard voices, so I looked out. I had the fan going, you know, I've got three fans going, but they're quiet. I heard a low voice, a man's voice, then a woman's voice, and then I just looked out. You know, as you do. You hear something, you just look. We're social creatures. I teach in the sociology department at NYU. Race and ethnic relations."

Shannon smiled, listening, also watching as the other two cops finished taping off the scene. The street was lined with parked cars. She asked the witness, "Ma'am, you said he put her into a car ... You mean a sedan?"

"No. Bigger. An SUV. I think so."

Caldoza cocked his head. "You think so?"

Jackson snapped a look at him. "This spot right here is in between streetlights. And I don't go to sleep with my contacts in or my glasses on. So? I don't know if it was an SUV for sure. I'm not sure I even know what an SUV is these days."

"Was it double-parked?" Shannon asked.

"Yes. That's right. He was parked in the street with his flashers on."

"You're sure it was a man."

Jackson stepped back and cocked her head. She said to Shannon, "Honey, I might not be able to see well at night, but I know a man's bullshit when I hear a man's bullshit. I've lived sixty-seven years."

Shannon was distracted when a vehicle, a white conversion van, slowed in the street. Caldoza excused himself and trotted over. The side door slid back and three people hopped out wearing white jumpsuits. The crime scene unit.

More bystanders had gathered. A uniformed officer remained with Shannon and the witness – the other three were spreading out to hold back the growing crowd. Shannon took the moment to scan the sidewalk for any signs. Nothing stood out. No blood, no dropped items. "Was there a struggle?"

"No," Jackson answered. "No, I wouldn't say there was a struggle."

Shannon pushed a little: "You said you could tell a man's bullshit ..."

"Oh, honey, I can smell it a mile away." Jackson stared at Caldoza, who was over with the crime scene people. Maybe she'd had some recent bad luck with the male sex. Maybe a lifetime's worth.

"You think he was giving her a line? Is that what you mean?"

"Mmhmm."

"In what way?"

"Just the way they was talking." Jackson seemed to resent the questioning. "I don't know, it just felt like it to me."

"Did it seem like they knew each other?"

Jackson tipped her head back and forth. "Maybe. I mean, he come up on the sidewalk, right about here ..." She turned around and walked toward the brick building behind her, stopped, then faced west, up the street. "Like this," she said. "And she was coming from that way."

The direction of the subway station. So far, it fit.

Jackson said, "And he's here and she's standing opposite, and he's talking – he's giving her a line – and he laughs a little. And then I ... I don't know. My mind wandered for a second. When I was paying attention again, he opened the back door of his car ..." The witness walked past Shannon to the street, stepped between two cars that were there, and opened an imaginary door.

Shannon said, "And she got in."

Jackson nodded. "Mmhmm. She got in, and he got in."

"To the front."

"No, to the back seat. And then he got *out* again, but she didn't. And he went to the front and got in."

"And, ma'am, this is very helpful – but if we put you with a sketch artist ..."

Jackson was already shaking her head. "I can't tell you what he looked like. I'll sit with whatever artist you need me to. I'll take whatever test. Put me on a lie detector. But all I can describe is white fuzziness."

"So he was white."

Jackson's eyes acquired a knowing look. "Oh, he was white."

"Does that mean something to you?"

"It means I've lived in this city all my life. Sixty-seven years. I know what a white man looks like, fuzzy or not."

Shannon swallowed and tried not to look at Caldoza. "Mrs. Jackson, I'm going to ask you not to talk to the press about this. Not even to any other witnesses – people in your building who might've seen or heard something. Okay? Doing so might contaminate the investigation. And this man – if he's the one we're looking for – if he knows what we know, it might change how he does things. It could make him harder to catch." She stopped short of mentioning that having all the information out in the public could make it harder to weed out false confessions – it was clear from Olivia Jackson's expression that she understood.

"Did I mention I've lived here sixty-seven years?" Jackson's mouth twitched with a smile.

"You did."

～

SHANNON CAUGHT A MOMENT WITH CALDOZA, just on the edge of the secured area. The crowd had swelled to fifty or more people.

Caldoza said, "I'm gonna pull every camera in this whole area. Every building lobby."

Shannon nodded, but was doubtful. "She can't tell if it was a Pathfinder or a Tahoe," she said about the witness. "She can barely be sure of the color. At one point she thought green, then she said blue, and then she was pretty sure it was green again. She says they got in the back, and the car moved a little, up and down – she thought maybe they were 'getting kinky.' Then he got into the front and drove away, fast."

"This sounds like Monica and our guy," Caldoza said. His eyes scanned the street, the buildings. He watched the people in jumpsuits and frowned. "I mean, Whitaker sent a crime scene unit. I don't know what they're gonna do."

"She didn't try to get away," Shannon said, still thinking about the witness's account of Monica's actions. "She stood there. Talking to him. Seeming unafraid. Jackson thought the man was hitting on her or making up some story."

"He's a charmer, I guess."

"Or she thought she was safe. Or she knew him. Or she was too afraid to run."

"We don't even know it's her yet," Caldoza said.

Shannon gave him a look.

Someone said, "Excuse me!" A female voice, calling from the street. Shannon picked her out: a blonde reporter pushing through the onlookers. When she reached the crime scene tape, she gave Shannon a million-dollar smile and said, "Hi. Jordan Baldacci, with the *Gazette*. I understand this is the site where Monica Forbes was abducted?"

Caldoza moved in front of Shannon, cutting his arms back and forth. "No comment right now. This is an active investigation. No comment."

The reporter leaned around Caldoza and smiled again at Shannon. "You don't look like NYPD."

Caldoza overheard. "Hey – what's that supposed to mean?"

Ignoring him, Baldacci asked Shannon, "Are you linking Monica Forbes and Eva Diaz? Is this about a killer targeting newswomen?"

"Hey," Caldoza said again. His forehead was shiny with sweat, dark spots showing under his arms. "I said this is an active ..." He trailed off, looking at the phone clipped to his belt. He plucked it free. "Caldoza." And he moved off.

Baldacci continued to home in on Shannon. "Come on. Just something. I can help you, maybe. If this is about media professionals being targeted, shouldn't we be warning people?"

"We don't know what it is yet," Shannon said, feeling the dampness on the back of her own neck. The spreading sunlight was starting to heat up the street. She thought a moment and added, "The information given at the press conference is what stands. If anyone has any information regarding the disappearance of Monica Jane Forbes, call the hotline. You have the number?"

"I do." Jordan Baldacci's mouth opened to ask another question, but something caught her attention. "Dammit," she said, taking out her phone.

Shannon saw it as an opportunity to break away. She wanted to talk to the witness some more. Jackson was outside the crime scene tape now, a gathering of passersby around her, but her lips were pursed and her arms crossed as Baldacci homed in on her.

Thank you for keeping quiet, Shannon thought toward Jackson.

Someone grabbed Shannon's arm. Caldoza pulled her close; she felt his breath against her ear.

"Her phone is on," he said. "It's pinging. We've got a location on Monica Forbes."

7

The Manhattan skyline loomed closer – Shannon picked out the Chrysler Building, the United Nations. The sights put them across the river from Midtown.

Caldoza pulled over and the two of them got out. Tall grasses buzzed with insects, the air held the scent of nearby water – the East River and Newton Creek – kind of metallic, kind of sour. Where those rivers joined formed Hunters Point, a section of Long Island City.

"108th is already here," Caldoza said, meaning another precinct. Shannon saw the NYPD officers he was referring to combing through the grass. An abandoned-looking construction trailer sat not far off, decorated with graffiti.

More cops arrived; doors opened and slammed shut. Caldoza checked the load of his Glock 17 and reholstered it. He popped the trunk and pulled out two bulletproof vests. "We don't know what this is," he explained. Shannon was happy to put hers on.

Caldoza looked around in the bright sunshine. Behind them were two massive construction sites, with nascent buildings several stories high. Things crashed and beeped and buzzed as men in orange vests and hard hats worked the machines and tightrope-walked the steel beams. Caldoza had to raise his voice as they neared. "Plans were filed for these sites a couple of years ago. Supposed to be completed in late 2022." More cops were moving through the sites, stopping construction workers and talking to them. Work was slowing, being halted by police. Shannon watched an unmarked car roll down Second Street and park. Detective Heinz got out.

Caldoza said, "Past these sites, to the east, are the railyards." He pointed up Second Street. "Right up there, Long Island City Yard." He showed her his phone and she got a bird's-eye view of the point, the streets, the railyards. "We're getting the cell ping in here, right in this area." He swirled his finger around the screen. "The problem has been, we don't have the call detail record yet. We're working off two low-range towers in this area, covering a few city blocks. What's helping us is that we're on a point. If she's out in the water, we probably wouldn't be getting a signal. So we're either going to find her or at least her phone right here on the Point, among these construction sites. Up Center Boulevard, up Second Street, or maybe over on Fifty-Fourth."

Heinz found them and they made a plan to start by moving up the East River. They fanned out, Shannon taking the route closest to the water's edge, feeling her pulse kick a little harder. Ten months in the field with the FBI, and this was her first potential serial killer case.

A sign declared *Hunters Point South Park*. She navigated a zigzagging walkway between the river's rocky edge and the long thick grass along the embankment rolling up away from the river to the groomed park. A couple of Jet Skis zipped around on the water. A ferry drew closer, going faster than she thought ferries ought, creating a froth. Shannon turned away from it all and watched the long mats of river grass as she picked her way along the asphalt walk. She felt excited, scared, but calm all at once. Maybe a little embarrassed. Because she was once a poor farm girl from rural New York State, and now she was thirty years old and a special agent with the FBI, working in New York City, and she felt the thrill of that – the pride of that – and she was afraid of pride, afraid of vanity.

Red flags marked a spot where someone – a conservancy group, probably – had posted a sign about bird habitat and not walking on the grass, but that was all she saw. She left the walkway where it ended at the ferry dock, people waiting to board. She moved faster, jogging now, as she left the river behind and moved down Borden Ave toward the Long Island Rail Road. She turned down Second Street, feeling a thread of sweat roll down her back.

She was going to head into the railyard when a news van passed her, trucking along Second Street. It turned onto Fifty-Fourth, just a block south. Shannon kept going that way, eyes on everything as she jogged. Two low-range towers? Monica Forbes could be anywhere. They could be looking for hours. Maybe days. And they might find only her phone – because what abductor let his victim bring her phone along for the ride? Anyone living in today's world knew police would get a warrant and ping the device. In most cases they'd be able to triangulate it within a few hundred yards. This area was an exception because, until recently, it had been mostly neglected.

Maybe Monica was alive. It was still possible that her disappearance wasn't related to Eva Diaz. That, despite what her husband thought, Monica Forbes had changed her routine, stopped somewhere for a few drinks, maybe tripped and fell on her way home. Were there any bars around here? Caldoza had pointed out some restaurants on the way to the Point. She'd also seen a few street vendors selling things like wallets and purses.

Shannon turned left down Fifty-Fourth and jogged past a low, redbrick construction supply company. People were out, unloading trucks: black men and Latino men and the occasional tattooed white man. She noticed these things because, growing up, you could count on your fingers the people of color in her hometown.

Someone was behind her. Still jogging, Shannon glanced back, saw another van rolling slowly along, unmarked. More press? The van passed her and slowed, then sped up again. Looking for something? How the hell had the media gotten here so fast?

Shannon passed a series of garages on her left, watching the van slow again. She almost caught up to it when the driver hit the gas and took off. There was an empty lot on her right; a sign – Pinnacle Realty – advertised it for sale, even though it was populated with vehicles – fifteen-passenger vans, transit buses, blue vans with "SuperShuttle" embossed on the sides.

She stopped running.

She glanced up the street to where the van had slowed again. It looked like it was turning around, the people inside it watching her. Waiting to see what she did.

The bright sun starred off the rows of commercial vehicles. The back of the lot abutted Newton Creek and was overgrown like the tip of Hunters Point, full of fast-growing cottonwood and ailanthus. Weed trees. An odor caught her attention – the kind of baked urine smell that wafts up from subways and homeless encampments under bridges and in certain parks.

Maybe Monica Forbes wasn't connected to Eva Diaz, no.

But if she *was*, Diaz had been found in a place like this one. The back lot of a building where a construction company parked its vehicles. Given the many arbitrary places to look, this was the better among them. Shannon entered through an open gate.

Caldoza called her phone as she walked in. "We've cleared the parks," he said. "We're focusing on the construction sites. Where are you?"

She gave him her location.

"Doing okay?"

"I'm good. I think I saw a news van. Maybe two."

"Yeah, they're all over. Somehow they're on it. Must've followed us from North Seventh."

Shannon only remembered one reporter at North Seventh and doubted that one would have given up new information to her competitors. Baldacci had struck Shannon as an "anything for the story" type of reporter. Maybe the type to listen to police communications and know ten-codes?

Still, it was very fast.

"Keep in touch," Caldoza said.

Shannon disconnected and put her phone away. The sweat was really running down her back now – the Kevlar vest was comforting but made her all the hotter.

She picked her way through the vehicles, getting closer to the weeds and trees on the creek bank. An urban environment, somewhat, but the trees and bunches of overgrown grasses evoked feelings of home. Hunting with her brothers. Turkey in the spring, deer in the fall. She'd had a thing with guns in her youth and had learned to hunt with a compound bow instead. Her first deer had been harvested that way, her arrow right through its lungs. It had run, forcing her to give chase. When she'd found it at last, the animal was dead and she'd said a prayer over it, even cried.

You didn't know what that experience was going to be like until you'd lived it.

Monica, she thought, *where are you?*

Shannon had worked her way all the way into the back corner. Concrete blocks supported a city bus without wheels. She started working her way back toward the street.

Then she stopped. Beneath the bus, something blue.

Monica Forbes had last been seen wearing blue.

Shannon pulled her weapon, heart rate speeding up. Instinctively: "Hello?"

No one answered. Construction rattled in the background. The white noise of traffic all around, but muffled by distance and heat. Shannon eased down into a squat for a better view beneath the bus. She was breathing a bit harder, aiming her gun, just in case.

The blue – a blouse, for sure – was attached to a body. A person.

Shannon pulled her phone out. Her fingers trembled slightly as she keyed Caldoza's number.

"You got something?"

She spoke; the words snagged in her throat. She grunted and continued, "I got her. I've got Monica Forbes." She looked in at the woman, at the marks on her neck, the way her head was bent back, eyes staring, seeming to look right at Shannon. Through her. "She's dead."

"On my way. Don't move."

Shannon dropped the phone on the dusty ground. She put a hand over her mouth, looking around a little bit more. *He dumped you here. Stuffed you under a bus like some discarded item ...* It couldn't have been for long. Maybe a few hours. Otherwise, some stray dog might've come poking around, or maybe the rats ...

Shannon heard a noise behind her, stood fast, and aimed. A redhead reporter and her potbellied cameraman stopped in their tracks. The reporter's eyes went wide. She tapped the cameraman's shoulder and pointed below the bus. He squatted down for a better angle and aimed the camera.

"Get back," Shannon said, chest pounding.

"Is that her?" the reporter asked.

"I'm going to need you to back up," Shannon said. She kept a grip on the gun but pointed it down. "This isn't safe back here. I want you out past the gate." She thought and added, "What are you doing here?"

The reporter and cameraman exchanged looks. The reporter said something to him, too low to hear, and they moved quickly for the street.

Shannon watched until they were out of harm's way, then faced the bus again. She dipped her head and was just able to see a bit of the body from this angle.

"Ah, man," Shannon said to the dusty parking lot. Then she said a prayer.

Keep her with you.

Keep her with you now. Don't let her go.

Sirens rose in the near distance.

THE CRIME SCENE unit had been just a few miles away in Williamsburg and so reached the new scene in minutes. In the meantime, Shannon had stayed with the body until NYPD dragged it carefully out from under the bus and covered it up, then roped off the area and closed off the entrance to the lot.

The media set up in the street. TV reporters with cameramen, a couple of photographers and half a dozen more newspeople standing around with their notebooks out. A feeding frenzy. Shannon recognized the reporter from North Seventh Street, Baldacci. Baldacci scribbled in her notebook as she soaked up the scene.

The medical examiner arrived and pronounced Monica Forbes dead. Shannon pushed through a growing crowd of cops and asked for time of death. "At least seven hours ago," the medical examiner said. He was an older man with wild gray eyebrows. "Maybe more."

It was noon. Seven hours ago meant just before dawn.

So the killer slips into the lot, dumps the body, shoves it under the bus. How? Carrying it?

The lot hadn't even been locked. He could've easily driven in.

"We need to be casting for tire tracks," Shannon said to Caldoza.

He raised his eyebrows at her. "I hear you, but this is a dirt parking lot for shuttle vans and transit buses. We need to focus on the body."

Shannon did: Monica Forbes had been strangled, according to the ME. A belt of some kind had been used. "But not leather," the ME said, "too much abrasion. Although that's just preliminary, to give you something."

Beyond that, Forbes would be autopsied and checked thoroughly for any fibers that rubbed off from the ligature. She'd also be checked for any fingerprints, hair, or touch DNA. Her hands were bagged – the pathologist would check under her fingernails. Had she clawed at her attacker as he'd tightened the belt around her neck?

But Shannon smelled it – she asked Caldoza if he smelled it, too, and he gave a sniff near the body. Caldoza asked, "Bleach?"

She nodded and stepped away, dialing Mark Tyler.

"Agent Ames," Tyler said, "been hoping to hear from you. What have we got?"

She explained the situation, a victim strangled, just like Diaz. Sanitized, also like Diaz. "The body is fully clothed," she added. "Like Diaz."

"I thought he cleaned them."

"He could dress them again. It's hard to tell – she was in an awkward position – but it could've been that the clothes were off. That the shirt was crooked."

"What else?"

Shannon was feeling keyed up, the adrenaline still

pumping through her from finding the victim. She flashed on the face of Ben Forbes, his sad eyes and stooped shoulders. This was going to devastate him. Eva Diaz was just as important, but at least she'd been unmarried, childless. Monica Forbes's children were going to come home from their idyllic little summer camps and learn that their mother was gone. No more hugs and kisses, no more of her soft eyes, her gentle touch, wafts of her perfume. Never again.

"Ames?"

"Now that we have a dump site – Forbes here in Long Island City, and we know Diaz was in Maspeth – just a reminder about that geographic proximity. The perp could be close, sir."

"Let's not rush to judgment. We need an autopsy, for one thing ..." Tyler went on and said something about getting ahead of the evidence, but Shannon only half heard him. She was watching the crowd of reporters beyond the lot entrance. The group had swelled to twice the size. She tuned back in as Tyler finished his spiel: "... to monitor and let me make the decisions whether or not we need to devote more resources to this, all right?"

"Yes, sir."

"It's not our job to take over investigations. That's not what we do. We offer assistance if it's appropriate, if we're asked."

The way he said it, it was almost like Mark Tyler resented these facts. But, then, maybe that was too hasty of her, too judgmental. "Understood, sir," she said.

"All right," Tyler said, and broke the connection.

Shannon put her phone away and reached the reporters. Cameras swung in her direction and microphones stretched toward her face. They started to barrage her with questions: "Are you NYPD?" "What can you tell us about what happened here?" "Is that Monica Forbes? Can you confirm Monica Forbes's death?" Shannon held up a hand to say, *That's not what I'm here for.* She also hoped that Ben Forbes wasn't sitting at

home, watching TV. It was local PD's job to call him – Caldoza
had said he would be the one. She hoped it would be soon.

Shannon looked over the group of reporters, zeroing in on
the redhead who had arrived first. "How did you know to come
here?"

Faces turned toward the redhead.

"I got a text," she admitted.

A woman near the back raised her hand. "So did I."

"Same here," someone else said – Shannon didn't see who.

Shannon asked, "A leak?"

The redhead shrugged and said, "I assumed it was someone
in the department. It happens. I mean, usually they like to get
paid, but sometimes they like to see themselves on camera ..."

Someone else in the group disagreed with this and it
elicited an argument. Half of the media group squabbled over
the intentions of sources, while the other half started lobbing
new questions at Shannon.

"We'll have another press conference," she said, looking
past them. One reporter was moving away. The one from the
Gazette, Baldacci.

Baldacci crossed the street, looking at her phone, and then
while she was looking, broke into a light trot. Where was she
going?

Shannon repeated, "Press conference will be soon. I'm sure
Detective Caldoza will fill you in on things. We'll, ah, we'll
know more in a little, ah ..." She was too distracted by Baldacci.
Moving away from the scene, headed down the street in such a
hurry, the reporter acted like she'd gotten some sort of emergency call. Maybe it was personal. Or maybe it was another
hot tip.

Shannon pushed her way through the gauntlet. "Excuse me
... sorry ..." By the time she got through, Baldacci was half a
block down, moving toward some dumpsters. The reporter

then stopped and did something else with her phone. Shannon realized she was taking video with it.

"Hey!" Shannon called. She glanced at the rooftops of the low brick buildings on Fifty-Fourth Street as she jogged along, reminded again of hunting, sitting with her brothers in the deer stand they'd built over two large boulders. *The Rock Stand*, they'd called it. From there, you had a deep view of the woods. One brother would put on a drive – he'd go through the woods making noise, hoping to flush out some deer – while another brother would wait in the stand.

Shannon glanced back at all the reporters gathered, a couple of them having admitted that they'd received an anonymous tip. Either that, or they'd been protecting sources. But if there was a killer out there who had it in for reporters ...

She returned her attention to Baldacci. The reporter had reached the dumpsters. She opened one and peered inside. She had her cell phone light on and shined it in.

A truck came rumbling down Fifty-Fourth and Shannon jogged out of its way. When it passed, Baldacci had moved to the second dumpster, in the middle.

"Hey!" Shannon called again.

Baldacci glanced over at her.

Shannon said, "Don't do that!" Her skin was crawling.

Baldacci turned away. She opened the next dumpster.

It was like getting punched by the wind. The explosion picked Shannon up off her feet and threw her backward. She hit the ground butt and elbows first. When her head struck the pavement, everything went black.

8

I n her dream, the water was icy cold. She swam in darkness, knowing the one whom she was trying to save was somewhere near. He was right there, just beyond the reach of her fingertips.

The water was so cold it seemed to burn.

She awoke in a bright room, chest exploding. After a few ragged breaths, she got her bearings. White walls, antiseptic smells, beeping machines. The hospital.

The skin of her arms and legs felt constricted. Touching her face, she felt bandages. The pain registered next, present but distant, like a storm muffled beyond thick walls.

The shuttle van lot in Queens. The three dumpsters across the street. Jordan Baldacci, hurrying to her death.

No one had even considered a bomb. The Reporter Killer – if he could be called that until there was something better – hadn't yet used explosives. His MO had seemed straightforward: abduct, kill, then dump in fairly plain sight.

Things to think about: who owned the dumpsters? When was the usual pickup time? How did the killer know someone else wouldn't open the lid first? What was the bomb made of?

How hard was that? How exotic were the components? But most pressing – why had Jordan Baldacci gone for the dumpster to look inside?

It had to have been another "leak."

Shannon tried to sit up and the IV tube caught on the bed railing and pulled taut. She freed the tube and searched for the lever to raise the bed. Once she was elevated, she clicked the call button for a nurse.

"You're awake," he said. Best-looking male nurse she'd ever seen, to get right down to it. But the appraisal was gone from her mind as fast as it had formed. He said, "How are you feeling?"

"How is she? How is ... the woman? Baldacci ..."

The nurse looked sorrowful. "I think you'll be ... I think someone is coming in to speak with you. They asked to be notified as soon as you were awake." He came closer, studying her with compassionate eyes. "Any pain?"

"Just tell me if someone died."

"Ma'am, I'm sorry. I'm not able to give you that information."

"Where am I? Are you able to tell me that?"

"New York Presbyterian Hospital. This is a Level 1 adult trauma center. They almost sent you into Manhattan, to Weill Cornell – that's where we have our burn unit. But your burns weren't that bad. You got lucky."

Lucky.

She wondered how lucky Jordan Baldacci was. Or if any of the other reporters had been injured. "Where's my phone?" Her mouth felt wadded with cotton.

"Your belongings are right over there, on that table. Though your service weapon has been locked in our safe. Don't worry, it will be fine there."

She felt sleepy and fought against it. "Can I have a drink?"

"Of course." He took a plastic cup and filled it with ice water and handed it to her. He stepped back and watched her drink and put a finger against the cleft in his chin. Jet-black hair, short but wavy, full lips, olive skin. The guy looked like Jon Kortajarena, the Spanish-born male model.

"What did you give me?" she asked the nurse.

"You're on painkillers and a mild sedative. Acetaminophen, diazepam."

Diazepam, she thought. No wonder she felt like ripping off his clothes. As a sedative, it tended to deregulate the libido a bit.

"Your burns are first degree and some second degree. You were concussed when the blast threw you back, and you've got abrasions on your hands and arms."

"Lucky," she whispered. The TV hung in the corner was dark, but as soon as mister male model nurse was gone, she'd be watching.

Baldacci had to be dead. If not, she'd wake up wishing she was.

The nurse smiled and said, "I'll go let your people know you're awake."

She turned her attention to the windows, the sky blocked by a hospital wing. "What time is it?"

"It's seven fifteen." Perhaps realizing she could be disoriented, he added, "P.m." Then he patted her leg. "Okay. I'll be back."

He left and she continued looking out the window. She didn't search for the remote, didn't turn on the TV. She only stared and felt the unexpected tears slide sideways down her face, and wiped them away, and then cried harder.

MARK TYLER WALKED into the room half an hour later. He looked more worried about liability than concerned for her well-being, but that was Tyler. Shannon knew he had his hands full. Running the resident agency meant he had six branches of the FBI under his roof, plus a small army of superiors and supervisors to answer to – from section chiefs all the way up to the Office of the Director.

"Shit," Tyler said.

"I'm fine."

He clasped his hands together like a pallbearer might and kept himself a body length from the bed. "Bomb squad is saying it was an ANFO blasting agent. Ammonium nitrate with about five, six percent diesel fuel and some other additives. Homemade – basically, an IED. He used a couple of sticks of dynamite as a booster to ensure detonation. Could've used Tovex, but didn't. This guy is old-school."

"Yeah. Really retro." The medication still pumping, she was unusually sarcastic.

"They said the detonator was triggered when the lid was opened; the fuse was set for a two-second delay. We're tracing it all back, looking for sales of high-nitrogen fertilizer to get the ammonium nitrate, looking into mining, quarrying, construction and demolition for the dynamite."

"Construction and demolition all over," she said. "Seems like Queens is one big renovation project."

"Yeah." He watched her and she knew he was waiting for the question.

For some reason, she couldn't bring herself to ask it. Tyler knew and answered anyway. "She was alive for about a minute. There wasn't much that anyone could do."

A silence formed, broken only by the beeping of her heart monitor, the murmur of voices in the hallway, beyond the closed door. "He took a risk," Shannon said. "Don't you think?"

Tyler glanced at his watch, then met her gaze. "I mean, maybe. Yeah. Someone coming and throwing in a bag of trash. But that place, though – Salt and Pepper Food, Incorporated.

That's the business there on Fifty-Fourth with the three dumpsters–"

"Everyone okay inside?"

"No one was there. Three employees scheduled. Two out making a delivery – they do deli and restaurant paper products supply. The other was at lunch. The place was locked up. The dumpsters get picked up on Tuesdays and Fridays. So maybe he was lucky; maybe he did his research. He must've prompted the reporters, and she was the first to walk over."

"Not the first," Shannon said.

Tyler frowned at her. "What do you mean?"

Shannon closed her eyes, cleared her throat, and tried to talk straight. "She was the *only*. She was the only one who went over. I saw her looking at her phone."

"Well, her phone is obliterated. But NYPD has the subpoena going in and they'll get her call log. Her texts."

"The reporters admitted there was a leak," Shannon said, eyes open again.

Tyler was nodding. "And we traced that number back – three of them had it – and came up with a burner. Which, you know, we can get the carrier, and the stores that carry the brand, and we can pull video, look for a purchase. It's a long shot. Like, a million-to-one. But we'll play it out anyway."

She felt the emotion rising again. She blamed the medicine when the tears welled up.

"Hey," Tyler said, "I'm sorry, but I've gotta go. This whole thing ... You know, you were the only FBI presence on the scene."

"What do you mean?"

"I mean this looks bad, Ames. This looks bad for the bureau. I've got a lot of cleaning up to do."

"I'm sorry," she said.

He just looked at her, then said, "All right. Well, this pretty much puts you out of things. I'll be in touch."

Tyler left.

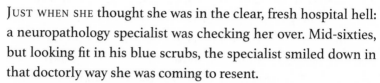

JUST WHEN SHE thought she was in the clear, fresh hospital hell: a neuropathology specialist was checking her over. Mid-sixties, but looking fit in his blue scrubs, the specialist smiled down in that doctorly way she was coming to resent.

She asked, "How bad is it?"

"You'll make a nice recovery – you'll heal. But with some scarring. Some on your arms, a little on your face and neck. But I'd like to run another CAT scan and an MRI."

She felt a flutter in her chest. "Why?"

"The initial CAT scan showed a subdural hematoma. Bleeding in your head. But sometimes the machine gets it wrong, sometimes the tech reads the data wrong. We're going to look again. And the MRI will show us if there's any other non-penetrating trauma. How is your side feeling?"

"It's okay."

"What looks like inflammation there, above your hip – to me, that says a lateral abdominal wall hematoma. It's gradually expanding and collecting on the left side of your back, expanding inferiorly into the left gluteal region."

"You mean the pain in my ass."

His smile showed teeth. "I'm glad you have your humor. Yes, the pain in your ass. Quite likely, deep to the posterior layer of the thoracolumbar fascia, but that's what the MRI will show us." He paused, as if giving the medical jargon a chance to sink in. Then another customary smile. "Let's get you looked at and we'll take it from there. Okay? Could be some PT in your future, lots of bed rest."

I can't rest. There's a killer out there, and I think he's just getting started.

What she said was, "Thank you, Doctor."

～

WHEN SHE WOKE AGAIN, it was out of black, dreamless sleep. She needed to pee. Carefully working the IV tube so it wouldn't catch on the bed rail, she left the bed for the bathroom, shuffling her steps. She sat in the dark, and her urine hit the bowl. She had yet to look at herself in the mirror. This was fear more than vanity. Fear that what Tyler said was true and not a threat – she was going to be benched for the rest of this investigation.

She wiped and flushed and rinsed her hands. There was enough light from the bright hospital room to see her face clearly in the bathroom mirror when she finally looked. A bandage covered her neck and jaw on the left side. She'd been told not to remove it, but undid the tape and pulled it back anyway to stare at the pink, twisted knots of skin there. She reaffixed the bandage and looked over the cuts and scrapes on her forearms, the serpentine burn snaking around her elbow, up to her triceps muscle.

Without expecting it, she dropped to her knees and threw up in the toilet bowl.

9

THURSDAY

Caldoza showed up with flowers. "Hey," he said from the doorway. "Is this where they keep the heroes?"

Corny, but she was happy to see a friendly face. He searched for a place to set the bouquet – a pretty arrangement of lavender asters, mini sunflowers and orange roses – and settled on the floor in the corner. He pulled a chair over to her bedside. She was sitting up and their eyes connected.

"How are you feeling?" he asked.

"I'm okay."

He waited to see if she was going to say more, and when she didn't, he pulled something from his bag. "All right. Wait until you see this. Just came in this morning."

He showed her paperwork from Jordan Baldacci's cell phone carrier. A list of texts. The last one, which had come in at eleven minutes past noon yesterday.

Forbes isn't the only one. I also took out some trash ...

Shannon looked up at Caldoza as her insides contracted. "You're kidding me."

"Nope." He reached around and tapped the right column of the page. "And it's the same number. The same burner number that sent the texts to the press, tipping them off to the location of the body. That's why they were there so fast. He wanted them there."

"Is she the only one?"

Caldoza was nodding. "So far. Couple we haven't gotten to yet, but yes – none of the other reporters from the scene got this text."

"He wanted her. Specifically her. I knew it."

Still bobbing his head, Caldoza said, "Looks that way."

IT WAS two more hours before the second CAT scan showed no intracranial bleeding. At least that was something.

But it was another hour before she could convince the specialist to release her, and forty-five minutes until they processed her and took her in a wheelchair to the front entrance, where Bufort waited in an unmarked.

He saw her and got out. Eyeing the pot of flowers on her lap, he said, "Nice."

She tried to hide her efforts to get out of the wheelchair, but it was too late; Bufort was looking at her in a way that mixed compassion with fear of contamination. Not of sickness, but of weakness. So when he held out an arm for her, she ignored it, limped to the car and got in on her own. She had to lift her leg with her hands and physically heft it into the car behind her before shutting the door.

When they were up to speed, threading through the Queens traffic, Bufort said, "You okay?"

"I don't know. Am I?"

He gave her a look and said, "No one else got to Monica Forbes first. You were the first on that scene."

"I got lucky."

"You were the closest to ... is that how you're going to play this? Going to have a pity party?"

"No."

He glanced at the flowers again. The orange container said *Bee Well Soon*, and three plastic bees on sticks jiggled amid the white daisies and leatherleaf fern.

"Secret admirer?"

"One of the NYPD detectives being nice. He probably got it in the hospital gift shop."

"Cute."

Bufort spoke with familiarity because they'd known each other almost a year now. He was in the National Crimes Branch, same as her. They answered to an assistant director out of the Manhattan field office and to Tyler, their supervisor at the resident agency. It seemed the FBI was always restructuring. The CCRSB – Criminal, Cyber, Response, and Services Branch – had been recently formed by the fusion of several smaller divisions, including the Criminal Investigation Division and the Critical Incident Response Group. But what it all meant was that Bufort, who focused on organized crime, was working out of the same resident agency as Shannon, for whom violent crime was the focus.

And anyway, like she'd told Caldoza, you went where they put you, did what they asked. She'd worked in the financial crime and civil rights sections, too.

"I'm not feeling sorry for myself," she said to Bufort.

"Good. Because, anyway – not that I have to tell you – but no one else was that close to Baldacci, were they?"

Shannon made no response.

"Thank you for not disagreeing," Bufort said. He flipped on his blinker and made a lane change; they were drawing close to her home in Rego Park. "And anyway," he said, "I mean, look at yourself. You practically caught fire putting her out."

Shannon was confused. "What?"

A sideways glance from Bufort, like he was testing to see if she was full of shit. "When you jumped on her and tried to put out the flames. She was already a goner. I mean, I've seen the footage. No one else will see the footage – that shit is not going to air *anywhere* – Tyler made sure of that. But *I* saw it." He waited, watching her, then said, "You don't know what I'm talking about, do you?"

"I was thrown back ..."

"Yeah, thrown back, hit the ground, and you scrambled onto your feet a second later. Rushed over to the reporter ... you really don't remember?"

The past twenty-four hours were a blur. She remembered a dream about drowning. Water so cold it burned ...

But that was about something else. Someone else.

Bufort said, "Yeah, I guess maybe you might've blacked out, there. But, so, okay – yeah, you threw yourself on the reporter, managed to put out the flames. But she was all ... I mean, there wasn't much left to do. She was gone. And then so were you – passed out." He pulled into the turnaround at her building's entrance and stopped the car. "Okay. I'd offer to help you inside, but I saw the way you looked at me at the hospital."

"Sorry." She grasped the door handle, then turned back to Bufort.

Bufort said, "He wants you rested, better. He said forty-eight hours."

She felt relieved. Tyler wasn't taking her off the case, just forcing her to pause. And maybe she could get around that, too.

"Thanks, Charlie."

"All right." He looked away.

She opened the door and got out. Bufort hit the gas and Shannon stayed in the street a moment, feeling the heat, smelling the exhaust and asphalt. She looked up at her redbrick building. Like the Forbes family, she lived on the seventh floor of a seven-story building. No concierge here. An elevator that squeaked as it ascended and smelled like pancake syrup. An apartment with one bedroom, one bathroom, no kids. But a cat.

"Hi, Jasper," she said as the feline twisted around her ankles. She set the flowers down in the kitchen and picked up the cat. As usual, he tolerated her nuzzling only briefly before bounding away.

She opened the door to her terrace and stepped out, took in the view and the air.

One way to look at the situation: it was good to be alive.

A TWO-SECOND DELAY. Shannon kept thinking about that. Standing in front of her open fridge, wearing only underwear and a tank top, drinking milk from the carton.

Why two seconds? You open a dumpster lid, and two seconds gives you just enough time to look in, maybe see nothing, but get your head in a little closer for a better look ...

As far as patterns went, this one clearly broke free. Diaz and Forbes were both abducted and strangled, their bodies scrubbed down, all within twenty-four-hour time frames. Serial killers were almost always sexual sadists – but when they weren't, there was still some kind of intimacy that came with an MO such as strangling. To strangle, you had to get close, had to touch. So while Diaz hadn't been raped, she was strangled. And Forbes was strangled, too.

But Jordan Baldacci had been killed at range, and in such a way that almost suggested another killer entirely. The only thing that linked her – she was another media person.

And that was, of course, a strong link.

It was on the news constantly. "Media under Attack." There was something in the eyes of the men and women reporting on the story, a kind of personal engagement that might not have usually been there. This was their turf; these were their people. If they weren't terrified yet, they were uneasy and getting scared.

Shannon sat and watched with her leg and hip iced down, her cat stepping in and out of her lap. Her phone had filled up with text messages and voicemails, and she'd yet to respond.

Forbes isn't the only one, the killer had texted Baldacci. *I also took out some trash …*

Shannon lingered over the choice of words. Obviously, the second sentence was a ploy to get Baldacci over to the dumpsters. Knowing she'd be on site – or at least, playing the short odds and risking it – the killer had lured her with simple bait. The first sentence suggested another victim, the second sentence that victim's location. The twist, then, was that Baldacci became the victim.

Shannon tried to remember more from that moment, but her memory stopped on an image of the reporter crossing the road, reading from her phone as she hurried in her heels. Her memory would just not go any further. She wanted to see the footage Bufort had mentioned. A cameraman from another network who heard Shannon calling out to Baldacci and turned just in time to see the explosion.

Had the killer been watching? There'd been no building over two stories high in the neighborhood. It was all supply companies and warehouses. Perhaps he'd been on a roof a half a block down, but she doubted it.

Had he been expecting to see it on TV, then? See his work on the news as it interrupted daytime programming? Killers often craved publicity. Maybe he wanted to see his handiwork displayed between Pepsi commercials and ads for the *American Stars* show finale, like he was part of the Zeitgeist.

But even if he'd felt confident someone in the press group would capture it on video, he'd have to realize it was too graphic for broadcast television. Maybe he'd hoped it would wind up on YouTube, but those chances were slim – the FBI had squashed it. And she thought she knew why. It would be graphic, yes, but since the explosion, Tyler was thinking about terrorism. An IED in a dumpster kicked open some more doors at the FBI. The National Security Branch was monitoring now. Backroom conversations were being had, playbooks consulted, worst-case scenarios considered, potential responses auditioned.

When her phone rang again, Shannon took the call. "Hi, Dad."

They went through it, and she told him what she could – which wasn't much – and assured him she was all right, in good health, and that everything was well in hand.

"I think about you down there in that city," he said. Thomas Ames had been a farmer all his life – he'd inherited the land from his father, but worked it like he'd paid every penny for it himself.

"New York is safer than it's ever been," she told him, remembering Caldoza's comment about rich women pushing strollers.

"According to whom?"

"The FBI."

She could hear hens clucking in the background. She asked him about the farm, the weather, her three living brothers, until she finally asked, "How's Mom?"

He hesitated. "Oh, you know, she's good. She misses you. Hopes you're well."

And that was it. Shannon returned two more calls – one to her good friend Kelly, whom she'd met at Quantico, and to Leslie, her best friend from college. Maybe in the old days you could get injured during the course of an investigation and not have people know about it, but not today, and not with a case ramping up to be as sensational as this one. One way or the other, everyone was seeing it, hearing about it.

Shannon sat up on the couch and gently kneaded her thigh. She painfully pulled on a pair of army-green shorts. She stood and limped to the terrace, thinking about an ultra-connected world. The terrace door was open, a warm midday breeze blowing in. Warmer than warm – it was going to be ninety-five again today. After standing a minute in the soupy heat, looking out over Queens, Brooklyn in the distance, she closed the door and turned on the air. She made a pot of coffee and opened her laptop on the dining room table.

She'd bought the place semi-furnished, and the furniture had looked like something you'd find on an old-fashioned ship. Dark wood with a natural, rough look. The hardwood flooring was a couple of shades lighter, the walls cream. Leslie would think it too masculine, maybe. Shannon's favorite part was a small antique desk with a high-backed chair with curvy legs. Buttoned-down leather upholstery. One of the few things she'd bought herself was the small glass dining table, which replaced the preexisting ugly, square white table.

Coffee ready, she got a cup and sat down, wincing at the pull of bandages still on her leg and arm. She began with Eva Diaz. Twenty-eight years old, originally from the Bronx. Diaz's death was mourned by a huge family; a picture of her mother, attending the burial, face twisted in agony, was particularly gut-wrenching. Diaz had been a reporter with Channel 2 for just four years. Even then, she'd only been an on-air field reporter for two of those years, covering mostly entertainment news. She'd started in the actual mailroom at CBS, according to her bio on the company website. A true story of a local girl who was a self-made success.

Her looks too, Shannon thought without cynicism, had to have helped her as well.

Forbes was older, more seasoned, but very pretty, too. Her college education and résumé were impressive. She'd spent many years behind the scenes working as a media producer before joining the ladies on *The Scene* and had been doing the late-morning show for almost four years now.

Shannon went to the antique desk, pulled out some paper, a pencil, and returned to the glass table. She started scratching out some notes, just dates, when each victim started working at the jobs they held when they were killed. She'd get more detailed information later.

She continued to mull over the locations. Forensics called it geographic profiling. But while all three victims lived in the New York City area, Diaz and Forbes lived in Brooklyn, mere minutes from each other. Baldacci had a Long Island address, a suburb called Melville. Almost an hour away.

Another difference: Baldacci was neither TV reporter nor TV news host. For the past six months she'd been a crime beat journalist for *Newsday*, a daily newspaper that primarily served Long Island counties, but also Queens. Though the paper used the more compact format of tabloid journalism, it had a reputation for being less sensational than its *Daily News* or *Post* counterparts. And Baldacci seemed the "serious" journalist; she also freelanced and had written articles for *Insight* and the *Gotham Gazette* – the last a daily online publication run by the Citizens Union Foundation, a government watchdog group.

Interesting.

In fact, if memory served, when Baldacci had first introduced herself on North Seventh Street, she'd said she was from the *Gazette*.

Shannon spent the next hour browsing recent articles from Baldacci, searching for segments featuring Diaz as the reporter on camera for WCBS-TV, and watching clips from Monica's show. Watching Monica was surreal. Because Shannon had just seen her beneath a bus, dead, yes. But also because of the way she looked on-screen. Like she was unable to completely hide the fact that discussing recent movies and hot new gluten-free recipes was a better job for someone else. She looked out of place. She looked like she belonged with Baldacci, in a way, chasing down the bigger stories.

Ben Forbes had said Monica was always trying to push the show content, to squeeze in a bit more of the intellectual. *Like what?* Shannon wanted to know more. Maybe dig into the thing with city hall that Forbes had mentioned.

Done for now, she stood up stiffly and gimped her way to the bathroom, using the walls to brace herself. She ran the tub and dumped in the rest of the Epsom salts she had beneath the sink. She lit candles. The plan was to soak for a full forty minutes, but she only made it halfway. She needed the water cool to keep from aggravating her burns, and lukewarm baths kind of sucked. Plus, she had to keep her arms out of the water.

After toweling off and blowing out the candles, she called Bufort.

"That didn't take long," he said.

"I need a car," she said to him. "I need, ah, my car."

"Not gonna happen. Not unless you want Tyler coming down on you. He's got you written off until at least Saturday."

"I just need to ... I need to look at a few things. My leg is ... you know what? It's fine. I'll take a cab. Thanks."

She hung up before he could say anything else. She ran a trembling hand through her damp hair. *Dammit.* She wasn't the type to get rattled like this. All her life, people had been telling her she had two gears: steady and steadier. She had the right temperament for this kind of work. But, then, so far there had been nothing holding her back.

Maybe she wasn't as perfect as everyone thought.

So be it.

She dressed and brushed her teeth, all of her movements slow and deliberate. She applied some burn cream and fresh bandages to her arm and leg. She removed the one from her jaw, dropped it in the trash, and didn't replace it. Instead, she used a little foundation makeup – a Christmas gift courtesy of her aunt Bernice. She pulled her hair back and added just a touch of eyeliner. Then a swipe of rouge and the subtlest lipstick.

There. It almost looked like she'd never been in a deadly explosion caused by a psychopath.

10

"Right here," Shannon said.

The cab pulled over. She was still half a block away, but wanted to keep her business private. She paid him and stepped out onto the street and waited until he drove off before she started down Second Avenue and turned onto Fifty-Fourth.

The walking was excruciating. After everything that had happened, it was her leg and hip, not her head, giving her the trouble.

The yellow crime scene tape became visible as she neared the Baldacci murder site. Two NYPD cars and an NYPD van blocked the street in this direction – there were more vehicles at the other end; they'd cordoned off at least a hundred yards of street. The lot where Forbes had been found was also protected. A handful of crime scene techs in white suits remained. One was scraping residue from the side of the Salt and Pepper Food, Inc. building, just beyond the ragged hole created by the blast. Two uniformed cops stood talking in the middle of it all, hands on their belts. And pressing against the crime scene tape, a latecomer reporter and camera crew.

Shannon stopped when she saw them, and moved behind a loading truck parked across the street. The last thing she needed was her own face splashed all over the news, especially when she was supposed to be standing down.

She backtracked to Second Avenue and walked around the construction site, thinking about explosives. Along Center Street, a guy with chest hair sprouting from his wide-open collar was selling men's shoes and belts. He tried to strike up a flirty conversation with her. She hailed a taxi and was saved when it pulled over and picked her up.

FORTY-EIGHTH STREET in Maspeth was much quieter, but the scene was eerily similar. Dylan Engineering and Construction sat on the corner. Forty-Eight ran north-south and Fifty-Fifth went east-west. Dylan had a large backlot where they kept a small squad of diesel trucks, equipment trailers, and massive refuse bins. Shannon peered in through slight gaps in the sheets of corrugated metal attached to a chain-link fence. Yellow crime scene tape remained in the lot, stretched from the back of the building to the fence at an angle, forming a triangle out of the overgrown southwest corner.

Shannon stepped back and looked up. The fence was only six feet high. Diaz had been found on the ground inside the fence. Found by one of Dylan's construction workers about fourteen hours after police believed she'd been dumped there. Dumped, it was determined, by being lifted up and dropped over the fence. Wrapped in black plastic garbage bags.

Which said a couple of things, Shannon thought, limping her way to the building's entrance, at least one of them for sure: that the killer was strong enough to lift a hundred-and-ten pound woman six feet in the air in order to clear her over the fence. The other thing it said, or at least suggested, was that he hadn't wanted this one to be found right away. Monica Forbes was under a bus, but that was perhaps just to give him enough time to get away – perhaps after double-checking his hidden bomb – and then make his anonymous tip to the reporters.

Shannon went into the building. A young woman sat at the only desk, a closed door behind her. The nameplate on the desk read *S. Martinez*. She was chewing gum and poking at an iPhone. Without looking up: "Help you?"

"Hi. Special Agent Ames, FBI."

A glance, then the young woman's gaze riveted back to her phone. "You want to see the place? Where she was found?"

"I was actually wondering if I could talk to who found her."

S. Martinez set down the phone. "Oh. Well, that's Alfonso. He's off on medical. Well, his wife is having a baby."

Shannon smiled. "Good for him. Is the owner here?"

"Two owners. Brothers. Tim and Jeff Dylan. They're in the city on a big project." Martinez shifted her gum to the other side of her mouth and looked Shannon up and down. At last, realization: "Oh, you here because of the thing over at Hunters Point?"

Shannon nodded. "Yes, ma'am."

"Crazy, right?"

"Yes."

"What's the deal? Someone got a thing for reporters?"

"Could be." Shannon pulled a card out from her inner jacket pocket and handed it to Martinez. "Would you hold on to this? Ask Mister ... ask Alfonso to give me a call when he has a chance?"

"Sure."

"How about you? Is there anything you could tell me about the discovery of Eva Diaz?"

"Oh yeah. Absolutely. She was wrapped up in garbage bags, for one thing. So, see, Alfonso was getting the trucks ready. That's primarily his job – we've got a lot of trucks, lot of equipment, and you need someone to keep all of that running smooth, right? So he's out there, four in the morning, he's checking the trucks, and he sees this lump of bags in the corner, goes to pick it up. Like it fell off a truck and didn't get into one of the bins. And he goes for it and he's like, 'shit' – sorry for the language – 'dang, this is heavy.' And he's feeling around, trying to get a grip on it, and he knows. In like, a couple of seconds, he knows. You can just tell the shape of a human body, right?"

"I think that makes sense."

Martinez nodded. "Yeah, and so he's like, 'shit, this is a body.' And he takes the top bag off, where he thinks the head is. It was like, a big heavy-duty contractor bag over the legs, one over the head, duct tape in the middle."

"And the police took all of that."

"Oh, yeah. Yeah, that was, um, the 104. Over in Ridgewood. Well, Ridgewood-Glendale. They service this area, I think. You never know. We've got police departments all over, but there's some places where it's kind of like a dark spot, you know? An area with bad coverage."

They talked for a few more minutes about the police response, about the condition of the body and Alfonso's reaction to the whole thing. Martinez also shared her theory – the Diaz killer, now the Forbes and Baldacci killer, too, was a Ted Bundy type who was former military. He got to Diaz and Forbes by using his good looks and charm, but when Baldacci didn't take his bait, he "blew her ass up," according to Martinez.

Shannon thanked the woman and left, thinking there could be a mote of truth to her theory – the bit about a charming killer. According to the eyewitness from North Seventh, the killer had approached Monica Forbes right there in the street. And rather than run away screaming, she willingly got into the back of his vehicle.

A Ted Bundy type? Or, perhaps more likely, someone

Monica knew? Someone she didn't find threatening? Could be. She didn't seem the gullible type to go for some killer's line about his lost dog or something. "Will you just hop in the back of my idling SUV and help me look?" No, of course it wasn't that.

Outside, Shannon called Caldoza from the corner and watched for cabs. "The witness at North Seventh – what was her name?"

"Hi, how you doing? Feeling any better?"

"I'm good."

Caldoza just breathed for a couple of seconds. "Okay, ah, you're talking about Olivia Jackson."

"How serious are we about her?" Shannon stepped off the curb and waved her arm at a taxi coming down Forty-Eighth.

"Considering her degenerative myopia and early cataracts? I mean, it's the right time for her to have seen Forbes. But we can't do anything with it. No real perp description, no vehicle description."

"I'm thinking more about the description that Forbes got into the vehicle willingly. Because I was wondering about something." The taxi pulled up, and Shannon slipped into the back seat. "Boro taxis are green. And the witness said green a couple of times." Shannon covered the phone and leaned forward and gave the driver her destination.

Caldoza was saying, "But Forbes was a block away from home."

"Yeah, right, I mean, I don't know what the scheme might've been, completely. It's just the idea that she trusted him. Maybe she called him. Maybe it was an Uber. Point is that either she knew him, or he was someone who caused her to let her guard down. Could even be a cop."

"Whoa now."

"I'm just saying we don't know."

"Well, it's just – we know where all our police vehicles are. We know where our personnel are."

"How about Ben Forbes?" Shannon asked after a moment. "Do we know where he is now?"

"He's here," Caldoza said. "I just came back with him from the Office of the Medical Examiner. He identified his wife from a photograph and birthmark on her thigh. I offered to take him back home, suggested maybe he start thinking about funeral arrangements, thinking about his kids, but he asked to come here."

"What's he doing?"

"He's been sitting in the lobby for an hour. He keeps coming back and checking in with me. The guy's a wreck."

"I'm on my way there," Shannon said.

"Yeah?"

"I'll see you in ten minutes."

IT TOOK SOME COAXING, but she managed to convince Ben Forbes to leave the precinct with her and go for a cup of coffee nearby. They took a booth overlooking the street. Forbes stared at the bandages on her hand, the visible burn on her jaw.

"Does it hurt?"

"It's okay," she said. "How are you doing?"

He looked all cried out, his face drawn, eyes underscored with dark smudges. "I had to say goodbye to my wife this morning."

"I'm so sorry."

He looked out the window and shook his head. "I don't get it. I don't get what happened out there." His gaze slid back to her. "This thing with the Baldacci woman, the reporter ... What's going on?"

"That's what I'm going to find out." They were silent a

moment, and then Shannon asked, "What can you tell me about that area?"

"Hunters Point?"

"Yeah."

"I mean, it's like a lot of places in the city, undergoing this kind of facelift." Forbes got a little more animated as he talked, some color returning to his face, life to his eyes. "It's gentrification, I guess, and you can say that in the pejorative, and it definitely has a downside – where there's no rent control, people get priced out of the neighborhood. Or, just, groceries get more expensive. Even in Williamsburg ... We used to go to a diner on Union and Metro. The whole family. The kind of place that home fries came out of a frozen box. You know what I mean? Cheeseburgers that have those individually wrapped slices of American cheese."

She was happy to let him talk, to live in the memory. "I do know what you mean."

"And then it gets new owners. Better food, but of course the costs go up. And I asked the waitress one day if the clientele had changed. And she said, 'Yeah, some people stopped coming. Just, that's it. Couldn't afford it, and they're gone.' And it's like, what do you do about that? Just shrug and say, that's change, I guess? That's progress? I don't know."

Forbes picked up his coffee for the first time and took a sip. His gaze drifted to the street again. When he looked at her again, he'd acquired a sheepish look. "Sorry."

"No. Please." Shannon thought a moment and said, "I'm interested. Especially in places like that, Hunters Point, getting this makeover, as you put it. This facelift ..."

Forbes nodded again, said, "A lot of these abandoned places in the city are going away. But you've still got railway stations, old colonial forts, psychiatric facilities, or places that just can't seem to work. They have these enormous water and power costs. There's mold, rot you can't get out – rats. Giant rooms, seventeen-foot floor-to-floor heights, everything dripping with condensation, streaked with rust, brick crumbling and paint peeling, abandoned." He shook his head. "But then, places like the Eagle Electric warehouse – different story. Something like that, you've got intrepid developers obtaining conversion permits and, boom, ground-floor retail units and expensive apartments on top installed within three months."

"Was that one of your projects?"

"It was."

Forbes seemed to have burned through his renewed energy and sagged again. He looked into his coffee, as if lost in thought.

"What did Monica think?" Shannon asked.

His eyes came up. "About the changing city and all that?"

"Yeah. About what you do, all of it."

"She thought it was ... you know. She was an optimist. But she knew, you know. People get left behind. She was compassionate." Forbes looked like he was going to slip off the deep end, the grief going to push him over.

Shannon said quickly, "Did she ever tackle that with her reporting? Or try to? You mentioned something earlier. About city hall."

Forbes had something in his eyes now, behind the nascent tears. He cleared his throat and took a quick look around, as if suddenly on alert for eavesdroppers. "Yeah, she was looking into that. It was kind of about gentrification, in a way, but really it was about something else. Something shady."

"Tell me about it."

"Well, I mean, I don't know everything. Just that maybe there was this city councilman, and he was doing a deal with the developer, and people thought the developer was into some stuff."

"Like what?"

"Like organized crime."

Shannon thought about it. "Interesting. And you're sure Monica was looking into this? No offense, but when we spoke last, it seemed like kind of an afterthought."

"I was in shock," Forbes said. His eyes had dried and his gaze was sharper. "But I'm telling you now – that's what she was working on."

11

In the 90th Precinct squad room, Shannon pulled down the New York City map from the ceiling. She used a red laser pointer she'd found at the podium. Heinz and Whitaker stared openly at her burns and the way she favored her right leg. At least Caldoza seemed genuinely interested in what she was about to say, waiting patiently.

Aiming the red dot at the map, she said, "This is where we found Monica Forbes. It's also where Jordan Baldacci was murdered. Site A. And over here, this is where a Dylan Construction employee found Eva Diaz dropped over a fence. Site B. Site A and site B are two and a half miles apart. Via Borden Ave, that takes eight minutes. I drove it."

Caldoza blinked. "I see where you're going. But you're talking about a very small data sample."

Whitaker added, "Plus – Baldacci is from Long Island."

Heinz snapped his fingers. "Shit. Listen to this. Baldacci is from Melville, right? That's in the Huntington Township on Long Island. And then Forbes and Baldacci were found – well, one found, one killed – near Hunters Point in Long Island City,

Queens." He glanced around. "I mean, pretty crazy with the names. *Huntington – Hunters* Point. Long *Island* – Long Island *City* ..."

Caldoza grunted. "All right, dickhead."

Heinz grinned.

Caldoza spoke to Whitaker. "Sir, she's talking about a hunting ground. We've all been thinking about it, even if Wonder Boy here wants to sound like an idiot."

Heinz blinked rapidly and touched his chest. "Me? I'm Wonder Boy?"

"I think we've got to give it a serious look," Caldoza said.

"Look how? Consult the serial killer playbook? Stick with the evidence," Whitaker said dryly. His eyes connected with Shannon. "Traffic cameras, eyewitness reports ... if you'd like to help, Special Agent Ames, we've got a shit ton of hotline calls to go through."

"I'll be happy to help there," she said quickly. She flicked a finger at the map. "My point is actually that two of our three victims are local. And our unknown subject abducted both of them. Which suggests – doesn't prove, just suggests – he could be local. He can nab the victims in his area, but a third one – Baldacci, who lives outside his area, he lures her in." She looked from Whitaker to Caldoza. "Speaking of traffic cameras ..."

Caldoza nodded right away. "We got the MTA video from Fourteenth Street. And I've seen her with my own eyes – Monica Forbes changed to the L train. We know she was on it. So that really puts the chances that our witness is, in fact, talking about Forbes when she describes the two people outside her apartment on North Seventh. Otherwise, we'd be looking at the world's greatest coincidence."

Shannon nodded. "Right. Thank you. And Monica Forbes got into the back of a vehicle. As bad as Olivia Jackson's eyes are, we can all agree it's hard to mistake someone getting into a vehicle. The sound of doors, the vehicle pulling away, the fact that no one was standing on the street any longer."

"No one arguing, either," Caldoza added. He looked at Heinz and Whitaker. "Though Jackson did indicate she thought the guy was using some lines on Forbes. Bullshitting her."

Shannon said, "Forbes was abducted. And Diaz was abducted – we don't know exactly how, if it was with the same method, but we know she was reported missing and then found two days later. We know she wasn't killed in the Dylan Construction equipment lot." Her eyes on Whitaker, she said, "That's what all the evidence tells us."

Whitaker scratched his head. "Okay. So what about Baldacci?"

Shannon ran the laser pointer east until she was off the map. "Melville, which is halfway down Long Island. She's the one victim from outside this area, so, again, he had to get her there. He leaked the location to the press, knowing she'd come. Or, at least, strongly suspecting. Not only does this suggest he's local, it suggests he's got a place he uses. Unless he's abducting these women and leaving the city and coming back and dumping them, he's in the area. And I've run the numbers. Between abduction and time of death, there's not enough time to go far. Heck – between abduction and *discovery* there's not that much time. We're talking a few hours in each case. So to clean them, he's got to be operating near the abduction sites."

"We don't have a definitive on when Diaz was abducted," Whitaker said.

"No, but we're close on it. She's last seen leaving work – just like Forbes. She's leaving work on a Monday, though, six p.m. She's discovered four a.m. on Wednesday the tenth, with time of death estimated at twenty-four to twenty-eight hours prior, so, roughly midnight on Monday, only six hours after she's last seen. That's a six-hour window in which she was abducted, killed, cleaned – or vice versa – and dumped. To do that, you've got to have a place close by."

"Like his home?" Caldoza asked.

"Sure. Or, this whole area, you've got these abandoned places. You have–"

Whitaker cut her off. "Agent Ames, with all due respect, if you think we're going to start going around to every defunct factory and warehouse–"

"No."

"I mean, *if* he's in the region and *if* he's using some space that he has access to, he's only using it once every couple of weeks. I doubt he's got someplace set up with a welcome mat and *Lair Sweet Lair* on the wall."

"Hey," Caldoza said. "Come on, Whit. You know she's making sense. You know it can't hurt to put it out at roll call, to have eyes on some of these places."

Whitaker scratched his head again, then pinched his nose. "Listen, let's say we run with this a second, let's say we go with a killer picking his victims because of their location–"

"I don't think that's the only criteria," Shannon said.

Whitaker shot her a look. "Okay. Their looks, too."

"Their looks," Shannon agreed. "Their profession. But there could be more."

Whitaker glanced around at Heinz and Caldoza, as if seeking moral support. He sighed and said, "Agent Ames, I appreciate your input. I do. But I've got a captain breathing down my neck, and a commissioner breathing down *his* neck …"

Whitaker trailed off as she left the map behind and approached him, her limp slight but still there.

"Then bring this to them," she said. "Tell them that the FBI special agent who's monitoring this case has started a profile on the killer. That he's selective, probably very strategic and organized, but also brutal. And that this FBI agent thinks he's right in our backyard."

~

"COME WITH ME," Whitaker said. He led her to a room at the far end of the precinct, closed the door, and dropped a giant three-ring binder on the table in front of her. "We sort the calls from A to D. Basically, from credible to nutcase-calling-with-nothing-better-to-do."

Shannon leafed through it. Over four hundred calls since the previous morning.

Whitaker said, "This is just the first phase, obviously. Everything goes into a database where you can search by keyword. I'll give you the access codes for that. You can network in with the precinct system, use your own laptop, or I can set you up – whatever you want."

She opted to use her HP laptop, pulled it from her bag, and got the necessary information. She thanked Whitaker and started going through the calls. On her first search, she narrowed things by geography. There were a hundred and sixty-four calls originating from Queens. People who thought they'd seen something suspicious, heard a noise, didn't trust their neighbor. About eighty calls came from within what she considered the likely hunting ground – an area of twenty square miles, from Ditmars-Steinway in the north, to Williamsburg in the south, Elmhurst to the east. The rest of the calls were outside of that, including Long Island and Manhattan, and all the way up to Putnam County and west into New Jersey.

She read one from Newark, a young man in his teens worried that his grandfather, who constantly ragged on the media for being "fake," might be someone to check on. A woman from the Upper East Side thought her perverted neighbor was the killer because of how loudly he played the evening news when, she suspected, he was masturbating. NYPD had given C grades to both these calls.

There were only two calls, out of the entire 433, that rated an A. And each had already been followed up on by a detective. In the binder, the reporters were initialed. Both "L.C.," for Luis Caldoza. The first was a thirty-five-year-old man who claimed he was the Media Killer – the official name given by the press. It turned out he was a schizophrenic, but not a killer. The second was Monica Forbes's college roommate. The roommate described a fellow student who'd been obsessed with Monica their senior year, to the point that Monica had had to lodge a complaint with campus security and local police. Checking into it, Caldoza learned that that man, now forty-two, living in Hoboken, had a credible alibi as a night-shift orderly at a local hospital.

Finally, with Ben Forbes's story in mind, Shannon searched for anything related to "land use" or "city hall" or "city councilman." She came up empty.

Her phone buzzed against her waist. Shit. "Agent Tyler," she greeted him, "how are things?"

"Special Agent Ames." He didn't say anything for a few seconds. "As long as you're feeling better, out and about, I'd like to see you in my office."

Shannon closed the hotline binder and stood up. "On my way, sir."

She didn't bother to ask how he knew. It was the FBI.

BACK AT THE Brooklyn-Queens Resident Agency, back in Tyler's office, he told her to sit. Bufort was there, too, chewing on a pen.

"So," Tyler said.

"So," Bufort said.

"Jordan Baldacci sometimes wrote for the *Gotham Gazette*," Shannon said.

"That's a real paper?" Bufort scowled.

"It's online. I just spoke to the editor over there who said Baldacci was working on a story about a big construction project going forward in the Bronx, suspected organized criminals involved, a city councilman issuing permits. And now, here's the thing – according to Ben Forbes, Monica Forbes was looking into that exact same story."

Tyler frowned. "She was? To bring it to her daytime talk show? They do in-depth reporting on dog grooming, not corruption."

Bufort asked, "Did Ben Forbes decide maybe his wife was working on this, too, because, like anyone could understand, he's a desperate widower hoping for answers?"

Shannon looked over at Bufort. "He brought it up first. I found out Baldacci was working on it *after* I talked with Ben Forbes."

That shut Bufort up. He studied his shoes a minute.

Shannon said, "I talked to WABC-TV and WCBS, and they've sent me everything our victims were working on going back a year. I figured I'd start there. Baldacci will take a little more work, since she was freelance. But she mostly wrote for *Newsday* and the *Gazette*."

Tyler pressed his lips together, the face he made when he was most skeptical. "I think that's a waste of time, Ames, to be blunt. This is about anti-media sentiment. We've seen it before, and we're seeing it again. Killings, bombs, hatred. You read the text message sent to Baldacci – 'I took out some trash.' You're talking about a serial killer, and technically – okay, if this is the same person, or group – it's a series. Otherwise, we're not seeing the hallmarks of a serial killer. Autopsy on Forbes is showing no sexual emission. Same as Diaz. This looks less like sexual coveting or sadism and more like hatred."

She was silent.

Tyler glanced away, then looked back at her. "There might be an element of proximity, yes – Whitaker shared your pitch with me. I'll give you that. These victims live near our subject – that's probably the case. But from there it's about hatred of the media."

Bufort spoke up. "I don't know, sir. I could see a psychopath who gets his rocks off killing hot reporters. Even if there's not an overt sexual component, that doesn't mean he's not at home jerking off as he watches this all on TV somewhere." He glanced at Shannon. "Sorry. I know you're Christian and everything."

Shannon said, "There's a call that came in through the hotline right along those lines," she said. "Maybe you want to follow it up."

He gave her a haughty look and went back to chewing on his pen.

SHE STARED at a wall in her office, feeling a headache coming on, feeling regret for how she'd behaved in Tyler's office. Sarcasm, insults – it wasn't her style.

On the wall: Baldacci story clippings, screenshots of Diaz in the field, Forbes on her talk show. Shannon built a database from victim employment records and felt a pulse of excitement when the first stories overlapped. Then there were more overlaps, and more, and more. A year was a long time. The average TV reporter covered two to three stories a week, and it was about the same for Baldacci's journalism. The excitement dwindled; it was too much overlap to be helpful.

At nine p.m., she went to the supply room and pulled out

some Aleve to work on her pains. By ten, the dosage had proved ineffective; her whole body ached. She headed back for more, then decided to give up for the day, took a cab home, and climbed into her bed. After a few minutes, Jasper leapt up beside her and found his spot by her feet. Sleep came fast and hard and dreamless.

W*hat's the matter with you?*
Josie entered her room looking at her phone. She locked the door behind her and flopped down on the bed on her stomach. A few seconds later, she dropped the phone on the floor.

It buzzed again. She hung her head off the edge of the bed and read the text on screen:

Are you coming out tonight?

She sighed. She rolled over and stared up at the ceiling. God. Why would she want to go anywhere? Especially if any of the people from her school were going to be there. She had to see them all school-year long as it was. Now during the summer?

It was because they were going to be seniors. The machinery was already starting up – exclusive parties for the seniors at Long Island City High, which were going to be all about bragging rights and looking down on the lower classmen. Parents knew about it, faculty knew about it – everyone thought it was cute. So long as it was inclusive of *all* seniors. Which it technically was, but practically was not. Not even close. You had to know where the good parties were, that was the thing. And it wasn't as if they were advertised on Instagram. No, you had to know somebody. Somebody who knew somebody, at least. And then – maybe.

For Josie, that somebody was Aaliyah. Aaliyah, who thought a good way to coax Josie out of her shell was to ask, *What's the matter with you?*

Real nice, Lee.

Anyone ever tell you that you catch more flies with honey?

But niceties didn't appeal to Aaliyah Joiner. Subtlety wasn't her style. And why should it be? She only wanted Josie along because she considered Josie less attractive. Josie was a "VA" – a value-adder. Which might or might not have been even true. Josie looked at herself in the mirror, presently, bared her teeth and looked at her curves from the side.

Or, where her curves would be, if she didn't have that extra layer. The nice layer she'd been adding over the past two years.

She let her stomach out, feeling like crap, and flopped onto the bed again.

She grabbed a pillow and moaned into it.

When was this going to go away?

She missed Charlotte like she never would have expected. Charlotte had been a real friend, and Josie had completely ruined it. To put it mildly. She'd ruined it to the point that maybe she ought to see a priest. Not that she believed in confession. But she needed something. Her parents were threatening therapy anyway. Her mother had said something to her father about Effexor. And her parents never talked.

She knew that Effexor was a drug for depression.

Because, yeah, she was depressed.

But she was smart, too, and knew that there were organic degenerative conditions in psychology – biological things you couldn't help. Chemical imbalances. And then, on the *other* hand, there were things that could cause a type of depression, a type of anxiety. Things like guilt.

Things like not dealing with your shit.

Things like walking around with a tremendous secret in your head. A secret you feel is like a bullet inside you, a poison working its way through your veins and into your organs, killing you.

Good times.

What's the matter with me, Aaliyah? I'm a horrible person, that's what.

And you *know it – you see it. Or suspect it, anyway. And then you exploit it – you know I'll do whatever you ask.*

But not tonight.

No. Not tonight. Maybe not even this weekend. Josie's mother was going out of town – maybe there was another way to spend her time besides trying to please Aaliyah Joiner.

Maybe she ought to please Charlotte Beecher. Maybe it was time to right a major wrong, to reset the scales. Time to come clean about everything – whether to a priest or a shrink or the public. Go online. That was how this whole thing started, anyway.

Josie stared up at the ceiling some more, hands folded across her belly.

Come clean, yeah.

Yeah, right.

The world would eat her alive.

13

FRIDAY

I n the morning, Caldoza called.

"Got two things for you," he said. "One – Jordan Baldacci was about to launch a sexual misconduct suit."

Shannon sat up in the bed, wiping her eyes. "Against whom?"

"Todd Spencer. He's another journalist. And it's not the first time it's been alleged that Spencer is too busy with his hands, but it's the first time he was getting taken to court."

"Interesting."

"Yeah. Interesting when you consider that it's all gone away now, with Baldacci's death."

"What's the other thing?"

"Raymond Tanzer. Former employee, WPXU. The TV station is called Ion and it's based out of Amityville. Guess where that is?"

"Long Island," she answered. "Huntington Township."

"Bingo." Caldoza sounded excited. "And guess what? Three weeks ago, Tanzer gets canned. And he has a fit. He rants and raves on his way out, carrying his box of personal effects. He goes on this diatribe about how TV isn't what it used to be, he's going on about the 'infotainment complex' and yada yada. This according to everyone we talked to down there."

She thought for a second. "How did you find out about it?"

"Heinz called around to all the area TV stations, big and small, looking for any signs of disgruntled employees."

"Smart," Shannon said, having perhaps misjudged Heinz as a bit of a ditz. Then, "My boss is going to love that one. What did he get fired for?"

"It's not crystal clear. Looks like he was just slacking off. But Heinz said there were rumors about drugs."

"Where's Tanzer now? When can we get him in?"

Caldoza paused. It sounded like he was chewing. "That's the thing. Tanzer is momentarily MIA."

Shannon swung her legs out of bed. "You really know how to get an FBI agent's day started, Detective Caldoza."

"Call me Luis." He paused, then asked, "What's your day looking like, Special Agent Ames?"

"I'm going into the city to talk to a council member," she said, ignoring his subtle bid to get them on a first-name basis.

"The story Baldacci was looking into?"

"Forbes, too."

"You want company?"

"I'm sure you've got a million things to do. Are you going to get Todd Spencer to come in and talk about his relationship to Baldacci?"

"I'm planning on it. I'll give you a shout."

"Thanks," she said. Then she added – because why not? – "I appreciate it, Luis."

SHE OPTED for the subway instead of driving into the city. The city hall area was so tight, the streets so narrow, it worried her to drive. But the subway turned out to be a nightmare – much of the red line was closed for repairs, and she ended up walking for several blocks.

It was another banner day, though: bright, unbroken blue sky. And the heat was holding off for the moment. She glanced up past the people walking and vehicles buzzing and beyond the buildings into that perfect azure.

Back home, the corn would be knee-high. Past it, by now. Her father would be out, side-dressing the crops – the corn, the soybeans, the popcorn crops – and managing weeds on the field borders. He'd have set up his fence row spraying rig and be driving along the outside rows of each field, applying herbicide. She could picture him bumping along as he rode the big rig.

And her brothers were likely hauling grain. You normally hauled the previous crop up until a couple of weeks before the next fall's harvest. Toward the end, when gravity wasn't pushing it out, you'd be in the silo, shoveling it out. You'd be checking for hot grain – meaning spoiled by moisture and mold – or bugs. It had been three years, yet she could picture her father and brothers working like she'd been home yesterday.

She could smell the dry, sweet grain, could hear the dogs barking and see their white shapes cutting through the high grass.

You never knew how good you had it. And wasn't that the damn truth.

New York City Hall was located in City Hall Park at the end of the Brooklyn Bridge. She could've just walked across the bridge and gotten here as fast. She went in from Chambers Street, up the wide steps toward the impressive four columns and three arched doorways of the entrance.

Paul Torres was one of the fifty-one council members who

primarily served as a check against the mayor. At the local level, the city council was to the city mayor what Congress was to the president. Council members approved the city budget, proposed and revised bills, monitored the performance of city agencies, and made land-use decisions.

Shannon put her gun and federal ID into a bin that was placed on a conveyor belt by a security guard. She stepped through the checkpoint, and another guard feathered a wand over her body, then waved her on. She collected her things.

Torres chaired the Zoning and Franchises Land Use Committee. In his late fifties, his public photo showed a man with thinning hair and a wide face, skin pockmarked from adolescent acne. His secretary had told Shannon he would be at city hall for most of the day, gone from his Bronx office. Shannon had obtained his cell phone number and called him, left a message. It was 9 a.m. – her proposed meeting time. Hopefully, the councilman had received the call and wouldn't stand up an FBI agent.

Then she saw him coming down the flowing stairs of the rotunda. She gazed up at the impressive dome ceiling, golden light pouring down, then smiled as Torres reached her and extended his hand. "Special Agent Ames?"

She shook hands with him – his palm was clammy – and said, "So nice to meet you, Councilman Torres. Thank you for seeing me."

"I only just got your message." His eyebrows twitched with concern. He was breathing heavy, wheezing a little with the extra weight he carried. "I tried you back but it went straight to voicemail."

"I was probably under the river, on my way here."

His eyes probed her. "Well, we have a few minutes before I have to get ready for session. Would you like to talk in the Chamber?"

"That would be great."

He smiled, though his eyes stayed serious, and headed back up the stairs. There were two stairways cascading down the round room to meet in the middle at the bottom. Like two waterfalls, she thought. "I've been here before," she said to the councilman's back as they climbed. "But I'm always impressed."

"It's such a beautiful building. Historic. Have you ever been down to see the original city hall subway stop? This is the birthplace of the New York City subway, you know. It's such a shame what we've been going through. Ever since Hurricane Sandy. Such a shame. Everyone is ready for this subway mess down here to get sorted out."

They reached the landing and she looked down into the circular room; Torres smiled politely at her and resumed walking. They passed more tourists taking images with their cell phones. Paintings adorned the walls – Revolutionaries in their white and blue uniforms, holding swords, straddling horses. Alexander Macomb. Oliver Hazard Perry.

"What are you meeting on today, Councilman Torres?"

He kept a pace ahead of her, his dark suit rustling as he walked. He smelled vaguely of mothballs. "Today is the Committee on Hospitals. We're meeting jointly with the Committee on Health."

"How many committees do you sit on?"

"Seven." He glanced over his shoulder. "And I chair two."

They entered the Chamber. Red carpet with white pointillism. Tall mahogany windows, blinds drawn. Gilded crown molding framing a white plaster ceiling; plaster carved into stars, eagles, scenes of civic virtue. The big painting was George Washington himself.

The balcony featured theater-style seats, most likely restored, but the main floor was populated by cheap-looking plastic folding chairs. They were alone except for two other people standing near the dais at the front. She checked her watch – it was now ten minutes past nine, and the meeting, according to the schedule she'd seen online, started at ten. Plenty of time. She looked at Torres. "Shall we sit?"

He cleared his throat and offered another smile – they seemed increasingly humorless. "Of course. Let's sit for a minute."

From the last row, she pulled a chair back and so did he, in order that they weren't side by side, bumping knees. She crossed her legs and got comfortable. Torres was looking everywhere but at her, as if seeing the place for the first time. Sometimes that happened, she thought, when you showed off otherwise familiar surroundings to an outsider – you found your appreciation renewed.

"Hard to believe the big restoration was almost a decade ago," Torres said.

"Have you been on the council that long?"

"I was. I began in 2007. But my time is up next year, I'm afraid."

Torres's gaze continued to wander. Shannon fell silent, thinking it would focus him. It did.

"I'm sorry," she said when he finally made eye contact, "this is right in the middle of your work. Last minute. Just a phone call and here I am. I do appreciate you taking the time, Councilman."

"Well, government has to work together. Right?"

"Wouldn't that be nice."

The next smile parted his lips. He was warming up to her. "What can I do for you, Special Agent Ames? You said in your message this relates to what's going on in Brooklyn?" He lowered his voice a notch. "This ... what they're calling the Media Killer?"

She was already nodding. "That's right. I'm wondering about two of the victims in particular. Jordan Baldacci and Monica Forbes – were you familiar with either of them, prior to this?"

His eyes stayed on her a moment, and then he glanced at the ceiling. "Hmm. Forbes. Okay. She had a show?"

"That's right, sir. *The Scene.*"

"I've seen that. Yes, I was familiar with her."

"And Baldacci wrote for *Newsday* and the *Gotham Gazette.*"

Torres did something with his lips, scrunching them up in a moue, which made him look like he was suppressing a fart. "Hmm, yes. I think she's familiar."

"Do you remember why?"

He grunted, as if clearing his throat. "She was writing a piece, I believe, about a property development in the Bronx. In my district."

Shannon nodded some more, feeling pricks of hot and cold breaking out over her skin. "That's right, that's what I understand. She was investigating the development of a new apartment building in the Bronx. The developer wanted to change the zoning to increase the number of units, which prompted the public review process. Is that correct?"

Another grunt. Torres glanced at the two other people in the room. "That's correct. I'm not sure, though, what the point is?"

"The public review process – that means hearings at the community board, the borough president, the city planning commission and you," she held out her hands toward him, "the city council."

"You're correct, yes." Getting annoyed now.

"But the council has the final say in whether the zoning is changed."

"Yes ..."

"And you're on the Land Use Committee, which has jurisdiction. So within the council, it's that committee."

"Correct ..."

"And you're the chair."

"Agent Ames? I'm sorry. I really need to prepare for this upcoming session. Is there something I can–?"

She rushed forward with it: "Baldacci's article alleges that the proposed apartment building, in Pelham Bay, ran up against some potential environmental concerns, since the park there is the largest park in New York City and is a habitat for a number of birds and animals. And Pelham Bay is, as I understand it, a middle-class residential neighborhood. The community was generally not in favor of this apartment building coming in. Nor did they favor the developer behind it, according to Baldacci's article, because he has ties to organized crime."

Torres had dropped all pretense of cordiality. While she spoke, his face had seemed to melt, his cheeks turning to darkened jowls, his eyes hardening to black points. He sniffed, then grunted, and said nothing for a long two seconds. Then, "Alleged ties to organized crime. In other words, gossip. But you're the FBI. Maybe you would know more than me."

"That's not my division," she said adroitly, having expected this. "I work violent crimes. And Jordan Baldacci is the victim of a violent crime, as is Monica Forbes. And according to Monica's husband, she was looking into this story, too, intending to cover it on *The Scene*. Only she never got a chance to, because she was murdered."

Torres stood up so fast the chair fell over. He picked it up and jammed it back into place. It drew the attention of the others in the room. At the same time, three new people, looking like council members, a man and two women, came in from the hall. One of the women made a concerned face. "Paul? Everything all right?"

"Everything's fine, Margaret."

Shannon stood up. "Hello. I'm Special Agent Ames, with the FBI." She shook with Margaret, who looked surprised, but then not, relaying looks between Shannon and Paul Torres.

Torres tried on a smile that didn't quite convince. "I'll finish this up and be over in just a minute."

Margaret glanced at Shannon again, then drifted deeper into the Chamber, taking the two other newcomers with her.

Having drawn the attention of the other council members, Shannon decided to ease back for now. She extracted a business card from her inner suit jacket pocket and held it out to him. "Mr. Torres, I thank you for your time. And again, I'm sorry to inconvenience–"

He cut her off when he stepped close, his whole face seeming to tremble as he spoke. "What about Diaz? Right? Wasn't there one of these murders two weeks ago? Was she making these allegations? Was she writing a story?"

"Diaz was a television reporter who covered mostly entertainment ..."

"I made a decision," Torres said. Little white curds were forming in the corners of his mouth. He was close enough that she could smell his breath – the egg and bacon he'd had for breakfast. "A decision in the interest of my district. We needed the housing. And I'm working with the park people, with the conservancy. We're going to protect the goddamn bird nests at the same time we're adding value to the neighborhood by adding that building. Everything was by the book; I didn't ram anything through. You want to check out the developer? You go ahead and–"

"I already did," Shannon said. "Please, Mr. Torres, step back."

He did, his lower lip and chin still wobbling, eyes glassy with adrenaline.

She said, "As I said, it's not my division, but I have access to everything on the developer. Nickolay Lebedev is the twenty-nine-year-old son of Victor Lebedev, who decamped the teetering Soviet Union some thirty years ago, came here, and made a fortune in gambling. Jordan Baldacci, without the resources I have, found that out for herself. And that both Nikolay and his father were known for leaning on people to get what they want. Baldacci questioned the manner in which the city council, in its wisdom, changed the zoning to allow for Nikolay Lebedev's Pelham Bay project."

"The manner?"

"*Hasty*, Councilman Torres."

"There was nothing that–"

"Jordan Baldacci questioned – she posed the question – was there intimidation? Was there coercion? And then she was murdered."

Torres shook his head and backed away. "I've seen everything on the news, read the articles – she was there at the scene of a crime. Anyone could have gone and opened that dumpster."

"No," Shannon said. "She was chosen. And we have the evidence to back that up." Shannon pushed her card at him. "Take it. Call me if you have anything you want to ..." She almost said *confess*. "If anything comes to mind. Anything you want to talk about. Day or night."

Torres stared at her. Finally, he snatched the card from her fingers, turned on his heel and strode away. He looked back at her only once he'd reached the safety of the other council members gathered in the center of the room, where they'd been furtively watching.

Shannon tipped them a smile and left.

14

Torres had a point about Diaz. And he was right. There was no record of the TV reporter covering property development in Torres's Bronx district.

"But maybe," Shannon said to Bufort, "there doesn't have to be."

They were in her office, Bufort eating a scone while he eyed the wall of notes, photographs, newspaper articles, and printed screenshots of TV news. Bufort brushed aside some of his blond bangs. "I think you've watched *Homeland* one too many times." He took a bite of the scone.

She explained: "There doesn't have to be a connection to Diaz if Nikolay Lebedev wanted it to camouflage his motives. If he wants it to look like something else, like hatred of the media. Consider how quick Diaz was, how Forbes took longer between abduction and death and discovery. Like she was questioned."

"No questioning of Baldacci."

"True. Or Diaz could've been killed by someone else, and Lebedev used *that* as the cover. NYPD was never quite able to clear Diaz's ex-boyfriend. He had a shaky alibi and a history of violence. So maybe Lebedev never touched her, but saw an opportunity in her death. Make the deaths of Forbes and Baldacci look like they were a part of something that ..."

Shannon trailed off, turning around to gaze at her wall, doubting her own theory.

Bufort voiced those same doubts: "But Forbes was only poking around in it. Baldacci wrote up a whole feature, questioning the motives of Torres, raising the question whether Nikolay Lebedev was a money-laundering Russian mobster. So Lebedev whacks Forbes? Leaks her dump site to the press in order to get Baldacci there and blow her up? If Lebedev is really connected, he doesn't have to do any of that." Bufort wiped his mouth with a napkin and said, "They whacked that guy last year, Lebedev's people. He was sitting at the McDonald's drive-through. One in his head and four in his chest. *That's* how they do it."

Bufort made sense, but it was too soon to let it go. More could come to light.

After Bufort left, she spent the next few hours getting additional background on Nikolay Lebedev and going through the Jordan Baldacci timeline. These crimes felt personal to Shannon. And while you typically saw that "personal" nature expressed in the type of victim – in this case, attractive female reporters – there was nevertheless something that felt perfunctory about their deaths. Almost clinical. Yes, two of the victims had been strangled. She tried to imagine the willpower it took to get behind someone, wrap a belt around their neck and squeeze. To maintain that pressure while they kicked and flailed, jerked and spasmed. She tried to imagine and couldn't. Because to carry through such an act typically meant you were born missing a key part of your brain. Or it meant you had experienced something so traumatic that it broke you. Changed you. Two of the victims had been strangled, but one had been lured into a trap and murdered in a violent explosion. That also took willpower, but of a different sort. It was a remarkably different MO – remote, technical, skilled. Suggesting – possibly – a killer with wartime experience, like S. Martinez had suggested. After all, humans did unspeakable thing to other humans in times of war.

Shannon tapped a pen against her thigh and consulted the wall some more. It was going on five o'clock in the afternoon. She stared up at an image of Jordan Baldacci she'd pulled from the internet. An absolute stunner, that Baldacci. A towheaded Italian woman with a voluptuous figure.

Beside her, Monica Forbes was also beautiful, but older, and dark-haired. If Baldacci was Marilyn Monroe, Forbes was Audrey Hepburn. And then there was Diaz, a Latina woman, a different look altogether. All three were attractive women, no question about it. But, then, TV people usually were. And Baldacci, not a TV person, but a journalist, could have just been incidentally beautiful. It happened! Pretty people *did* occupy other professions as well.

Shannon realized she was getting a bit punchy. She needed to eat; maybe that would help ground her. But she kept looking over the wall, not moving, letting her mind wander through it all.

If Lebedev had gotten so up close and personal (manual strangulation, bathing a victim) and so brutally violent (taking off a victim's head with a dumpster bomb) – it suggested more than "just business," but something personal. Which was what she was looking for. And the thing about young Nikolay, she'd learned – he was a hothead.

One of his properties was a Bronx nightclub. About eighteen months previous, a customer had ostensibly made a pass at one of the club bartenders, and Nikolay had beaten the guy so badly he'd put him in the hospital for a month. They'd settled out of court for $750,000, a big price to pay for having a bad temper, a misplaced sense of gallantry.

It was one reason she wasn't ready to let go of the lead. Guys like Lebedev, who acted so overprotective of women, were often also possessive of them, too. It was more about property, about ownership, than it was feminism or equality.

Yeah. The more she studied him, the more she could imagine Nikolay Lebedev so undone by Jordan Baldacci's reportage, so enraged that a woman would write such things about him and his planned apartment building – that the community didn't want it or him around, for one – he wanted her dead. And in a big way.

And then when he found out Forbes was looking into the same story, considering getting into it on *The Scene* and reaching even more people, that was the last straw. Lebedev concocted a way to get them both, and to make it look like something else.

The phone rang, startling her. "Ames."

"We got some rubber," Caldoza said.

"From Fifty-Fourth?"

"From Fifty-Fourth. Right outside the SuperShuttle lot."

"How much?"

"A bit. It's going for processing. I'll let you know if there's anything solid – obviously there's lots of trucks coming and going through there – but wanted to let you know."

"Nothing else? Foot impressions?"

"Not yet. I was hoping for a torn piece of paper that said 'I did it' with a name and address, but we're going to have to keep looking."

"Thank you, Luis."

"You eaten anything since yesterday morning? Besides hospital food?"

She thought back and realized she couldn't remember much beyond the nuclear-green Jell-O brought to her in the hospital bed. "I probably should."

"You like cold pizza?"

"I eat anything."

"A woman of discerning tastes. I like it. Well, we've got pizza down here at the station. And guess who's coming for dinner."

"You wrangled Todd Spencer?"

"Yes, ma'am. Roped him and tied him. He's on his way from the city, and he's going to be here in, like, an hour. Thought you'd want to get in on this."

"I do."

"I'm coming to get you. We'll swing by Fifty-Fourth and get back here in time."

She started to protest, but Caldoza had already hung up.

DOWNSTAIRS, he stood next to his car, a black Mustang.

"Oh, you're one of *those* cops," she said, giving it a closer look. She knew a little about cars from her brothers. The Mustang looked sixth generation. Boxy but sleek, with silver Hot Rod rims.

"Yeah, I guess so." A smile played at the corners of his mouth. The sun was getting low, but the day was still busy. Traffic rushed all around – Queens Boulevard, Jackie Robinson Parkway, Union Turnpike. The way it whooshed and swirled around the building in Kew Gardens could make you think the FBI satellite office there was the center of the world.

Caldoza's smile faded as he watched her walk. "How you doing?"

"The doctor said 'lateral abdominal wall hematoma collecting on the left side of the back and expanding inferiorly into the left gluteal region.'"

"Pure medical poetry," Caldoza said. He moved to the back of the car and pressed a button. The trunk lid swung slowly upward. Caldoza leaned in, his body blocking her view. He retrieved an item. "I got something for you."

For a moment, she was speechless, feeling both flattered

and uneasy. Then she took the cane from him and tested it for length. "Where did this come from?"

"My grandfather. Had shrapnel in his knee. Hated the cane, but he'd use it when no one was looking."

She looked up at him, still feeling those mixed feelings. This was incredibly thoughtful, but could cross a line. "Won't he miss it?"

"He's not vertical anymore. He's over in Rosebush Cemetery, been there for fifteen years. I got all his old stuff. Only grandson. I thought you could use it, and he'd want you to have it."

The cane had a curved wooden handle, well worn, atop the metal alloy rod. She leaned her weight on it and took a step, alleviating some of the pressure. Caldoza watched, looking pleased.

"Luis," she said, "I, ah ..."

His expression sobered, and he gave a slight shake of his head and raised his hand. "Hey, listen. I'm not, ah ... I had it, okay? I saw the way you've been gimping around."

She watched him for a moment, waiting for signs she'd wounded his pride, but either he was being on-the-level platonic or had an excellent poker face. "I'm sorry," she said. "I'm just ... you know?"

"Hey, say no more. I get it. Handsome guy like me, you don't want to give the wrong impression." He winked and opened the door for her.

Good grief, it still felt like a date. Caldoza went around to the driver's side as she got in.

He drove fast but not too fast, engine growling, and they reached the crime scene in less than ten minutes. He then slowed once they reached Fifty-Fourth. They jostled over potholes, past a barrier of corrugated metal sheets on the left, a sagging chain-link fence on the right. Then they were back in familiar territory – the SuperShuttle lot – the place she couldn't quite get at yesterday with all the press around. They were gone now.

Out of the Mustang, Caldoza lifted the crime scene tape and Shannon ducked underneath. She was using the cane and feeling awkward about that, but to be honest, it was better.

Numbers marked evidentiary spots on the road. Caldoza squatted near one and opened his hand. "Right here. Someone pulled out of the lot and hit the gas hard, left a little rubber behind. Crime scene got some with a gelatin lifter. They're trying different tires on paper, looking for pattern matches with what crossed the dirt there in the lot. But preliminary findings, it's from an SUV."

From the angle, Shannon couldn't see the bus. She didn't need to. She could see Monica Forbes clearly, lying on her stomach, head to the side, eyes open, lips parted, neck bruised.

Shannon touched her own face and neck. Caldoza slowly rose, watching her.

The lowering sun was now behind the Manhattan skyline. The light around Shannon left no shadow.

TODD SPENCER WORE his hair in the pompadour style, shaved on the sides, high and greased on top. A middle-aged hipster, with the eyeglasses to match; thick black frames on top, rimless bottoms. He looked bored, sitting across from Detective Heinz. Shannon watched through the one-way glass, Caldoza and Whitaker beside her.

"Okay," Heinz said, "Mr. Spencer, thank you for coming down."

"Mmhmm."

"We've, ah, we've asked you here today because, as you know, we had a situation Wednesday afternoon ..."

"You could say that, yeah."

Heinz, who seemed to Shannon the picture of unflappable, leaned back a little in his chair. "Would you call it something else, Mr. Spencer?"

"I mean, really? Fucking IEDs going off in the street? Blowing up reporters? It's a fucking attack on the fourth estate is what it is. It's some alt-right lunatic out there, someone who thinks Donald Trump was sent by baby Jesus."

Heinz nodded a little, as if this made sense, as if he'd given it his own serious consideration. "You aware, though, that Ms. Baldacci filed a lawsuit against you? For sexual harassment?"

"Am I aware?" Spencer glanced at the mirror, perhaps checking his own reflection, or thinking about the persons on its other side. "Of course I'm aware. But it's bullshit."

"It's bullshit," Heinz said, his head still bobbing up and down. "Unfounded."

Spencer smiled. He rocked back in his chair a little, then set it down hard on all four legs and jammed his finger at Heinz. "You're something. I mean, you ask me to come in. You say it's because you're 'getting a picture of Jordan Baldacci's life.'" He hung air quotes around the phrase. "You think I don't know? What it means that you're getting some background on me? Jesus Christ. *Yes,* there is a fucking lawsuit pending. *No,* I did nothing to warrant those allegations. Baldacci is ... well, I'm not going to speak poorly of someone who's passed on. Okay?"

"But she brought it on herself, or something? Is that what you were going to say?"

"Listen, I don't need this shit," Spencer said. He pushed the chair back, the legs making loud scrapes. He stood. "Let me out of here."

On her side of the glass, Whitaker leaned down and spoke in Shannon's ear. "Do me a favor?"

She looked up into his cool blue eyes.

"Get in there?" he asked.

Caldoza was watching.

Shannon said, "Why me?"

Whitaker looked her up and down. "Honestly, because he'll probably like you. Maybe he'll give something up."

Caldoza stepped in. "That's bullshit. Lieutenant, all due respect, that's sexist."

The two men stared at each other as Shannon left the room. She'd already decided for herself it was a good idea. She rounded the corner from the viewing room and knocked on the door. Heinz said, "Come in," and she opened it on Todd Spencer, his face twisted with anger. He saw her and his expression smoothed and he said, "Who are you?"

"Special Agent Shannon Ames. Can I talk to you before you go?"

He looked her over, then he stepped back and held out his arm, suddenly the cordial host. "Be my guest."

"Thank you," she said, and stepped in, but not far enough to let him close the door. She held out her own hand, offering Spencer a seat. His mouth hooked into a smug smile. She closed the door behind her as he sat, and then she walked toward the mirror and got a good look at herself. She licked her lips, knowing the two men were watching on the other side. Heinz stood up and moved to the door. Spencer never took his eyes off Shannon as she sat down.

They watched each other across the table. She could smell his cologne, something overly musky.

"So, Mr. Spencer, you're a journalist, like Jordan was."

"Yes ma'am." He quickly added, "Well, not *like* her ..."

"What do you mean?"

"Oh, I don't know. I don't want to be a ... you know. She just ... She worked very hard. I'm not sure she was writing to her strengths, though." The corner of his mouth went up again.

"How do you mean?"

He glanced at the ceiling and sighed. "You know, just, out of her field. Women's fare. Baldacci tried too hard. She tried to be something she wasn't, and I think it just came through in the work." He barked a laugh. "She wasn't an intellectual, but she tried to be."

"Do you feel you are, though? Writing to your strengths?"

He made a face she thought was meant to evoke humility. "Oh, well, it's not what I think, really, now is it? That's not how we're judged."

"And how are we judged?"

He made an exaggerated shrug and held his hands out, palms up. Then he waved at the air, a dismissive gesture. "Look – at the end of the day, what we do is, we report the news. And we try to get it to as many people as possible. Whether it's a little prettier or not in its presentation, who really cares, right? The point is to get it out, get it wide. Reach as many people as you can. I switched from running cameras to writing, and I've had a decent reach with my work. And I think that's because, yes, I've been writing to my strengths. Writing about the stuff that suits me. Someone like Jordan – and again, I don't mean to speak ill of the dead, I think she wrote what she *thought* she should be writing – still, that can hurt a writer. It really can. And when she came to me, and we talked about this, that's what I told her. Honestly, I don't think she liked hearing it. I don't think she could deal."

"You're referring to a dinner you attended with Baldacci. A little less than two months ago."

"Yeah. Right."

"The night she claims you offered to help her career if she slept with you. You'd put in a good word, you said, with an uncle of yours who works at the *Times*."

First the twitch of a smile, then he broke out in the full Flatbush cemetery, teeth ivory white and Chiclet big. "That's what she claims, yes."

"She also claims that, after she said no, a little later, in the back of the restaurant, you groped her while she waited to use the ladies' room."

The grin faltered just a bit, but Spencer persisted with it. "Crazy world we're living in today, isn't it? When people can just say whatever they want?"

"Well, we've lived in that world for a while now. Isn't that free speech, Mr. Spencer?"

He dropped the grin and stared at her. She glanced at Heinz, who lifted his eyebrows, as if to say, *I think you've made him mad.* It was true she'd quickly shifted from charming Spencer to baiting him, but it was deliberate. She sought his pressure points. What would his reactions reveal?

"You know what I mean," Spencer said. "I understand all about the court of public opinion. But that's not a function of what I do. That's what *people* do – they make up their minds before due process. Like you, sitting there right now, judging me. What I said a couple of minutes ago – it's other people who make the judgments."

"Mr. Spencer, like you – a journalist with integrity – I traffic in facts. Things I can prove."

"Traffic. That's a good line. You should be a writer."

"And what the facts are here is that Jordan Baldacci filed in civil court just days before she died in the explosion. That's number one."

Spencer leaned forward in one quick motion and stabbed the table with his finger. "You think I rigged some fucking explosives because of a sexual harassment case? Boy, where did they pull you from, huh? Some corn-fed town in the Midwest?"

From behind him, Heinz said, "That's enough."

Spencer ignored Heinz, but he sat back, simmering, still clocking her.

"Fact number two," Shannon said, "is that you also knew Eva Diaz." She took the photos she'd been holding onto and tossed them onto the table. "You worked at WCBS-TV until a little less than a year ago. As a cameraman. And while Eva Diaz never filed a lawsuit, she did lodge a complaint."

The room went silent, the air heavy; Spencer breathed with a mean energy.

Shannon said, "And finally, fact number three – you have no alibi for Wednesday afternoon."

"I was home writing."

"Yes, that's what you told Detective Heinz."

"Check my laptop. I was online. Look at my searches. Time stamps." There was a bead of sweat running down his temple.

"That would be very helpful," Shannon said. "But, of course, anyone could have been on your–"

"So look for fingerprints. I didn't do this shit, bitch."

"Hey," Heinz said, stepping forward.

Spencer spun around on him. "Go ahead, motherfucker, and touch me. Go ahead. I'll sue the shit out of you and this whole piss-stained facility. Come on. Put your hands on me. Do it in front of the federal fucking agent, why don't you."

Two such wonderful personalities, Shannon thought, Torres and Spencer, and in just one day.

THE THING WAS, being a sexist pig and a prick weren't charge-able offenses. And while Todd Spencer didn't have an alibi for Baldacci, his daughter could attest to his whereabouts when Eva Diaz was abducted. Spencer was divorced and shared custody with his ex. Spencer had been with his daughter during the hours of Eva Diaz's estimated time of death.

"A daughter," Caldoza said after Spencer was gone. He slumped against the wall in the viewing room. "How does a guy like that have a daughter? What's wrong with the world?"

Shannon had just finished a phone call. Tyler had wanted to fill her in. He also had given her a fresh assignment: "These people, these media people, they have their annual awards thing tomorrow night. Put together by an organization called the Crunchtime Club. It's in Manhattan at the Harvard Building. I spoke to the AD at the field office, and he's in agreement – we'd like you to go. NYPD is going to be there, bomb-sniffing dogs, extra security – the whole nine yards. Getting a lot of pressure on this. Two days, and we have no solid answers and people are starting to panic. You go, you put on a nice outfit. You know, smile at some people and assure them the FBI are on it."

It was a mouthful, but she'd gotten the picture: go to the journalism awards dinner and make people feel comfortable. Make them feel heard.

"Yes, sir," she'd said.

Caldoza was still stewing about Spencer, and when Shannon shared her supervisor's request with the detectives in the room, Caldoza widened his eyes and jerked a thumb at the window on the now-empty interview room. "He's gonna be there, you know. This Spencer guy is going to be there at this awards thing. He's a presenter."

"Good," Shannon said. "I was hoping I'd get to see him again. Be around him. There's something about him that kind of grows on you."

Caldoza just gaped at her until the humor penetrated. Heinz waggled his eyebrows and Whitaker headed for the door, saying, "All right. Looks like we're all going to the newspaper-fucking-Oscars, or whatever it is."

15

I t was an excuse to dress up.

Since she'd been living in the city, Shannon had gotten fancy only one other time, and that had been to celebrate her own graduation and subsequent induction into the New York City division of the FBI. A friend from back home, plus one from college, together with Shannon, had painted the town red. Which for her meant four drinks instead of two, and staying up all the way past one o'clock in the morning. Life in the fast lane.

She still had the outfit, a black number called a Cold Shoulder Little Cocktail Party Skater Dress. The name was long, but maybe the dress was too short. She showed it off in front of the mirror in her bedroom. The hem was above her knees. It hadn't bothered her to celebrate with friends in it, but representing the FBI at a public event?

But that wasn't really what bothered her, or why she covered up with a black sweater. Bandages and burns didn't complement a skimpy dress too well. At least the marks on her face and neck were fading, and the makeup took care of the rest.

If Tyler wanted her there looking good, then this was what he got.

~

CALDOZA PICKED HER UP, eyes bugging out. "And with the cane," he said, holding the door for her, "you're killing me. I'll never think of my grandfather the same way again."

They made small talk as they drove out of Brooklyn. As they crossed the Williamsburg Bridge into a thousand sparkling lights, the conversation drifted to serial killers.

Caldoza said, "I always thought these guys kept trophies from their criminal acts. Or at least some way to relive, replay things. Dahmer with his freezer of body parts."

She watched the people thronging the streets as Caldoza drove them north through Manhattan. "Bundy didn't, and he was one of our most prolific."

"Why'd he do it?"

"Bundy? Because he was evil."

Caldoza jerked his head back, glancing at her as he drove. "Wow. Didn't expect that."

"Why?"

"I don't know. You don't seem like the type. What did you, ah, go to school for?"

"I double-majored in psychology and sociology. Got my master's in mental health counseling and worked as a psychiatric social worker for three years at a county clinic."

"Did you evaluate violent offenders in jail?"

"I did. Sometimes."

"I got a cousin who does that. Same type of thing."

Shannon said, "Environmental factors can switch genes on and off – abusive homes, trauma – there's that. Some killers have chemical imbalances. They might have tumors. So there's reason for compassion. There's reason to say, it's not the perpetrator who's evil, it's the act. I've spent years looking at all of that."

Caldoza looked at her again. "But?"

"I'm okay calling it evil, too. Because if there was evil, why wouldn't it use these things to get the job done? The fact is, I don't know. I'm not going to know. But a little shorthand can help get the job done. And that's what I'm here to do – get it done."

"Ah shit," he said.

"What?"

"I just realized you're smarter than I am."

"Stop it."

"It won't be a problem. I can handle it." He grinned and darted a playful look at her.

"My point is that you have to have some principles. Some things that are hard ground under you. And I understand – trust me – you've got to check your assumptions from time to time. But you can't be a couch."

"A couch?"

"A couch just bears the impression of the last person who sat on it."

Caldoza was silent a moment, pondering, then broke into a raucous laugh. He gave her another look when it passed. "This is the most I've heard you talk all week."

A FEW MINUTES LATER, her eyes devoured the scene: a red carpet and sweeping skylights, their beams sliding over the steel and glass of surrounding buildings.

Midtown Manhattan. Times Square was a block away. They were surrounded by it all: Rockefeller Center, Radio City Music Hall, Grand Central Terminal. Limousines were dropping people off. Valets were handling the rest, parking the cars as far away as Bryant Park. It felt more like the opening of a new dance club than an awards night for journalists. She'd been expecting something a bit drier – not quite conference tables and PowerPoint presentations, but more in that direction. And there was a strong police presence. Like Tyler said, extra security. Guys in black suits, white cords curling out of their ears. Most of them older, like ex-cops. A K9 unit was posted at the entrance, bomb-sniffer dogs getting a whiff of every guest coming through, in case any of them had C-4 in her purse.

Shannon showed her ID to security and was waved through. A coat-check room, a small lounge, a larger bar. The crowd was currently three persons deep.

"There's our boy," Caldoza said, in her ear. "Two o'clock. In the double-breasted suit."

"I see him," Shannon said. She'd spotted Spencer half a minute before Caldoza had pointed him out. Spencer looked over, as if sensing their thoughts. He met her eyes and smiled in that smug way he had. Shannon said to Caldoza, "I'm going to go say hi."

"Good luck. Tell him I'm pulling for him."

"Thanks. Yeah, will do."

"I'm serious. One look at you and he's done for. Putty in your hands. He'll confess everything."

She flashed Caldoza a smile and then made her way through the throng of people until she was next to Spencer. "I didn't know journalists were such rock stars," she said.

Spencer gobbled her up with his eyes. "Oh yeah," he said. "We all have huge egos." She could see him calculating. Wondering where he stood after his antics the day before. Wondering, perhaps, what else he could get away with. "What are you drinking? Or are you on duty?"

"I'll have whatever you suggest," she said, giving him a long blink and another smoldering smile. Not quite her best one –

she was withholding that for later – but her third best. It was enough to blow away the skepticism he showed in his face.

"Vodka tonic," he said. "All I ever drink."

"Sounds good." She looked around, as if already bored. Setting the hook deeper.

Spencer said, "You really off duty?"

"Put it this way," she said, gazing at the people around them, all the mahogany and candle-colored lighting sconces. "I'm here to be a presence. Like you said last night, this is an attack on the fourth estate, an attack against free speech. And so it's the opening salvo in an attack on our republic, as far as I'm concerned." She met his eyes and said, "The FBI doesn't tolerate that kind of shit."

"No? Didn't Thomas Jefferson say something about the tree of liberty and the blood of patriots?"

"He wasn't talking about cowards killing women."

For the first time, Spencer's bravado flickered. He glanced down. "I got a little upset last night ..."

"I know," she said.

He started to say more, but noticed an opening and moved in on the bartender. He leaned close and shouted his order over the music. He didn't look at her while he waited for the drinks. She spotted Caldoza talking to Heinz, who was dressed a little more casually in jeans, a white button-down and a dinner jacket. Tyler would be around somewhere, too. Tyler would want to introduce her to people. People he thought were important and needed to be both assured and impressed by such an attentive law enforcement presence.

Was she already getting cynical?

Spencer pushed a drink in her hands. He moved the red straw aside in his own glass and took a swallow. They moved away from the bar, to more open space near a grouping of high round tables. She caught Caldoza's eyes as she went.

She asked Spencer how he'd gotten into TV and journalism, and he started talking. The awards show officially started at nine, and it wasn't yet eight fifteen, so there was time for him to rattle on. He told her how he'd started out his career not knowing where he fit in. How he'd worked as a cameraman for a time. Then Spencer said abruptly, "I know why you're here."

"Oh yeah?" Trying to be coy.

"I'm a suspect, I get that."

She took a sip of her drink. *Help me*, she thought, *only someone like Todd Spencer would actually say things like that.*

"You're amazingly beautiful," he said with a put-on smile. "But it takes a lot more than a little batting of your eyes and having a drink with me. I mean, you're pretty obvious."

"You know two of the victims," Shannon said, setting her drink on the table. "And you have a lawsuit pending with–"

"I know all *three* of the victims," Spencer said. He leaned closer to Shannon, getting in her face. "I worked with Monica Forbes a bunch of times when she was a producer. And I've had Diaz on camera. I've had Forbes on camera – just for focus and white balancing, but whatever." He gave her a big wink, and his trendy glasses flashed in the lights. "So? How do you like me now, Agent Ames? Am I a major suspect because I've spent time with all of the victims? Let me tell you, this is a small world. Everybody knows everybody in this business. We bump into each other while working, or at things like this. So just relax. Enjoy yourself."

Something brushed the back of her dress. A split second later, she had his hand in hers. She used a little move where she dug the sharp knuckle of her middle finger into the pressure point on the outside of his thumb.

"Ah!" He jerked his hand back and started rubbing it. "Jesus," he said, his eyes bright with surprise and anger.

"It can get worse," she said. "Touch me again."

She was impressed he maintained his calm. But then, maybe he didn't want to draw any more attention. She spied two women at the nearest table who seemed to have noticed things, and if anything, they looked ready to cheer her on.

She picked up her drink and downed the rest of it, keeping her eyes locked on Spencer's. He knew all three victims, small world or not. He'd made a move on her, an FBI agent considering his potential guilt in a serial killing case. Maybe it was only meant to piss her off, or make her feel cheap. Maybe it was a cry for help. A narcissistic prick who couldn't stop himself and his terrible impulses. Touching women, harassing them, threatening them, strangling them.

The music continued to thump, and the din of voices grew louder as more people arrived, as more alcohol loosened inhibitions and raised volumes. Spencer moved close enough for her to hear him; he spoke in a voice just above a whisper. "Fuck you," he said. "You fuckin' farm girl."

She stepped away from him, found his eyes – smug bastard eyes if there ever was a pair – and nodded once at him. "I'll be seeing you again, I'm sure," she said. Then she left the table and submerged into the crowd.

16

"He's *what*?"

"He's the emcee," Caldoza said.

She'd just given Caldoza a quick version of Spencer's loathsome behavior, and now they were in the next room, the massive dining room with its high ceiling and enormous chandelier, thirty tables, two giant projection screens. Everything glittered and clinked and smelled of garlic and red wine. She and Caldoza sat at a table on the end of one of three rows. "He's the host for the whole night," Caldoza said. "The piece of shit."

The music lowered and a voice said over the system that there was ten minutes left before the start of the evening; would people start making their way to their seats? Shannon watched a few guests begin to drift from the bar in the next room, but the music and din of voices from the bar were still going strong.

While waiting, she found herself entertaining a scenario in which Todd Spencer was friendly with Paul Torres: Torres wants to shut down negative news coverage of the development deal in Pelham Bay. Maybe he's getting pressure from Nikolay

Lebedev. So he turns to Spencer, a friend from the media. Spencer has names, phone numbers, addresses ...

Or maybe Spencer was just a psychopath who belittled women, who verbally and physically abused them. Diaz and Forbes had been cleaned – there might've been a sexual component to the crimes after all. Diaz and Forbes – he performs some sick act on them, then washes it away. He strangles them. But with Baldacci, because she would see him coming, he had to do it another way. Or maybe he did it that way because it was extra violent. How dare she file a lawsuit against him? He would show her who was boss ...

Shannon looked down at her bare legs, seeing the goosebumps. It was cool in here, for one thing. But drawing out the poison in Spencer had worked faster than she'd anticipated, and had left her slightly shaken. Not with fear, or the humiliation Spencer had intended, but with anticipation. He was really fitting into the role of prime suspect.

"I can see him doing it," Caldoza said. The detective's gaze roamed the room, more people trickling in, bringing their drinks and conversations with them. People from *The New York Times*, VICE, BuzzFeed, the Associated Press, Reuters, ProPublica. *Newsday*, where Baldacci had worked. "I can see him cleaning them."

She thought she could, too.

She tried to settle in and looked over the list of awards. There were more than thirty. Everything from *Newspaper or Digital Beat Reporting* to *Opinion Writing* to *Spot News Photo* and *Local Television Spot News Reporting*. The gamut was covered. She'd never seen so many newspeople in one place. She recognized several faces from TV, and more from the investigation. People who had worked with Monica Forbes. A photographer whose images often accompanied Baldacci's reporting. No one associated with Diaz, though.

Mark Tyler joined them. He had his wife with him. A pretty

redhead in her late forties, she looked stiff and unhappy to be there. Heinz emerged from the bar with a Heineken. Caldoza made a remark about it: Heinz drinks Heineken.

Waitstaff came around and took orders. There were three to choose from: steak with roasted red potatoes and asparagus, salmon with lemon rice and broccoli, or vegetarian lasagna. Each came with a salad and bread. Just as they finished ordering, applause rippled through the room. Todd Spencer picked his way through the round tables. He reached a podium between the two giant screens. From here, he looked like a handsome, hip, thirtysomething journalist.

Scumbag.

"Good evening," he said. The sound levels were good, the acoustics were good. The audience, mostly black tie and gowns, a few rebels like Heinz in more casual wear, were hushed. Spencer said, "Thank you for being here tonight, at the Forty-Eighth Annual Crunchtime Club Awards Dinner!"

The crowd erupted into more raucous applause and cheers. Spencer grinned wide and launched into a spiel about how great it was to be hosted by the Harvard Society. He went into the history of the Crunchtime Club – founded sixty years prior, back when "New York City had twenty daily papers, three wire services, eight radio stations – and no TV stations."

The audience rippled with laughter. Flashes of bright white smiles. Heads leaning together, nods, more laughter. Ah, the good old days before TV.

"Back then," Spencer continued, "new members were inducted in a special ceremony. Black robes and lighted alcohol lamps. The initiation ritual included dedicating one's self to the pursuit of truth. 'He who serves truth serves best' – that's the motto."

The applause began and grew sharply and loudly, and people got out of their seats. Clapping vigorously. Whistling. Nodding to Spencer, nodding to each other. When it gradually died down, Spencer said, "And we have always been forward-thinking. Though both the national and local organizations accepted only male journalists as members for the first seven years, that rule was abolished in 1967–" It was hard to hear him over the fresh eruption of cheers and applause, until Shannon could make out the words, "–was a broadcasting pioneer and we saw the first woman sworn in as a Crunchtime Club member."

Ugh, she thought.

Spencer let the applause subside before continuing. "In those early critical years, we met in the old Times tower. Later, we met in various newsrooms and venues around the city. New York University, Columbia University ..."

Caldoza looked at his watch. Then he found Shannon's eyes. "Can we arrest him now?"

Tyler overheard, and Shannon explained that Caldoza wasn't being literal. In her mind, she was thinking of a saying her father used: "It's not set in stone, but we're carrying bags of mortar."

Spencer said to the room, "Each summer for the past forty-eight years, the club has honored excellence in New York journalism at this, our annual awards dinner."

More applause. Would they ever get through it alive?

"What I'd like to do now," Spencer said, "is take a look back at last year's winners."

He stepped away from the podium and watched the screen on his right-hand side. A waiter set out salads at Shannon's table as the lights went down and the screens flickered. Shannon watched Spencer – he sat at a nearby table. The room grew still and quiet, properly reverential.

Someone screamed.

Shannon looked up from her salad. Dominating the two screens was a familiar face, tearful and bruised. She was dressed in a dirty sheet and tied to a medical gurney, propped upright.

She was the woman Shannon had found dead beneath a bus.

On screen, Monica Forbes, in a trembling but strong voice, said, "Hello. I have a message to deliver to you tonight. A message to deliver to the country."

Shannon was on her feet. Caldoza was up, too. Tyler pushed his chair back and stood, saying, "Shit. What is this?"

Nobody moved. They'd had discussions about how they would respond to another event – an explosion like the one in Hunters Point – but this was a video.

What did it mean?

Monica Forbes said, "For too long, the media has gone unaccountable. We have never had to apologize for the fear we sell. Never apologized for the way in which we influence elections and trials and congressional investigations. The way we spread fear, generate outrage, and disseminate disinformation."

Shannon's mind worked fast: this had happened between Monica's abduction and her murder, a longer period of time than with Diaz. The killer had put a camera on her, attached a small microphone – even the lighting looked good.

Shannon started moving through the room. Everyone else was riveted. Somehow he'd hacked in to the system? Or – he was here, and he'd put a damn DVD into the player feeding the two screens?

Someone shouted, "Shut it off! Shut it off!" But Monica's voice continued to boom through the room.

"As many of you no doubt know, network news was once a loss leader. But once corporations started buying those networks, the news needed to become profitable. So you focused on violence. You focused on fear. You focused on political scandal. It's not a problem that you divide people with your partisan coverage, it's the point – the division is good for ratings."

Shannon found a door at the back, which led to a small control room. The second she opened it, a young man wearing black, looking panicked, was coming down the stairs so fast he nearly plowed into her. "How is this up there?" Shannon asked. Others had gathered behind her – Caldoza, and two of the evening's organizers, a man and a woman. "We need that shut down *now*," the man growled.

The young tech spread his hands. "I didn't do it."

Shannon asked, "Is it a DVD? A flash drive?"

He was stuttering, nervous. "Laptop. PowerPoint. Video is embedded. Someone changed the video."

The organizer crowded in. "Well, shut it off!" he growled.

The tech looked scared. "The door is locked. My key is gone."

"What?"

"Someone took my key ..."

Shannon put it together: the tech was terrified because whoever had altered the presentation to play the Monica video was among them. Here, at the dinner.

Spencer? Maybe, but he'd been on stage. Working with someone else, then?

She quickly scanned the faces of the people beside her. Everything was new, like she'd stepped through an invisible door and into this parallel universe where everyone was a suspect. "Relax," she whispered – to herself as much as the people surrounding her. "We don't want a panic ..."

And to Caldoza, the faintest whisper: "We need to get to Spencer right ... now ..."

On screen, Monica Forbes continued, speaking through tears, her face streaked and haunted: "You've become sloppy, breaking a story before it's confirmed. Others then reference the first story as fact, leading the public on wild-goose chases.

Yet you take no responsibility. You shape civil discourse in this country, you influence policy, you shape culture – you shape *lives*. You barely even understand the consequences of this. Instead, you celebrate. You behave like celebrities in a gross display of narcissism. If you won't hold yourself to account, the people will. This is a reckoning. This is the beginning of your atonement. This is ..."

Monica Forbes stopped talking and looked off camera, fully crying. "I can't," she said. "I won't say that ..."

Shannon moved closer to the screen. People were mumbling, some were crying. "Quiet!" Shannon called. She strained to hear – Monica's captor might say something, give her a vital piece of information about who he was, where they'd been, a clue as to where he might even be at this very moment.

But the only information came through Monica's eyes, shining with fear.

She swallowed, pulled herself together, and finished.

"Ladies and Gentlemen, there is a bomb in this building rigged to detonate in sixty seconds."

Cutting her off in mid-sob after she'd delivered this news, the video ended. The screen went black, plunging the room into darkness and screaming chaos.

YOU COULDN'T BLAME people in a panic. Couldn't expect them to behave rationally. The amygdala took over, the struggle for survival. They became, in a way, the animals they once were. That people slammed into her, Shannon expected. That they screamed and trampled and clawed their way out of the building was normal. What surprised her was the deep sense of calm she felt, as if it had all happened before.

Maybe it had. Maybe getting locked in the silo that one

summer as the corn came pouring in, that experience had burned the panic right out of her. Nothing could ever compare to a drowning cascade of grain, a waterfall of hard pellets, dust quickly choking your lungs, stinging your eyes, so that the death portended was blind and deaf and suffocating.

All with that dry, semi-sweet stink of corn, an odor she hadn't been able to stop smelling for weeks afterward.

"Shannon!"

She saw Caldoza in the dark. He used a flashlight as he cut across a river of fleeing people. She checked her watch: twenty seconds were gone.

She looked into Caldoza's eyes. He said, "I can't find Spencer. We need to get out."

She nodded at him and followed as he led them into the crush of people headed for the main exit. But at the last second, she peeled off and moved into the emptied lounge, needing a quick moment to think. Caldoza didn't see her go.

Flickering candles lit the copper-topped surface of the bar, just enough light to see by. Would the Media Killer detonate a bomb here? He'd been specific up to this point, seeming to target individual members of the press. There had been little to no collateral damage. Unless you counted an FBI agent. Damage to her face, her arms ...

Think ...

She went behind the bar and had a hasty look. Spencer had been in this room when she'd arrived. Had he stuck an explosive somewhere nearby? Then a light grabbed her. "Ma'am, need you to get out of there, now! There's a bomb in the building."

She left the bar and approached the security guard. "I'm FBI."

"I don't care if you're the French Foreign Legion. I'm evacuating this building."

It was inevitable. He took her arm and she let him draw her

out of the room. She joined the river of people still moving toward the exit, checked her watch: forty seconds had passed since the lights went out. She could see the exit up ahead. Someone screamed. Fresh panic rippled through the escaping group, changing the direction of their movement; people were avoiding something up ahead. The security guard surged past her, and Shannon got behind him, drafting him. More screams as people discovered whatever it was in their path that alarmed them.

By the coat-check area, Shannon saw it: a man on the ground, his feet slightly kicking. Then she saw the blood. It bloomed out from beneath him in a widening pool. She held her breath. She knew the face, knew the clothing, knew the man.

Todd Spencer made gurgling, choking sounds as the ragged slash in his neck spit out more blood. He had his hands around his throat. His wide, terrified eyes jerked in their sockets until they fixed on her.

Shannon dropped to her knees. "Ambulance, now!" She put her hands on Spencer's throat and was instantly covered in his blood. The security guard who'd yanked her from the lounge stood by, his face blank with shock. Others who'd stopped to look kept a distance. Most kept moving outside. Only fifteen seconds were left before they were all blown sky-high, maybe ten. "Help me!" Shannon yelled. She got around behind Todd Spencer and took his shoulders, tried to lift him, drag him. A man in a tuxedo joined her and grabbed one of Spencer's legs, the security guard took another.

The security guard was yelling, "Move! Move, people! Move!"

Five seconds left. No more.

The air hit her, hot and thick and smelling like New York City summers. They moved down the steps of the building and into the street and kept going.

Two seconds left.

They reached the other side of the street. People were everywhere. Others had joined in to help with Spencer. Shannon barely had something to hold onto now. Her eyes stung with tears.

But still calm.

One second.

Up onto the sidewalk, moving ever farther away. Figures all around, getting away, running or walking fast. A man in a wheelchair, people running him right down the middle of the street.

And then things slowed a bit, and they reached the end of the block. Her hands and arms were covered in blood. Some of it had smeared across her bare legs. She said, "Okay," to the people holding Spencer. "That's good. That's enough. Let's put him down. Let's set him down."

Her back was to Sixth Avenue whooshing with noise and traffic. They had this little bit of quiet on Forty-Fourth Street, this light from the Chase Bank on the corner, and the group of them lowered Todd Spencer to the ground. His eyes remained open, the blood still leaking from his gashed neck, but slowing. His hands formed claws at his chest, his face a frozen grimace of pain and surprise. There was no breath.

Todd Spencer was dead.

Shannon looked back down toward the building with its neo-Georgian façade of brick and classical columns. The building still stood unmolested. No smoke roiling out. No bomb. Nothing.

Shannon located Caldoza on the street in front. He gaped at her, rushed toward her.

"It's not mine," she said about the blood. She pointed down the street. "Someone got to Spencer. Opened his neck." She swallowed over the lump in her throat and said, "He was here, Luis. If Spencer wasn't ... Luis, our guy was just here."

Caldoza put an arm around her, but she pulled away and started pacing.

When Tyler found them, Shannon insisted on going back in. He shook his head, adamant. "Not until the bomb squad clears it."

ONLY SECONDS LATER, the sirens wailed. The fire department, emergency services, local NYPD, and NYPD Bomb Squad. Within minutes after that, the lights were back on inside – the blackout had been nothing more than a flipped breaker. Shannon sat on the curb, cleaning herself with antiseptic wipes, going over it and over it in her mind: the killer had been there with them all along.

Not Spencer, no – but one of them. Someone from the group of journalists and TV people who'd been attending the gala dinner. Someone who was taking aim at the whole system.

She crumpled up a wipe covered in Spencer's blood and threw it in the trash on the street as she watched Tyler, farther down the block with Bufort and other FBI.

She knew where Tyler would take this now.

17

SUNDAY, EARLY MORNING

Hours spent at the scene, then a hasty trip home to
shower and change and eat, then back to the scene
in the predawn. New York never slept, but it did
slow, just a little, for the ditch hours of three and four a.m.

Shannon sipped a coffee and waited until the NYPD cop got
the word to let her in, and then she went through the doors
she'd entered almost eight hours earlier. It seemed like a lot
longer – a week ago, maybe.

Tyler and Bufort were set up in the library with three other
agents she didn't recognize. Tyler made quick introductions,
explaining to the other agents that she was an agent on her
probationary period, whom he'd asked to monitor the Monica
Forbes missing person case.

"We're working with Midtown Precinct South to get statements from every single person who was here last night," he
told Shannon. "*Someone* who was here last night got into the
system, swapped the video, and killed the lights."

"Do we still have it?"

Tyler glanced at the other faces in the room, then his gaze

came back to her. "The video? Yes, we do. It's not going anywhere."

Bufort stepped closer. "But we've got a situation. Someone who was in the crowd got it all on their phone and already uploaded it. It's incomplete, starts a couple of seconds after the disruption began, but it's out."

Tyler said, "We're getting to that source and we're going to shut it down. In the meantime, we had over three hundred people here last night. In an hour, we're going to start the interviews." He started to turn away.

"With whom?"

Tyler squared his shoulders. "People on our list. Agent Ames, this is an act of terrorism, and we're treating it as such. Every single employee and contractor and person involved with producing this event is being questioned. I don't care if it's a waiter or janitor. But we have certain individuals who are going to get a little more attention."

She looked between Tyler and Bufort, puzzling it out. Did he mean someone connected to hate groups, or some kind of disruptor organization? It was hard to imagine someone like that embedded in the group of journalists and TV people here last night. Foreign terrorism, then, with one or more sleepers in the Crunchtime Club? But she didn't ask. She could see it in Mark Tyler's eyes: terrible as this all was, this was the kind of national attention he wanted, a case that was going to put him in the books. Get him that promotion.

Tyler said, "I need you working with local PD, obtaining the statements, conducting the interviews. Okay?"

"Yes, sir."

His attention left her again, and she asked, "Sir?"

He turned back. "We'll get to the rest of it, Agent Ames. I know what you're thinking. Right now, I want those statements while people are fresh."

"Yes, sir."

IT TOOK MOST of the day. Using every agent and officer available, the FBI and NYPD recalled 298 people from the previous evening's activities. Most were happy to report on what they'd seen and heard and felt. Some were angry – hungover, perhaps – to have to relive the harrowing event. Several cried as they remembered. The few who knew Monica Forbes personally were flagged. Many were already working on reportage of the evening, preparing articles and evening news stories. And some invitees hadn't attended the event.

At 3 p.m., the dusty window high in the cramped NYPD interview room blazed with light. An air-conditioning unit made lots of noise, but put out little coolness. Shannon took a break, checked her phone, scrolled through Twitter. News of the event was everywhere, but links went to a "content no longer available" page. Tyler had gotten the video taken down. She was glad that a victim's terrible suffering wasn't on display for the world to see, that a terrorist – of sorts – wouldn't get that gratification. Like Caldoza had suggested, it was a trophy from his criminal act. But she also wondered about the public's right to know.

It was a sticky subject.

Her phone buzzed. "I was just thinking about you," she said to Caldoza, then winced. *The heck are you saying?*

The smile came through in his voice. "Oh yeah?"

"Thinking about this video getting taken down. What that might mean to our unknown subject."

He seemed to sober. "Ah. Yeah." Caldoza paused. "I mean, you gotta think he would've expected it. Seems like a smart guy."

"Are you back in Brooklyn?" she asked.

"Been here all day. Just drowning in paperwork. Thought I'd check in on you. You're taking statements? Where do they got you?"

"A precinct on the West Side. But what I want is to be looking at that video."

"Your supervisor – Tyler – he's sent around a call for a meeting at your resident agency tonight at six. You going to be there?"

She hadn't been notified. "I think so." *Tyler has sidelined me for some reason.* She could've said it to Caldoza, gotten a sympathetic ear, but she'd be undermining her boss. A boss was a boss. What she said was, "I've been thinking about the first victim. Diaz."

"Yeah?"

"It's just ... everything they taught me in school was how an offender's first crime tends to be the most revealing. You focus on that first crime, because that's where he makes the mistakes he later learns from. That's where he does what's easiest and most comfortable. The crime is close to his home or his job. And he's rough, underdeveloped."

"So what does the Diaz murder tell you?"

"Well, it could tell us a lot if this was a typical series of crimes. If this was the same MO, if this was the same type of victim. But the victimology here is that these people all work in the same field. So that's a different direction. And his methods are changing. Strangulation, IED, then a box cutter? That's not perfecting technique as he goes through victims."

"He's sort of just getting the job done," Caldoza theorized with her. "Doing whatever it takes. Being practical."

"Right, but also, everything he does seems to have purpose. I mean, to do Diaz like that, then two weeks later, to abduct and strangle Forbes in the same way? That was deliberate and precise. That was to present the illusion of a typical killer, an expected type of killer – one obsessed with attractive reporters. Then dumping Forbes where he did served to get Baldacci where he wanted her. But the abduction of Forbes also served him in this other way – it gave him the ability to make this video of her."

"And now his motive is made known."

There was a knock on the door. Shannon rose and opened up. A uniformed cop stood with another guest from the awards dinner. The woman looked tired and sad and wore yoga pants and a light hoodie. "Come on in," Shannon said. To Caldoza, "I gotta go. See you tonight."

"Hang in there."

She ended the call with him and smiled at the woman. They went through the night, where she was sitting, what she saw and heard. Anything suspicious? Anyone you noticed go up to the control room? Anyone at work seem to harbor resentment against the profession? And so on, and so on. Shannon did her job, but as sure as she was that the killer had been at the awards dinner last night, she was equally sure that they weren't going to find him. He was going to blend in.

He was any one of them.

STILL, the police got a picture of things: an NYPD beat cop named Jablonski took the statement of a newspaper photographer named Gordon Gay. Gay had heard the victim scream. He'd seen Spencer clutching his neck, and a second later, had seen the first spurt of blood jettisoned by the pulse.

Gay wrote on the statement: *Then he sort of dropped to one knee. He went down. I looked around, but I didn't see anyone else. I mean, there were people around, everyone was running, but it was dark...*

Tamika Monroe-Wells, a journalist with *The Forward*, was the first person to try to assist Spencer as he went from on one knee to falling onto his side.

I reached for him, Monroe-Wells wrote in her statement. *I tried to help him back to his feet because I was thinking about the bomb. We had to get out. He was in shock, and then so was I. And when I couldn't lift him, I just left. I'm so sorry and ashamed to admit it, but I left him there ...*

Each guest wrote out their statement like this, and they also met with an officer – whether Shannon or another agent or someone from NYPD – and sat for a recorded interview. Monroe-Wells broke down crying on camera during her interview. The interviewing detective brought her some water.

Everyone was shaken up. "I thought that was for real," Andy Rothstein, another journalist, said. "I thought I was going to die. I was at the back of the room – I mean, we were the *furthest* table from the exit. And people were just piled up. Stampede, man. I thought, *There's no way I'm getting out of here in sixty seconds ...*"

"What did you think of the video?" Shannon asked.

"What did I think of it? Sick. Depraved. Horrible what they did to her. She looked like ... Hannibal Lecter or something."

"What *they* did to her?"

"I mean, this is ..." He cocked his head, frowning. "This has got to be a group, right? I mean, one guy doing all this?"

"You don't think one person could do this? Why?"

Rothstein backtracked. "Well, there was no bomb, though. Right?"

"It took three hours, but the entire place was swept clean."

"So, yeah. Scare tactics, then. To get people all riled up. Get them panicking. Then, in the pandemonium and darkness, you get Todd Spencer. Cut his throat."

Shannon had watched Rothstein closely. The journalist

studied his hands. She asked, "What did you think about Todd Spencer?"

Rothstein's head came up quick. "A chauvinist. A narcissist. One of the most obnoxious people in the business." Rothstein hooked her gaze and held it for a moment.

"Thank you," she'd said to him.

18

SUNDAY EVENING

The dread formed a nauseous churning in Josie's stomach. The longer she watched the TV coverage of this bomb-scare thing, the worse it got.

Todd Spencer. His name went through her head over and over again. When they showed his face, when they said he'd been murdered, his throat slashed open, her veins turned to ice.

But there was no one to turn to. No one to tell. She was home alone, and she couldn't drag herself away from the TV. She was riveted to it – the flashing lights from all those emergency vehicles, that crazy building with its gargoyle-looking things on the windows. All the people in the street, watching. And when the one man, with light eyes contrasting his brown skin, Caldoza or something, when he gave a statement, they put that number at the bottom of the screen again. *If you have any information ...*

She did.

She had information.

The line rang, and she waited, bouncing her leg, chewing her nails. Her house felt stuffy and oppressive in the late-day heat, the lowering sun blazing around the edges of the drawn blinds. This was a nightmare that just kept getting worse.

"New York Police Department tip hotline," a female voice said. "Can I have your name, please?"

"Josie. Ah, Josephine Tenor." She was nervous, her voice light and scratchy.

"All right, Josephine, and your location?"

"Astoria Heights."

"What can I do for you today, Josephine?"

She almost hung up. It was hard to even speak. "I'm ... I'm gonna ... I'm gonna be killed. I know it. I'm gonna – he's gonna come for me. Because of Charlotte."

"Wait – sorry? Are you talking about the suspect in the–"

"Yes," she said suddenly, forcibly. "All of it. The guy doing all of it. He's going to come for me. He's going to come for me and he's going to kill me just like all these other people he's going to–"

"Ma'am? Josephine? I'm gonna need you to calm down. Josephine – how old are you?"

"That doesn't matter."

A silence. Voices in the background, chattering. Probably other police taking calls like this. Cops who were on probation, or got in trouble for something, they were the ones who had to field these calls.

"Sixteen," Josephine said at last.

"Okay." The cop cleared her throat. "I'm going to put you through to talk to an investigator, okay, Josephine? We're over-loaded with calls, so it might take a minute. Stay on the line."

Josie sighed. "Okay."

There was a click, and then some bad music, a distant, distorted version of some old-timey crooner guy, like Ray Charles or someone. Josie held the phone, her family's land-line, and watched the TV. A helicopter shot swept over Midtown, showing the cluster of emergency vehicles and flashing lights, dozens, if not hundreds, of people in the street, kept back by barricades and police. It was showing what happened yesterday, but when it cut back to the news anchor, he was saying how this had become a joint investigation between NYPD and FBI. Even the Department of Homeland Security had gotten involved.

"The city is holding its breath," the anchorman said, "as this 'Media Killer' investigation has taken a turn towards terrorism."

Terrorism, she thought. That was huge. New York didn't lie down for terrorism. The taste of blood on its tongue like that, the FBI and all the rest of the cops would never stop. They'd look at everything. People would be getting stopped in airports.

The bad music kept jangling away in Josie's ear. Frustrated, she hung up the phone. And instantly regretted it. She hadn't even given her phone number to the woman. "Well, they got your name and the town you live in," she said aloud to herself. "They can find it."

She thought of calling back. She chewed her nail. She dialed the same number and waited for what seemed like forever, and a man answered, "New York Police Department tip hotline." He sounded even less enthused.

She was ready this time. "My name is Josephine Tenor." She gave her phone number and her house address, just in case. "I know who he is," she said. It felt like her heart was going to beat out of her chest.

"Who *who* is?"

"The Media Killer."

"Okay. Let me put you through to an – oh. I see you here on the screen, Miss Tenor. Yes, we have your call, it's on file, and someone will get back to you as soon as possible."

"He's not going to stop," she blurted. "He's going to get everyone."

After a moment, the male cop said, "Okay, miss. Ah, just

stay calm. Is this, ah – where did you say you were calling from? Astoria?"

"Astoria Heights. The man who is doing–"

"Okay, listen, they got a guy they like for this, okay? Nowhere near where you are. I'm not really supposed to tell you that, but just to comfort you."

"They ... got someone?"

"Looks that way. They're getting real close to someone. Okay? So you should try to relax."

He hung up.

Josie held the phone a moment before putting it back down. The news changed to a TV commercial, an advertisement for arthritis medication that was blaringly loud. She left the living room, feeling stiff in her own joints, and walked down the hall, to the window by the front door, and looked out at the street. Pretty, the sun slowly sliding away for the day. The middle of summer. High, hot summer. She should be enjoying it.

Maybe she was wrong. Because how the heck would she know what was really going on out there? Just because she recognized some faces, some names – these were journalists, TV people. Their names and faces were everywhere. They were plastered on the sides of buses, for God's sake.

She stood looking out at the street, the familiar houses, the narrow path between two buildings that cut through to the next street over, and she thought about Charlotte.

Guilt, she realized. *That's what this whole thing is about. You've been driving yourself crazy because of all the guilt.*

It had been a good five years or so since she'd done a confession. She'd made her First Communion, and confession was a required part of that. She'd skipped it ever since. Her parents didn't seem to mind. Her mother was gone half the time anyway. Today was Sunday, and where was she?

Off in la-la land with her new boyfriend.

Leaving Josie home alone, feeling guilty, being paranoid.

"You're not gonna die," she said.

When her cell phone buzzed in her back pocket, she jumped and let out a little yell. But then she realized what it was, pulled it out and saw the message from Aaliyah: *u still being a whiny beotch?* It made Josie laugh with relief, and the smile felt good on her face.

19

"Everybody checks out," Shannon said to Caldoza on the phone. "I don't understand it. All the waitstaff and hospitality, the security team, and every guest seen so far has been cleared. Or close to it."

The city flashed and pounded outside the cab window. Midtown was typically choked with traffic. It was marginally better south of Penn Station. The cab kept them headed for the field office downtown.

Caldoza asked, "Did your people have a look at my guy? Tanzer?"

"I'm told we're looking into it."

Shannon was glad to talk to Caldoza, but her mind was wandering, buzzing. Ben Forbes had called her office twice. She'd accessed the messages from her cell – he'd sounded terrible. Desperate.

"Luis, I've got to make a call."

"No worries," he said. "Talk to you."

She got a little air when the cab sailed over a road boil, reminding her of her gluteal aches and pains. Her body swung right with the momentum as the driver whipped around a bike messenger with dreadlocks and fingerless gloves. Shannon braced herself and keyed a contact in her phone. "Mr. Forbes?"

"Agent Ames." He sounded calm. A good start. "Thanks for calling me back."

"No problem, Mr. Forbes. So. How are y–"

"I understand you were there last night. I've heard all about it. Monica was reading something. Something this guy made her read. That she was tied to a chair or something ..."

"No one is supposed to be talking about that, Mr. Forbes. I'm sorry that you–"

"No one is supposed to be ..." he started to repeat, and then broke up laughing. A humorless sound. Not menacing – overwhelmed. "Right, well. The point of being a journalist is to talk. To promulgate. To disseminate ..."

"Mr. Forbes, how are you? Is there anything I can do for you? Anyone I can call?"

"Anyone you can call? You can call Monica's parents. Because I don't know what else to say to them. I don't know what else to say. Their daughter was at their house in Connecticut last weekend. Last weekend we were there, and then we drove over to the camps and saw the kids. And now she's in some video, tied up, giving speeches against her profession."

She waited, letting him vent.

His voice was barely audible. "I still haven't told the kids. They don't watch TV up there at camp. They're not allowed internet. So they're safe."

She thought she understood his meaning – Monica's children weren't in danger of finding out about their mother's death before their father had a chance to break the news. But something in the way he'd said it, the tone of his voice, gave her the unnerving idea of a killer who killed through screens, like a contagion, affecting those who watched or read.

She could hear Ben Forbes softly crying. It was half a

minute until he spoke again – the cab was cruising past Union Square, catching a rare run of green lights. "Did you check into the thing with the land deal? About the councilman in Pelham Bay?"

"I did. I am."

"Yeah ..." His voice grew stronger. "And? Isn't this just like those kinds of people would do? This fucking Russian mobster and his fucking father and a goddamn city councilman on their payroll?" He paused, just ragged breathing coming over the connection. "I'm sorry."

"Listen to me, Ben. I want to make sure you're okay. Would you like someone to come by, just ... talk? See if they can help you? We have grief counselors. We have people who–"

"I'm fine. No, I am. I know it must seem like ... but I'm okay. I'm gonna miss her, but ... but I ..."

He broke down crying, his final words lost.

Whatever generic suspicion remained against Ben Forbes – for being close with a victim, for lacking an alibi – drained away with the sound of his weeping. As the cab jockeyed around downtown traffic, Shannon wiped her eyes with her thumb and forefinger. The cabbie glanced at her in the mirror.

"Ben," she said, mustering conviction, "we're going to get this guy."

"Yeah ..." He sounded a million miles away.

She repeated it with a slight amendment.

"Ben – *I'm* gonna get this guy. I promise you."

THE BIRDS WERE CHIRPING in the pin oaks on the sidewalk when Shannon stepped out of the cab. The forty-story building loomed above her, grayish-beige, its hundreds of windows reflecting the powder-blue sky. FBI's New York City field office was massive, took up five floors, and was run by the assistant director in charge – Ronald Moray.

Upstairs, Moray's head was so polished it gleamed. His silver glasses looked fused to his skull. Shannon had met him twice before, but Moray didn't recognize her as he approached her and Tyler in the hall. He was neck-breaking tall with long, spidery fingers that gripped like a Terminator. He smiled down at her and then turned to Tyler, and the smile vanished. "Are we just about ready?"

"Ten minutes."

"See you in there." Tyler hurried away, checking over his shoulder that Shannon was following; she was.

"You doing okay?" Tyler asked.

"I'm good, sir."

His expression said he didn't trust it. "You eaten?"

"I'm all set."

He stopped then and stepped close, so that she moved back toward the curved hallway wall. She had a partial view of an open area – a common area with lots of desks and a ceiling three stories higher. A young man with a box in his arms glanced over at her and Tyler.

Tyler said, "We're going to present to thirty people. I need to know that you're in good shape."

"I'm in good shape."

He continued to gauge her with his eyes. Finally he relented, opening up a little space between them. "Okay."

The room to hold the briefing had been arranged with theater-style seating, a laptop, projector, and screen. Tyler moved quickly to the back of the room, opened his leather valise, and pulled out a sheaf of papers. "Hand these out. Thirty-five of them. Just set them in the seats."

It was the killer's words, a transcript of what Monica Forbes had been forced to read on camera.

She distributed as asked, and agents were filing in by the

time she was done.

Tyler began the presentation. "I've given you all a copy of what we're calling the manifesto," he said. "We're going to start with two things to focus on. One, digital forensics. If you don't know Special Agent Amy Dodd, there she is."

A blonde agent blushed and raised her hand.

Tyler said, "While digital forensics studies the video for clues to the type of equipment used – camera and lights and microphone – they're also looking for any tip-offs on location. Exact time of day, all of that. They can listen; they can judge the acoustics. Get a sense of how big the room was. Everything. While they're doing that, we're also pulling apart this manifesto. We're studying the words. I've had top forensic linguists looking at it all day. Special Agents McIntosh and Gowarski – they're our linguists."

People looked around at a skinny man and a heavyset man, who both nodded and looked like they preferred the attention to be elsewhere.

FBI agents: shyer than you'd think.

"And over there in the corner is Special Agent Stratford. Agent Stratford specializes in hate crimes, hate groups. He's going to help us as we go through this line by line. He's going to run every expression, turn of phrase, and idiom against the groups we know about. Their rhetoric, their slogans, their bumper stickers. Everybody got it?"

There were murmured agreements and nods. Across the room from her, Ronald Moray looked pleased, overhead fluorescents shining off his head.

Tyler said, "What we're going to do now is, we're going to all watch this video."

Someone dimmed the room. Tyler hit a button on his laptop. The projector beamed colored light onto the screen. It was a recreation of the previous evening, in a way.

It was the first Shannon had seen the video since the

awards dinner. She'd been distracted then, focused on locating the source of the disruption, then getting people to safety. She could sit now and watch.

As before, Forbes read from the sheet of paper in her lap. She would look up at the camera every once in a while, like the trained public speaker she was. It was clear she struggled to be strong. *She thinks she might get out of this*, Shannon considered. It was in her eyes, in her voice – Forbes was trained to be on camera, to have poise, but in this situation the thing motivating her was the promise of getting back to her life, back to her family. To survive. Anyone would try to rationalize a horrific situation like that. Anyone would hope for humanity in her captor.

When it was over, McIntosh said, "One problem. We don't know if she's reading verbatim. She could be straying from what he's given her."

"I'd say she's probably pretty close," Shannon offered. "She's used to cue cards. She's familiar with the camera – even as unusual and scary as it had to have been, this comes naturally to her."

McIntosh was nodding agreement. "That's true, I'm sure, but as we get into the very fine details of this, I'm saying it's dubious to build our analysis off this transcript." He shook the paper in the air. "Because it's ultimately her interpretation. Even if it's ninety-nine percent accurate." McIntosh pointed at the screen. "But how do we know? Right near the end, for instance, she says, 'This is ...' but she doesn't complete the thought. After that, she delivers the line, 'Ladies and Gentlemen,' et cetera. All we can really evaluate is her performance."

"All right," Tyler interjected, "but–"

McIntosh cut him off. "I'm saying that might work to our benefit, too. As a professional, Monica Forbes could be a step ahead of her captor. She could be anticipating where this is going to go – out to the public, where law enforcement will sit in a room and do exactly what we're doing – she could be giving us clues. What we *need* to do is get together with the video team and say, 'Okay, at fourteen seconds, she glances up and blinks twice. Or, at seventeen seconds, she looks off camera.' We need to analyze this for anything she might be trying to communicate."

Tyler was nodding, but hastily, darting looks at Moray, and he said, "Right, okay – I understand all of that. But I don't want to miss the forest for the trees."

"Of course not," McIntosh said.

"This is a terrorist's mission statement," Tyler said. "Okay? It's right there in front of us. She says – *he* says – 'this is a reckoning.'" Tyler looked over their faces. "He's punishing." His eyes lingered on Shannon. "Don't you think he's punishing?"

She didn't have a ready answer. Not because she hadn't thought about it – she'd been thinking about it for a day – but because her theory was still brewing, and she needed more to back it up. "I think he's preaching," she said. "I think it's punishment. But it's not necessarily punishment for what he's preaching."

All eyes locked on her at that point. So much for holding back.

Tyler scowled. "What are you saying?"

"I'm saying if it was truly punishment for the sins of the media – for everything he's saying through Monica Forbes in that video – then there *would* have been a bomb. There wasn't. There was one victim – Todd Spencer."

Tyler shook his head. "There was more than one victim, Agent Ames – everyone was terrorized. He caused an absolute panic. You were there, weren't you? You don't call three hundred people running for their lives, nearly trampling each other to death, a form of punishment?"

Bufort spoke up from where he sat near the back of the room. "And this is his whole thing. Pick 'em off one at a time.

It's no fun to just blow up a whole room of journalists. Right? He's got to drag it out, torture them."

Shannon turned around to face him. "Maybe, but why them?"

Bufort stared back at her. "I feel like we're going in circles. Why them? Because those are the people he's seen on TV. The people's names he's seen in black and white."

She shook her head. "I think it's more than that."

"Okay, so let's get to it. What is it?"

"I'm working on it."

Tyler waved his hands in the air, redirecting attentions his way. "All right, fine. That's all fine. But, Agent Ames, I think you're so hot to get into your own theories, you're missing what's right in front of us." He meant the video; he meant the *manifesto* Monica Forbes had been forced to recite. Forbes, on the screen right now, frozen in time, paused just before she delivered her tearful threat: a bomb in the building.

There was no question that the effect of that threat – the entire video – was terrorizing.

The heat rose in her cheeks. "I'm not missing it," Shannon said.

Tyler glared at her. She realized she was dangerously close to arguing with him in front of Moray, the man on whom Tyler wanted to leave a positive impression.

Moray said, "This is good. I think you want multiple ways into something like this." He began to stand up, pausing to brush some invisible detritus from his pants before unfurling to his full height. "Keep me posted," he said, his gaze landing on Shannon, and then he walked out.

SHE RODE the subway back to the Brooklyn office. It was where Tyler wanted her – out of sight, out of mind. She didn't want it to be this way; she respected Tyler, but there was a tension between them, competition. *Multiple ways into something like this.* Tyler surely registered this as a tacit endorsement of that competition. As if Moray was saying, *May the best man win.*

Whatever. It didn't concern her. What concerned her was the promise she'd made to Ben Forbes. The one she'd made to herself, and to the public, when she'd been accepted into the FBI.

Back in her office, pictures of Monica Forbes, Eva Diaz, Jordan Baldacci – and now, Todd Spencer – covered her wall. Professional headshots of each, plus some candids found online, and of course, clippings from their work. A still photo of Diaz in the field, standing in front of a movie theatre premiering the latest Scorsese picture. Monica Forbes sitting on set with her three co-hosts of *The Scene*, discussing a school flooded from a broken water main, indicative of citywide budget problems (probably Monica's idea).

The picture of Baldacci showed her on the steps of city hall. She had one foot up on a higher step, her arms folded – a power pose. Baldacci looked like a force to be reckoned with, no question.

Shannon turned to her laptop. She studied the database she'd been creating: each victim and all the projects they'd worked on. The silver lining to Todd Spencer's murder? It narrowed things down. It helped, in a twisted way; the more victims there were, the fewer stories that could be cross-referenced. So if the murders were related to something like Paul Torres and his shady rezoning deal, she'd be getting closer to finding it.

But that was a big *if*, a theory not shared by Mark Tyler. Bufort didn't buy it, either. The two of them were full steam ahead on domestic terrorism.

Tyler had uploaded the video to a secure FBI server. Shannon navigated there and entered her password, then a separate access code for the video. She didn't want to watch it again, but she had to.

The video began with the image of Forbes on the upright gurney, covered in a blanket. Behind her, slightly out of focus, a bluish-gray wall. Dirty or possibly paint-chipped, cracked. Maybe all of the above. Shannon leaned close and studied Forbes. Forbes said, "Hello. I have a message to deliver to you tonight. A message to deliver to the–"

Shannon hit pause. She'd noticed it before, but now that she was able to scrutinize, Monica Forbes's wet hair was confirmed.

According to the National Weather Service, the New York metropolitan area had been experiencing a run of sunny, hot weather. It was humid, but hadn't rained in over a week. Monica Forbes's hair was wet because the killer had cleaned her first before recording her recital. And the blanket, wrapping her, because she was naked beneath. Because she'd just been bathed, for God's sake.

Why clean her up before recording the manifesto? Why not after he'd killed her and all was said and done?

Most investigators were assuming the cleaning occurred posthumously, to remove trace evidence, but Shannon had never been sure. It could have happened immediately following the abduction; a kind of preparation for what came next. Plus, both autopsies had revealed traces of sevoflurane, an anesthesia, in the victim's bloodstreams. Sevoflurane was similar to chloroform, but faster acting and with greater potency. The victims were drugged. Incapacitated. Pliable. Perhaps he washed them while they were unconscious.

Shannon backed up the footage to the beginning. "Hello," Monica Forbes said. "I have a message to deliver."

McIntosh had a point, voicing concerns over how to interpret the video – where did its content and Forbes's performance diverge? Had the killer, for instance, written *hello* into his manifesto? Or, with her brain in pure fight-or-flight panic, had Monica Forbes reverted to a kind of newscaster persona and ad-libbed the word?

What was also interesting, along that pathway of thinking, was what she *didn't* say in the video. She didn't say, "Hello. I'm Monica Forbes. I have a message ..." She hadn't identified herself.

Why not?

Had the killer written the manifesto with a specific speaker in mind? Could that be determined based solely on whether or not the speaker formally introduced themselves?

It was dizzying, the questions Shannon knew she could ask and never have answered.

Monica Forbes said, "For too long, the media has gone unaccountable. We have never had to apologize for the fear we sell ..."

McIntosh and others were analyzing every choice of word, regardless of Forbes's possible distorting effect. McIntosh hewed to the idea that, as a professional, Forbes would be delivering the manifesto with close to 95 percent precision. And so, he studied how the sentences were structured. What that might say about the killer's background, his level of education, his intelligence.

Others were drilling down into the technical aspects of the video itself, from the frame rate to the depth of field and potential lens used, while still others were studying the wall behind her, the gurney, the type of blanket wrapped around her – every conceivable clue that might shed light on the location, or that might lead to revealing the killer.

Toward the end of the ninety-second-long video, Forbes delivered the threat: "If you won't hold yourself to account, the people will. This is a reckoning. This is the beginning of your atonement."

The beginning of your atonement.

Atonement – a kind of frou-frou word. Suggesting the killer either used such a word unconsciously, or he'd splashed it in to convey tone. But beyond that, the message seemed cut and dried: anti-media sentiment had been percolating through the culture for decades, but it had gotten acute over the past few years. However, the killer didn't make any specific references to public figures or political parties, the grievance was broad – a dressing-down of the media at large. An indictment of the for-profit model; the massive advertising industry tangled up in the news – what some called the "infotainment complex."

Was the killer anti-media, or anti-corporatism? Did it matter? It might matter, since people on both ends of the political spectrum had their bones to pick with the seeming corporate takeover of society. Where had he gotten his ideas? A political family? A local culture? How about academia? Thinkers like Marshal McLuhan and Neil Postman warned against a Big Brother-like state of mass media. Controlled not by central governance, but by private entities. Did the killer agree?

There were no answers. Shannon watched the video several more times, made copious notes, and finally relented. She left her office, went down to the Starbucks on the main floor, and got a coffee. It was 10:16 p.m. The morgue was still open. After all, it never closed.

∽

THE SIGN near the rows of human freezers read: *Remember – Always Load Bodies Head Out.*

On duty tonight was a medical student looking all of twenty-two. The fresh-faced kid said, "Forbes, here we go," and opened the small stainless-steel door. Grunting with the effort, he rolled out the body encased in an opaque bag. Then he glanced up at Shannon, kind of shyly, and said, "You want me to open it?"

"Please."

The kid reminded her of Gabe, one of her older brothers. The way he was when Shannon had still been a young girl. Delicate, somehow. Strong, tough, but always quiet.

Wearing blue latex gloves, the attendant carefully unzipped the top of the bag.

Monica Forbes looked like they all looked after a few days' refrigeration – a kind of bluish-purple, bones prominent against the skin, eyes glued shut.

"Thank you," Shannon said.

He offered a slight smile. "I'll leave you to it, ma'am."

As she stood looking down at Monica, considering the snaking bruise around her neck, Shannon read from the autopsy report she'd gotten from upstairs. She knew most of the material it contained. Time of death, cause of death – strangulation. It had come to include her last meal (a slice of pizza) and the toxicity of her blood, which was negligible. No drugs, no drinking. Just the sevoflurane.

Touch DNA had yet to be determined; DNA took a long time. But a swab of her neck had gone to the lab and came back as bearing trace elements – fibers – of a synthetic material called Cordura nylon. This material was so widely used, from belts to backpack straps, military wear and performance apparel, that on its own, it didn't help much. What she knew was that such fabrics were considered highly durable and resistant to tears and abrasions. Only a minute amount of material had been found embedded in the victim's flesh. Microscopic.

Shannon set the report down on a nearby tray table. She stood looking at Monica Forbes. Then she lowered her head and closed her eyes.

I want to help this woman.

I maybe just need a little help. A little help to show me the way ...

20

She ventured out into the night air, grateful to be free of that cloying, formaldehyde stink of the preserved dead. The heat had barely let up, the humidity oppressive, but she didn't mind. She sat on one of several concrete benches near the Medical Examiner's Office, listening to the muffled traffic surrounding her, and watched the blinking red/green lights of a low 747 coming in for a landing to the north, LaGuardia Airport.

She went through it one more time:

Forbes had been killed almost a week ago now. Diaz was two weeks before that. Baldacci was killed right on the heels of Monica Forbes, no lag in between. And the most recent murder, Spencer, came a few nights later, because of the awards dinner. Baldacci and Spencer were killed at that time and place for a reason. The other two? Were the times of their deaths arbitrary?

Serial killers were known to speed up. Like drug addicts, their needs increased as their patience decreased. They got a high from the killing, or the reliving of the killing, then developed a tolerance to that high, and needed to up the stakes to achieve the same chemical satisfaction.

This wasn't that. This killer was organized. He was so good, he'd killed a man in cold blood with two dozen cops *right there.* Right in the same place.

"He's got to be there," she said under her breath, thinking about the three hundred guests at the awards dinner, the employees. But, like she'd told Caldoza, everybody was checking out.

How was that possible? They'd missed something. Or there was someone they'd yet to see ...

Maybe Tyler and Bufort were right. This was terrorism, plain and simple. Someone who hated the media, hated corporations, hated America – et cetera.

On the other hand, maybe Ben Forbes was right – this was payback for reporters not only covering a story, but for having information dangerous to someone like Nikolay Lebedev. The story about the Pelham Bay apartment building wasn't in Spencer's employment history, but that didn't mean he hadn't been working on it.

She needed to get to his house, go through his things.

SPENCER HAD a tiny but chic studio apartment at the southernmost tip of Manhattan, right near Battery Park. After deciding to man up and drive herself this time, she handed over her identification to a positively ancient Asian man, who scrutinized it and made several soft grunts before unlocking the sixth-floor space. He stood in the doorway as she walked in.

The Statue of Liberty, dark and just barely visible, took up a small space within one of the two front windows. A Murphy bed was enclosed in the wall. A handful of dishes – coffee cup, bowl and spoon – sat in the sink. On the fridge, a picture of

Spencer and his daughter, a pretty teenaged girl, possibly of mixed race. They posed in front of the entrance to Disney World, in Florida. There were more pictures of the daughter from when she was younger – riding a bike in what looked like Central Park, sitting on stage with a small band, playing the oboe. An English test, graded A-plus, adorned the center of the fridge door. *Nice Job, C!* was written in red.

Huh.

Spencer was a proud father.

Shannon pushed around some mail on the table, but it was the laptop she was here for. Spencer's phone was already in custody, but no one, not Tyler or Moray, not NYPD, had sent a unit to his house to bring more personal items into evidence. He'd been a person of interest for about a minute, then a sudden victim, and it had only been twenty-four hours since the switch. Law enforcement was struggling to keep up.

The laptop was a MacBook Air. She tried a few passwords, and it shook her off each time. Shannon smiled at the landlord still guarding the doorway. She pulled out her phone and called Tyler and requested they get a unit over to Spencer's to pick up his devices and give the place a thorough sweep.

"The hell are you doing, Ames?" Tyler sounded angry but distracted.

"I'm trying to pick up some slack, that's all. I know how busy you are – everyone is."

"You're out there running your own investigation."

"I just think there are things ... Maybe Spencer knew the killer. And I don't have everything he was working on, since he was freelance. It could help."

Tyler made no response.

"Sir?"

"Fine. I'll sign off and get someone over there in the morning. But please remember your place here, Ames. I know we've moved beyond simple monitoring, but you still need to run everything past me. Or at least check in with Bufort."

"Yes, sir."

She hung up, gave Spencer's place one last look, and left. It was midnight. Time to go home, feed the cat, and try to get some sleep.

∿

THUMP-THUMP-THUMP.

The pounding on her apartment door startled her awake. She groped for her phone, but it wasn't on the bedside table.

Shannon threw the sheet back and swung her legs out of bed. The floor was cool beneath her bare feet. She scuffed toward the door, rubbing away the sleep in her eyes with the heel of her palm. Her gun and badge were on the table. Her phone, too. Still in silent mode from the briefing. *Shit.* But it wasn't even five a.m. Who the hell was here?

Thump-thump-thump.

She grabbed the gun and cocked it, then peeked through the glass peephole while keeping most of her body – her vital organs – away from the center of the door. A training habit.

Bufort's head looked abnormally large through the convex glass. He stood in the hallway dressed in a Kevlar vest. Another hung from his grip. "Ames, open up. It's me."

"Hang on," she said. She was still only dressed in her underclothes. She grabbed a blanket off the couch, wrapped it around her waist, set down the gun, and unlocked the door.

He came in, looking at her, checking out her place.

She asked, "Why'd you come up?"

"I've been calling you."

"I was deep asleep, sorry. What's up?"

"We've had guys looking for Ray Tanzer."

Caldoza had just asked about Tanzer the day before. "Tanzer is the guy who got fired from Ion?"

"And made a big stink on his way out, ranting and raving about how he wanted to see the whole media establishment take some bitter medicine." Bufort glanced down at her bare feet. "Get dressed. We can talk on the way."

Tyler's voice in her head: *Remember, you're an agent during her probationary period.*

When she didn't move, Bufort said, "Unless you want to sit this one out."

She stuck a finger in the air. "One minute. Tops."

21

MONDAY MORNING

Fifty-two seconds later, they were riding the elevator down as she affixed the Kevlar vest. She'd dressed in jeans, a white T-shirt, and sneakers. These vests, though, were starting to give her a bad feeling.

Bufort watched the numbers. "So Stratford went through the manifesto all night long, line by line. The big thing, at first, was how Forbes kept saying 'we.' At the beginning of the manifesto, she's saying 'we this' and 'we that.'"

"Like it was written for her. Or at least to include her as a media professional."

They reached the bottom floor and moved fast through the lobby, Bufort saying, "Well, right – but then it goes into accusation mode." He pushed through the glass doors and Shannon followed. A black Tahoe with tinted windows idled in the faint light. Bufort squeezed the fob in his hands to unlock it.

Shannon looked around. "Where is everybody else?"

"On their way."

"Why did you come to get me?"

He glanced at her. "You want to learn? This is an experience."

He jumped into the driver's side and she entered on the passenger side, and they were rolling before she got the door fully closed. Bufort cranked the wheel and they shot down her street, redbrick apartment building rapidly shrinking in the mirrors. "So," he said, "you can interpret that we/you switch multiple ways, the switch from inclusion to accusation, but Stratford had the idea this manifesto was really written stream-of-consciousness. He has all sorts of reasons for it, but whatever – point being, it was his professional opinion that this was someone in the media. Either actively or formerly."

"Was Tanzer at the awards dinner?"

Bufort cut her a side look. "Bingo. Now you're thinking. He was on the list. Either they forgot to take him off after his firing, or it's just not their policy."

"I never saw the guest list."

"That was a decision made way at the top," Bufort said. "To keep that guest list from getting into anyone's hands, in case our suspect was on it. National security guys wanted it quiet, too. Anyway, we looked through video and didn't see Tanzer, but we talked to one of the witnesses, someone who saw Todd Spencer spurting blood, and gave her an image of Tanzer, and she thought maybe he'd been there."

After several rapid turns, Bufort got on the Southern State Parkway and they barreled southeastward. "But that's not what clinched it. What clinched it was this group called Blackout. American-based, anti-media, government watchdog group. Their big thing is in boycotting media – no social media, no mainstream news, no newspapers. They use virtual private networks and DuckDuckGo for their internet searches. They think *everything* is suspect. Facebook, Google, all of it. They're paranoid that reality has disappeared and we're just living in a world of stories produced by corporations and governments. Stories capitalizing on and exacerbating existing divisions for maximum revenue – so it says on their website, right next to the part about spreading fear, generating outrage, and disseminating disinformation."

She felt a chill. That was a direct line from the manifesto.

She asked, "You think they're dangerous?"

He was silent a moment. "Agents Stratford, Lonsdale, and Stemp are about fifteen minutes ahead of us," he said, dodging the question. "However long it took for me to come get your ass. They've got local PD out there backing them up."

"So Tanzer was home?"

"Yeah. We posted a guy out there as soon as your fella over there at NYPD – Caldoza – as soon as he sent the information over to us."

"It was Detective Heinz who found the guy. NYPD."

"Whatever. So Tanzer's not there Friday night, he's not there Saturday – the night of the awards. But he shows up at his home last night about three a.m., at his residence in Amityville. Our guy says there's others in there with him – he came in with three other guys. Middle of the night. So we're not taking any chances." Bufort reached for a Snapple iced tea in the console, popped the top and took a long guzzle.

They passed JFK International Airport, and then they were due east, cruising through places like Valley Stream and Malverne, headed deeper into Long Island, headed toward the breaking dawn, the sky bronzed with haze.

Bufort walked her through the plan. Traffic was light, the agent's foot was heavy; they were there in thirty minutes.

TANZER'S PLACE was a small brown house with solar panels on the roof. A chest-high chain-link fence surrounded the front yard. Not much else to see yet from a block away – Bufort had parked behind a dark gray van. One of their own, Shannon recognized. Bufort had a two-way radio and he clicked the transmitter twice.

A moment later, two clicks came back.

"They're still waiting," he told Shannon. "Must be local PD aren't here yet."

Everything was still in the early-morning heat.

The radio blew static. Then, "I want to just do this," a voice said. Stratford.

Shannon tried to see into the van parked ahead of them on the street. No good, but she could imagine it: three guys with itchy trigger fingers who wanted to get their man. "All right," Bufort said into the radio. "Let's make it happen."

The van doors opened and the agents poured out into the bright day. Bufort opened his door, paused, and looked at Shannon. "Just hang back a bit, okay?"

"Sure." She exited the vehicle and crossed the road behind the men, who were moving faster. One undid the chain-link gate and headed up the walkway toward the front door. Two men flanked the house on either side. Bufort came up behind Stratford, watching his back. As they moved, as if sharing one mind, they all drew their weapons. Stratford reached the door as Shannon reached the edge of the lawn. She stayed in the street, getting the wider view on things.

Stratford knocked. He kept away from the door, off to the side. He jabbed the doorbell next. Shannon could just hear it, a telephone-like ring from deep in the house. Something caught her eye in one of the upstairs windows – the flip of a curtain. "Got something," she called. "Second floor." Her pulse hit harder as she drew her weapon. She glanced around the street. Not yet seven in the morning. People were just getting up, getting ready for work. Families pushing their kids towards the door. It was fairly quiet now, birds chirping, a dog barking in the distance. But in a few minutes things would start to liven up, people leaving for their commutes.

She gripped her gun tightly and watched as Stratford rang again. Something felt off. Was this correct procedure? Just rolling up on a suspect like this without an arrest warrant? Bufort had said "just talk," but with NYPD presence. This seemed rushed. Aggressive.

The radio Bufort carried made noise. Someone whispered something, but Shannon was out of earshot. Stratford looked at Bufort, twirled his finger, and Bufort nodded. He started jogging around the house, his shaggy blond hair flapping. He looked at Shannon as he went, and held out a hand, palm down, fingers splayed, *just sit tight.*

But she felt exposed down here on the street at the end of the walkway. This wasn't the way that–

The blast made her jump. It sounded like two things at once – an explosion and shattered glass. Stratford went down. Where he'd been standing, the window was blown out. Shannon ducked and ran for cover. Another blast followed. Bits of dirt and grass sprayed her. Someone was firing a shotgun and the last load had just hit the lawn beside her as she ran. Reaching the corner of the fence, she crawled behind the thick hedgerow bordering properties. She was breathing hard, her mind racing.

It's okay. It's okay ...

Her hip and leg beat an alarm of pain in time with her accelerated pulse as she peered through the vegetation. Stratford wasn't moving. Shouts rose from the back of the house. More gunfire. Shannon heard a noise behind her. She was on the edge of another yard, and the homeowner had stepped out onto the porch, looking curious. He saw her, and Shannon made shooing gestures. *Get back in the house!* He understood and quickly disappeared.

She couldn't stay here. No one seemed to be exiting the front. She wanted to help Stratford, but there was no cover coming at the house from the front like that. What'd they been thinking? She moved along the hedgerow on the neighbor's side until she was flanking Tanzer's house. From the porch around front, Stratford's radio burst with static, then some unintelligible shouts. They hadn't even given her a radio.

She pushed through the juniper hedge. No easy feat. It was thick, with tons of tiny branches scratching her face and forearms. On the other side, she ran fast to the house and slammed her body up against the wall. *Get control of your breathing.*

Now, to see about Stratford, she moved toward the front of the house, went around a chimney, and reached the corner. She risked a quick look. The elevated porch was chest level. She could see straight down to where Stratford was. He stared right back at her. Blood covered half of his face and made trails down his nose and cheek to his mouth. There was no sign of life in his wide eyes. A kind of cold stone slid down into her stomach.

She heard thumping from inside. Bufort had said three men, plus Tanzer, had arrived in the middle of the night. Someone had gone out the back. But there was nothing coming from the rear of the house–

Wait, there it was. A car engine just fired. Voices, two of them – "Turn it off! Turn off the ignition and step away from the–"

More gun blasts. Shannon ran toward the rear of the house. She slowed when she got to the back corner. Directly in front of her, three trash bins. She took cover behind these as she watched the shoot-out in the driveway – two men in a Dodge minivan were exchanging fire with agents – Bufort and either Lonsdale or Stemp – she didn't know their faces yet. Bufort, standing in the back doorway, took a hit in the upper body and fell inside the house. The other agent was in a four o'clock position behind the minivan, firing into the vehicle. Glass shattered. Bullets punched plastic and metal. The driver of the minivan hit the gas in reverse and Lonsdale/Stemp jumped out of the way.

Shannon stood up. She took aim on the vehicle windshield and fired four quick rounds. The windshield cracked badly but didn't fall in. Driver visibility would be greatly reduced – the glass was practically opaque with fractures – but the driver managed to back into the street. Shannon left the bins and ran toward the vehicle. She only had seconds before the passenger would have a direct shot on her. She aimed for the tires and unloaded her magazine. Then she dove into the open garage and out of range just as the driver put the minivan in gear and jerked forward. She was sure she'd punctured the front right tire with at least one round.

Nothing happened for three full breaths. Just Shannon, on her ass, in the oil-smelling open garage, staring across the driveway at the house, the rear doorway into which Bufort had fallen. She didn't see him. After the final breath, another agent stepped into view in the doorway. He startled when he saw her, then quickly pointed his gun away.

The first sirens rose in the distance.

"Fuck," the agent said. "This is bad."

Shannon pushed herself up and gained her feet. "Is the house clear?"

He nodded his head. "It's clear. Nobody in there."

"Agent Bufort?"

"He's okay. Took it in the vest. He's just getting his wind back."

"The other guy ..." she said.

"Stemp," the agent answered, making him Lonsdale.

A loud screech and violent wrenching crash-boomed in the distance. Both Shannon and Lonsdale got moving and trotted down to the street, weapons ready, aimed at the sky. Straight down, two intersections away, the minivan had collided with another vehicle. Stemp was running in that direction.

Lonsdale got going, but it was hard for Shannon to keep the

pace. She started to say *go ahead* to Lonsdale, but someone got out of the minivan and opened fire.

"Shit!" Lonsdale ran off the street to the right. She limped to the left, behind a containment wall that provided cover. Stemp shot it out with the man, and Stemp got him – the man holding the shotgun dropped to the road. A second later, another man ran. Stemp tracked him, but the man was clearly hurt badly already. He dropped too, just a few yards away.

Stemp moved in. Lonsdale returned to the street and ran to join the other agent in order to back him up. Shannon got to her feet again, and she walked. There was no running left in her. She looked down her gunsights as she approached, watched as Stemp got the driver's side door open and grabbed the driver. Lonsdale aimed his handgun into the vehicle as he circled around the passenger side, then yanked that door open.

The sirens were louder now. An NYPD car took a corner at speed and raced toward the scene. Another followed seconds later.

Shannon got closer and positioned herself behind Lonsdale. A man she'd never seen before, never met, was the passenger, his head lolling to the side, mouth hanging open, a bullet wound in his neck. Shannon didn't need a ballistics report to confirm it; the knowledge twisted her stomach: the bullet inside this man was one of hers. She'd just killed a human being.

Feeling suddenly dizzy, nauseous, she stumbled back from the damaged minivan and turned her attention to the other vehicle involved in the accident – a sleek SUV.

She almost couldn't look. Didn't want to know. But as the NYPD cars screeched to a halt and doors were flung open, footfalls beat toward the scene, Shannon forced herself to peer through the glass into the interior of the civilian vehicle at the man behind the steering wheel.

He looked back at her, bewildered, shocked, blinking. Breathing. Relatively unharmed.

She nearly collapsed. Caught herself against the SUV; forced her spine to straighten. *Thank you, God.* She grasped for the handle of the SUV driver's door and swung it open. "FBI," she said to the man. "Are you hurt?"

"They just came out of nowhere," the motorist said, slack-jawed and staring. "I just came to the stop sign, stopped, started rolling forward, and they just came tearing through, clipped me right in the front there. My God. Who are they? What's happening?"

"Someone will be right with you, sir. Just sit tight."

She needed air. Even though she was outside in it. She stumbled away, taking another look inside the minivan and the person she'd never met, gone from this earth.

Then someone had her by the arm, and he was talking to her, but his voice was coming from a long ways away ...

22

MONDAY AFTERNOON

"God," Bufort said. "What a thing."

Shannon sat in the SUV she'd arrived in with Bufort. Hours had passed like minutes. Of the four criminals, two were dead. Two were alive – Tanzer, who'd run from the vehicle and collapsed – and the driver, James Paddock.

The deceased were Winston Hitchcock and Manuel Lopez. All four had records; all four had drug charges. Tanzer's jacket was the lightest – one possession of marijuana charge from five years before. He'd managed to deal with it and keep his job at Ion. Of the other three, two had done time for opioids, one for heroin. They didn't exactly seem like intellectual revolutionaries.

And Stratford was dead, too. The medical examiner said he'd succumbed within seconds of getting shot, most likely by Hitchcock, the one with the shotgun, the only weapon the group possessed besides a snub-nosed revolver found on Paddock.

Bufort's arm was in a sling – but only because of the sprain he'd sustained falling through the door. The bullet was lodged in his Kevlar vest. He'd refused a trip to the hospital and said he'd check himself in that afternoon, back in Queens.

Shannon thought the whole thing was nuts. They should've watched Tanzer for a couple of days, got something on him they could use, then brought him in. As it was, his house was practically empty. Not a stick of furniture, just boxes. They could ask Tanzer why, if he was moving to a new residence or what the story was, but he was at the hospital with multiple internal injuries.

"Fuckin' Stratford," Bufort said, watching the street, watching Tanzer's house, the porch where the agent had succumbed. "He shoulda waited."

"What was he acting on?"

Bufort shook his head, saying, "He was on this all weekend. Tanzer has ties to Blackout ..."

She shifted in her seat, trying to get more comfortable. It wasn't working. "Blackout isn't a terrorist group. They don't murder journalists, make bomb threats. They're paranoid intellectuals."

Bufort shot her a mean look. "Hey ..." He held a finger in the air. His mouth worked, but all he ended up saying was, "All right?"

She relented. Stratford was gone. They had Tanzer. As soon as he was able, they'd question him. It all seemed unnecessary to her, but maybe this was how it was out in the real world. You followed procedure, but part of that was making judgment calls. Tanzer was a former TV guy who got fired, left on bad terms, and Agent Stratford had connected him to a group with ostensible motives for systematic attacks on the media. It didn't fit with what she believed, but then, she wasn't sure exactly what she believed. And anyway, it wasn't about criticizing someone else's operating theory, it was about coming up with your own that was better.

~

THE REST of the day was spent talking to people.

Doctors: *Can you feel this?* Yes. *Can you hear this?* Yes. *Follow the light, please.*

Department of Justice: *And then what happened, Special Agent Ames?* Then the minivan started to back up and I fired three times into the windshield. *Were you aiming for one of the suspects?* I was ... I just tried to ...

Tyler: *What the hell were you thinking?!* Bufort is a senior agent, sir. You said– *I didn't say abandon all good sense! Now I've got the DOJ so far up my ass they're going to find my tonsils. Bufort is suspended. You're lucky I don't suspend you, too ...*

Finally she was home. She fed Jasper and watered the plants, and when she sat on the couch after a shower, the cat came to her and jumped into her lap. It purred, looked at her, then leapt away suddenly, as if spooked.

Night filled the window and she drew herself into the fetal position on the couch and pulled a blanket over her head.

The guilt for killing Winston Hitchcock was going to destroy her if she let it.

She sat up, wiped her tears, and picked up the remote. She watched TV for the next twenty minutes. Every channel covered the Amityville event. *Serial Killing Terrorist One of the Media's Own?* Profiles on Tanzer. Video footage of him storming out of the Ion offices three weeks prior. "Just days before Eva Diaz was found in a pair of garbage bags," one commentator noted.

Shannon watched, and she remembered the words of the manifesto: misinformation and wild-goose chases. Reporting on other stories as if they were facts.

No court or judge or jury had convicted Raymond Tanzer yet. No law enforcement member or body had made definitive connections between Blackout and the killings, the manifesto.

But the media was. Rather, they posed the question. They put the idea out there, got it rolling through viewers' heads.

Dissemination of disinformation ...

Shannon got off the couch. It was late, the eleven o'clock news concluding, but she felt suddenly wired. She almost called Ben Forbes – his kids were coming back from summer camp this week – but she didn't. Terribly inappropriate. She used Caldoza's cane and got up off the couch, then set out a yoga mat and did some leg stretches. Her hip and buttock flared with pain. She gritted her teeth and worked through it.

Who are you?

She imagined Raymond Tanzer standing in the street as Monica Forbes walked home that night. The man somehow convincing her to get into his car. Because she knew him? *Ray? What are you doing here?* Once she was lured into the vehicle, he attacks. After regaining consciousness, she finds herself bound to a gurney. Given a script to read. Words that sound eerily similar to the statements made on the Blackout website.

Shannon finished stretching and brought her laptop down onto the floor and scoured that site. She bit her thumb and read. Blackout feared and loathed the "establishment media." There were no pictures of Tanzer, of course – all members of Blackout were anonymous – but Stratford had connected him to the murders. Because Tanzer was on the guest list at the Crunchtime Club awards dinner. And because Tanzer was a disgruntled, fired employee who knew people from Blackout. How?

She closed the laptop and rolled over and stared up at the ceiling, hands across her chest. She would learn more tomorrow.

The cat found her, climbed up onto her, purring, and she stroked his soft fur.

This time, he stayed.

23

TUESDAY

Two days, and no one was getting back to her.

Two days. Because her call meant nothing to them? Because they'd checked it out and found no cause for concern? Because they were so overwhelmed with everything that was going on?

It had to be the last one, Josie thought. Had to be, because this thing had spread all the way out to Long Island, to Amityville, for God's sake, where a bunch of Secret Service–looking cops had just had a shoot-out with some crazy terrorist group.

Terrorists.

That was the word buzzing through the beehive at present. Reporters were hazy on the details – big surprise – but in the early hours of that morning, the FBI had "moved in on" a house owned by Raymond Tanzer, a former cameraman at WPXU, Ion Networks. It must've been the guy the hotline cop said the police were interested in. "The Federal Bureau of Investigation sought to question Mr. Tanzer in connection with the bomb scare during the annual awards dinner for the prestigious Crunchtime Club in Manhattan on Saturday, and the brutal slaying of freelance journalist Todd Spencer that same evening," said a platinum blonde TV reporter standing in front of Tanzer's little brown house in Amityville.

Josie watched, eating ice cream out of the container, as further shots showed a car accident in the street, a sheet draped over a body, a gathering of concerned citizens (there was even a woman in hair rollers, dear God) – but no one from the FBI did any talking at the scene. Still, Josie had seen glimpses of a woman with some kind of burn on the side of her face. A ridiculously attractive cop, if that's what she was, burn or no burn.

"I like girls," Josie said, digging the spoon for further excavation. "So what are you gonna do about it?"

She spent a little time upstairs after the ice cream, with her T-shirt hitched up and tucked under her chin, pinching the fat around her stomach. She looked at her butt in the shorts she was wearing. She changed into yoga pants. Even less flattering. Not that it mattered. No one was going to see her. She hadn't left the house in days. At least, she figured, it looked like they'd caught the guy.

But later there was a press conference, and some middle-aged dude who was trying to look like a millennial with his high hair gave a statement on behalf of the FBI. He said that they were not only still thoroughly investigating the deaths of Eva Diaz, Monica Forbes, Jordan Baldacci, and Todd Spencer, but they were running an internal investigation into the nature of the events on Tuesday morning.

Josie saw the woman again, standing off to the side, her hands folded in front of her. So she was FBI, then. Brunette. Light brown eyes. Damn cute for FBI.

The reporters off camera started lobbing questions, and the dude with the high hair said he couldn't answer since it was a sensitive investigation. Josie heard things asked having to do with the "anti-media group known as Blackout" and "Is it true that Mr. Tanzer spent a week with them the previous winter?" and "Are these attacks on the media being considered hate crimes?" but none of them were answered.

"How's that make you feel?" Josie asked the unseen reporters on the giant flat-screen TV.

Yeah, she definitely needed to get out. She was talking to people who couldn't hear her, couldn't talk back.

How appropriate, though. What a theme for her life.

When the news paused to advertise *American Stars* – yet another summer season coming to a finale for the TV talent show that just wouldn't die – she clicked off the TV. Talk about a horrible, ugly reminder.

She walked into the kitchen and threw the ice cream spoon into the sink with a large clang, then threw the empty pint container in after it. For a moment, like a goddamn ghost, she saw Charlotte's face, big as life, hanging suspended in the gloomy kitchen. Smiling.

24

Shannon walked down the hallway toward her office. She started past the conference room, hearing voices. Half a dozen agents were gathered inside. Domestic terrorism specialists, hate crimes specialists. Tyler was just shutting the door. He glanced at her, said, "I'll be with you in a bit," and then closed off the sights and sounds.

In her office, she booted up her computer and opened the spreadsheet database with stories covered by each victim. She sat looking up at the photographs and news clippings she'd amassed.

She ran a search for Winston Hitchcock. The man she'd killed was a former truck driver. He'd spent two years at Rikers Island for distribution of OxyContin. He had three children, two teens and one little four-year-old girl. His mugshot made him look hardened, a typical criminal projecting strength, but she couldn't ignore the pain in his eyes.

She shut it down. Grabbed the cane, left her desk and went back down the hallway. Out.

～

NYPD's 90TH precinct in Williamsburg. She found Caldoza and Heinz in the bullpen. Their desks faced each other. Caldoza had his hands behind his head, feet up. Heinz was blowing his nose. Heinz noticed her, wadded up the tissue, and threw it at Caldoza. Caldoza batted it away, got angry, started to grumble something, and Heinz nodded in Shannon's direction. Caldoza looked, saw her, then stood up fast, nearly knocking over his chair.

"Agent Ames, how you doing?"

"I'm okay."

She was acutely aware of Heinz watching them, noticing their body language, the vibe Caldoza was putting off. But it wasn't why she was here. "What are you boys working on?"

Caldoza scratched the back of his neck. He had his badge hanging at his chest, gold against a black T-shirt. He wore blue jeans and blue cowboy boots. He looked at Heinz. "Well, ah, you know, we're following up on everything here and ..."

"The hotline calls?"

Caldoza kept avoiding her eyes and darting looks at Heinz. Heinz adopted a smug look, sitting there in his gray suit. "The Ray Tanzer thing ..." he started to say.

She held up a hand, nodding. "I understand. We took it and ran with it."

Caldoza moved a little closer, at last engaging her with his eyes. "You had quite a bit of action out there. You okay?"

"Yeah."

Heinz asked, "Tanzer awake yet? I heard he's having complications."

"They've induced a medical coma because his brain is swelling. No one has been able to talk to him yet."

Heinz opened his hands, did a half shrug. "I mean, he's good for it, right? What about the other guy? What's his name? Paddock?"

"They're going to grill him today." She looked between the

city detectives. "Why aren't you guys still working the Forbes case?"

Heinz shrugged again. "Talk to Whitaker. Talk to your boss, there, Tyler."

"I will," she said. She turned on her heel and headed for Whitaker's office, going by memory.

Caldoza hurried to catch up with her. "Hey, we've really had no choice here ..."

"Who's on the hotline calls? They're still coming in?"

"Yeah. Yeah, there's still calls coming in. We're checking them."

"Anybody heard from Ben Forbes?"

"The husband? No ... look, you're going to sprain something. Slow down ..."

She turned and pushed into him, suddenly seeing red. They were in the corridor just beyond the bullpen, still in sight of half the precinct, and people were watching. She didn't care. "Why does nobody give a shit about the Forbes case anymore?"

"I give a shit." Caldoza held up his hands in peace. "I do." He added, "But it's out of our hands."

"Why?"

"Why? Like Heinz said, maybe you need to ask your supervisor. As soon as that video played at the awards dinner, your team took over. The whole thing moved into domestic terrorism territory. We're just superfluous. No one is looking at Monica Forbes as an isolated homicide." He added, "Or even as some serial killer's second victim."

"I am."

He searched her eyes and said, "Well, maybe I'm with you, but we're alone."

She had him pinned to the wall. Not touching, just pushing with her aggression. It dissolved away and she stepped back, using the cane for support.

Caldoza's voice was low. "Have dinner with me tonight."

She looked closely at him, saw the sincerity, the attraction. And she said, "I'd like to see the hotline calls."

"You've already got them," he said. "Everything was transferred over to the FBI early this morning."

She turned and headed for the exit, then stopped. "I'll let you know about dinner."

∼

TYLER WAS IN HIS OFFICE. The conference room was empty. She'd tried to center herself on the way back from NYPD, but this intense frustration remained. She knocked once on Tyler's open door, stepped through when he looked up, then shut it behind her.

He got a look at her, then sat back. "What Bufort and Stratford did was reckless."

"That's not what I'm here about."

He folded his arms. "Okay. So ..."

"You're sure it's Blackout?"

"No. I'm not sure. Nobody's sure." Tyler used his palms to smooth back his already-slicked hair. One of the agents called it *Gavin Newsom* hair, governor of California. "But Tanzer is a hot item. He's been recorded making threats during his firing. He's on the guest list for the awards dinner. He's–"

"How did Stratford connect him to Blackout? The guest list I wasn't allowed to see? That's it?"

Tyler glared a moment, as if incredulous she'd cut him off, or for her insolent tone. He answered, almost growling: "Tanzer did a segment on them – on Blackout – for WPXU. For Ion. I'm surprised you haven't found that out yourself, with all of your moonlighting. He embedded with Blackout for a week. He had a small TV crew and everything."

"Why did they let him? A group that hates the media?"

Tyler said, "I don't know, Ames. Because they want recognition like anyone else? And Ion Networks probably loved the ratings a show like that got them." He looked at her, cooling a little, then pushed back his chair and stood up. "We're interviewing Paddock in an hour. Sit in on it. See for yourself. It wasn't perfect – we lost an agent. There's been some poor decisions – but this is how it gets done sometimes. Life in the big city."

She felt more cynical than she could remember, and grunted a laugh. "Life in the big city seems a lot to me like predrawn conclusions leading the search for evidence to fit them."

She turned, opened the door and left before he could respond.

∾

SHIT.

Ten minutes later, in her office, sitting with regret. For letting her emotions get the better of her. For being insubordinate.

But then she considered that, too. She'd been second-guessing herself this whole investigation. What it felt like sometimes was gaslighting. People telling her what she saw wasn't there, what she'd heard hadn't made the noise. They were gaslighting her, and then she was gaslighting her own damn self on top of it.

Enough of that. She looked up at her wall of victims and their stories. Then she logged in to the system and navigated the hotline calls database. Lieutenant Whitaker had showed her how to work it a few days before. She entered keywords – *Blackout*, *Tanzer*, *media*, and others, and came up with little.

When it was time for the Paddock interview, she went down one floor and stood in the viewing room with several others. Moray was there, along with some unfamiliar faces. Agents from the National Security Branch with somber, flat expressions and dark suits. They watched through the glass as Tyler grilled the suspect.

"I don't know what you're talking about," Paddock said.

"You don't ... Then why were you at Raymond Tanzer's house yesterday morning?"

"I want a lawyer."

"You don't get a lawyer for terrorism, James." Tyler was having a moment, showboating a bit. Oh well.

"I told you, I'm not a fucking terrorist."

"Tell me about Blackout."

"I don't know what that is."

"Okay. Okay. Then how about we talk about why you picked these particular victims?"

Paddock just turned his head away. He was a solidly built man, balding on top, tattoos on his arms. He looked into the mirror on his side, which on Shannon's side seemed as though he was looking right at her.

"I'm done talking," he said.

An hour later she was back in her office, chewing painkillers. Paddock hadn't admitted anything. Tyler remained focused on making it fit – finding the undeniable connection between Blackout and the murders.

"This is your chance," Tyler had said. "This is where you can tell me that Tanzer was on his own. Maybe starting his own terror cell, modeling it on what he'd learned from Blackout when he embedded with you six months ago, to do his story."

Paddock had made no response.

The next move was to round up anyone else associated, now or in the past, with the anti-media group. Question them as well. Wait for Tanzer's brain to stop swelling; wait for him to wake up. Shannon went to the hospital where he was being treated, showed her ID to be let through. She didn't know why she was here, what purpose it would serve, but felt drawn nevertheless. Maybe just to look at him and see.

Tanzer's eyes were closed, a tube stuck in his mouth. He was a smaller man than Paddock; a few too many cheeseburgers had expanded his midsection. She watched his chest rise and fall. The window beyond his bed was dimming, specks of rain hitting the glass.

Outside, she sat in the car in the hospital parking lot as a thunderstorm bore down, the rain hitting the roof like a dumped bag of dimes. No insights from visiting Tanzer. No epiphany.

When her phone buzzed, Caldoza calling, she ignored it.

For a few seconds.

"Hey," she said.

"This weather, huh? We needed it. Break the humidity."

"What can I do for you, Luis?"

He made a *tsking* sound. Then, "Come on. Just dinner. Just talk."

She sighed. "Okay. Where?"

SHE KNEW the word *prego* was Italian and probably meant, in this case, "have some more," but the name of the Italian restaurant nevertheless made her grin, thinking of the euphemism for being pregnant. When she realized she was smiling, she decided this had been the right choice. She'd needed to take a step back.

The night was wet after the storm, and still warm. Inside the place, with its burgundy and navy blue color scheme, it was cold enough to refrigerate beef. Having anticipated it, she pulled on the zip-up hoodie she'd brought. "Sorry," Caldoza said. Then he lowered his voice and said, "You want to go?"

"No. This is great."

The waitress was quick to bring them water and bread.

They ordered a calamari appetizer and declined the wine list and settled back.

"So how are you doing?" he asked.

"I don't like it. I really don't think Blackout is behind this."

"I meant *you*. How are you doing?"

"I'm fine."

"Still got the cane."

"Yes, thank you. It was very nice of you."

He swept his hand through the air. "That's not what I meant. I meant, how's it going? You doing the PT?"

"I haven't been."

His eyes stayed on her, and then he nodded and looked away. After a moment, he asked, "So you're from the Adirondacks?"

"I grew up near Westport. That's where I went to school."

He nodded. "Westport. I've actually heard of that. It's a stop on the train, right? There's a train you can take out of Penn Station? Takes a long-ass time. Takes like nine hours or something."

"Yeah, but that's all the stops," she said. "It's not nearly that long by car. It's like four, four and a half hours."

"So you been back? Recently?"

She hunted for his agenda, staring him down. Finding none, she said, "Not for a little while."

"How long's a little while?"

"Three years," she said.

"Yeah. Okay. I feel you."

"Everything's okay. It's just, you know, work. I've been on this probationary period, so working holidays, trying to make good. Before that I was finishing up in Stafford, there was training at Quantico ... So it's been a bit."

He studied her. "Yeah, sure. I get it."

She cleared her throat, feeling like she'd just rambled. "How about you? Ah, are you close with your family?"

"Sure. My ma. Two sisters. Lots of cousins." He re-situated himself so he had his back to the wall, one of his feet up on the bench seat on his side of the booth. "I'm from Philly, originally. But my parents divorced, and my dad took a job in the city. Here, I mean. Working for the MTA, actually, as a transit cop."

"No kidding."

He bobbed his head. "Yeah. And then, you know, years later, my dad had squirreled away a little bit of money and he bought some property up there."

She forgot about her nerves. "Really? Where?"

"Port Kent?"

"Sure. I know right where that is."

"So I was in school – maybe seventh grade – and my dad would go up there, sometimes for a couple of days, and he was messing around with this little piece of property. One time, I took the bus up there and met him. Bus was worse than the train. I told him. So the next time, I took the train. I remember Westport because I was terrified I was going to miss the stop for Port Kent, so I paid attention, and as soon as I heard Westport, I was like this ..." He put his feet down and sat up rigid-straight and widened his eyes in mock alertness, making her laugh.

"And the land?"

"Yeah. It's still up there. See ..."

They were interrupted when the waitress came with their calamari. "Ready to order?"

Shannon picked up her menu. "I'm so sorry, I haven't even looked." She glanced up at Caldoza. "Should we ... do you have anything you recommend?"

"One chicken piccata," he told the waitress, but then asked Shannon, "You eat meat?"

She nodded.

"One chicken piccata, one roast beef au jus." He handed the waitress the menus and said to Shannon, "We'll share."

When the waitress left, Caldoza sipped his water and said,

"My dad had these ideas. He thought everyone is going to leave the city. Not necessarily in his lifetime, but in mine. By the end of mine. People would be leaving the cities and getting back to the land." Caldoza looked at her then frowned and shook his head. "It wasn't like a climate thing. I don't think my dad thought about sea level rise or storms or anything. He just thought people wouldn't be able to keep it up. Society was going to be breaking down, and it was going to be this mass exodus back to the land. So he wanted a little piece of property, a little peace of mind." Caldoza shook his head and shrugged. "Something like that."

She waited. "And? Does he live there?"

"My dad lives the same place my grandfather lives. Rosebush Cemetery. The property is still sitting up there. I've got the paperwork at my house. I haven't been back up there since he died. So, eighteen years."

"Wow. So your grandfather outlived your dad, huh?"

"You remember that?"

"Yeah, you said fifteen years."

"That's right." He nodded and had some more water. "Dad was a drinker. Grandpa was not. They say sometimes it skips a generation. But just to be on the safe side, I steer clear of that stuff. Plus, I'm kinda always working."

He gave her a big smile, genuine, and she realized she liked Luis Caldoza. She respected him, found him genuine.

"You?" he asked. "Got family up there?"

She thought about her brother John first. Always first. She saw him in her mind the way she saw him the last time in life, beneath the water. Ice all around. John in the middle of it, through it, in the blackest of water, his skin white in the lights that the cops were shining in. Cops who knew him well. Cops who were his own men.

But she didn't need to tell Caldoza about any of that right now. She could talk about the good things, about her living brothers, about her father. She could even talk about her mother. And she opened her mouth to start when her phone buzzed.

At the same time, Caldoza lifted his waist to grab his own phone.

"No, it's mine," she said, pulling it out of her hoodie.

But he held his up, looking at the screen. "It's me, too."

Shannon answered, "Hello?"

25

Josie's phone chimed with an incoming email. She picked herself up off the floor and opened it.

The subject heading read: *Influencers get influenced.*

The body of the email contained a livestream link. She followed it and waited for the video to load, or buffer, whatever it did, with her heart beating a little faster.

She didn't know who CrazyEights88 at Gmail was. She didn't know why she was so quick to follow the link, not worrying about viruses or anything, instead acting on automatic pilot. Or acting like someone controlled by fate. Like she'd always known this was coming.

Like she'd just been waiting for it.

The video revealed two people, a man and a woman, both attractive and in their thirties, and both with nooses around their necks.

Josie covered her mouth with her free hand. She started sucking air through her fingers. Too fast, she was already breathing too fast ...

The couple were alive. She knew who they were. Half the world knew who they were. The nooses around their necks were slack. The camera – cell phone or whatever it was – widened out just enough to show them standing on stools. A second later, the person with the camera moved in, focusing on their faces, on the strips of duct tape covering their mouths.

Oh God oh God oh God ...

The cameraman then moved around behind the couple, first showing how the woman's hands were tied behind her back. He kept the shots tight, revealing little of the surroundings. The man's hands were tied too.

Oh God, I know what this is ...

Josie finally dragged her eyes away from the screen and read the text below:

'Like' what you see? This video is 100% real. And if it receives 100,000 likes, guess what? The stools they're standing on will be kicked out from under them.

Her breath came harder as her heart slammed against her ribs. She mumbled, "Jesus ... Jesus, this is *insane*," and her phone buzzed in her hand, making her jump and scream.

It was a text from Aaliyah. *Are you seeing this? Did you get this email?*

The next text had a link to the same video, *Influencers get influenced.*

Someone had apparently abducted the most popular Instagram couple in the country and was going to publicly hang them.

Josie texted back. *Yes. Watching now omg omg omg*

The phone vibrated. *I mean WTF? Is this real?*

Says it's real.

Maybe it's some stunt and they're trying to cash in likes.

Josie hadn't even noted the number of likes on the live video yet. She went back now and checked: 13,423. Before her very eyes, it ticked up to 13,429.

What the hell was wrong with people?

Then again, this was pretty much what had happened with

Charlotte, now wasn't it? People piling on, people too isolated and desensitized to realize the real-world impact made by their online actions.

She'd been one of those people. She'd been one of the worst ones.

Aaliyah kept texting, but Josie ignored it. The strangest thing – as she watched the video, her lips went numb. As she stared into the wide eyes of the influencer couple – the cameraman was showing their faces up very close – her ears and neck tingled, felt cold. All she could do was watch. Watch as the likes continued to roll in. Up to over 14,000 now. Climbing faster.

15,000, half a minute later.

Josie dropped her phone on the carpet. She ran into the kitchen. "Mom!" In her shock, she'd forgotten her mother was still gone. She thought about calling Robbie, her older brother, but what she really needed to do was just dial 911. Forget the stupid hotline.

She picked up the house phone and hit the three numbers. She waited.

An automated voice said, *"Due to a high volume of calls, your call is being redirected to a Public Safety Access Point. Please stay on the line."*

There was a click and a pause and a ringing.

Josie walked slowly back toward her phone, which lay faceup on the floor. She bent down, feeling tremors in her legs.

In her ear, the line kept ringing.

And ringing.

oving fast. The air outside the restaurant hitting like a wall. Running again. At least her hip and leg seemed to be recovering. Caldoza opened her door, even though the date was over. She sank into his Mustang as he ran around to the other side. Once in the driver's seat, engine ignited, growling, he said, "Get your seatbelt on."

The tires squalled as they pulled into traffic. "Where are they?" he asked. "SoHo?"

"Yes." She was already plugging it into the GPS.

"You called your people?"

"Computer forensics will try to trace it to an IP address. But we should go straight to their residence."

The couple on the video were James and Evelyn Priest, married thirtysomethings whose lives were broadcast nearly twenty-four seven for public consumption. Two very beautiful people, paid millions through advertisements and product placements. Part of a new and growing market, their job was to live their lives, and people tuned in. The more people "liked" and up-voted their exploits across a variety of social media platforms such as Instagram, Twitter, YouTube, and Facebook – the more money they made.

As Caldoza navigated Brooklyn traffic, heading for Manhattan, she watched the livestream on her phone.

"What's it up to?" He craned his neck to see.

"Eyes on the road. It's at thirty-two thousand." She scrutinized the image. Their faces looked horrified. Sweaty, eyes wide and crying. The nooses around their necks weren't rope, but something else. Like straps. Shannon would bet they were made of Cordura nylon.

"Ah, God," Caldoza said. "*Why*? I don't ... why are people liking it?"

She couldn't answer definitively, but thought at least some of the people liking the video must have thought it was fake.

Caldoza took a fast turn and she had to drop the phone and brace herself.

~

THEY CAME into SoHo with NYPD already on the scene, Wooster Street blocked off, emergency lights stuttering red and blue against the brown brick buildings. She'd checked it out on the way over – the Priests' lavish loft had been purchased two years before for a cool ten million.

She and Caldoza moved behind NYPD and fellow FBI agents – two from the New York field office – through the building lobby, up the stairs, to the sixth floor. The penthouse. The bomb squad checked the door for wiring. Shannon's skin tingled in the cloying heat. Heavy breathing filled the stairwell. One of the bomb squad guys said, "We're good," then SWAT rammed in the door.

SWAT first, guns out, followed by the bomb squad, still assessing for potential threats. Shannon and the rest of them had to wait.

The agent next to her introduced himself as Glenn Morshower.

"Shannon Ames."

"I know." Morshower looked at Luis. "And you're Caldoza."

They shook. Everyone was quiet after that, guns out, waiting. The bomb squad came back. "Clear." There was a collective exhalation of relief, followed by fresh tension: where were the Priests?

She pulled out her phone and called up the link. The video had jumped to sixty thousand likes in the last ten minutes.

LAW ENFORCEMENT SPREAD out through the couple's posh home. It was impossible to discern the Priests' location from the video. While others were scrambling to source the livestream, Shannon's job was to search their residence for any clue to where they might be.

Wherever it was, Shannon was sure it would be the same place where the Media Killer had put Monica Forbes on camera. Where he'd taken her and probably Eva Diaz, too, washing them of evidence before they served their function. But this was Manhattan, so she could be wrong; they could be nearer.

She moved slowly through the place with Caldoza close by.

The first level of the loft featured five large windows overlooking Wooster Street. An enormous living room had two L-shaped couches situated opposite each other, inlaid shelving against one wall. Shannon quickly browsed the titles before moving onto a large framed black-and-white photo of New York City.

"Where is that?" Shannon asked.

Caldoza stared for a minute. "Not sure."

"Hell's Kitchen," someone said.

Behind Shannon was an NYPD officer in uniform. Older man, graying around the temples. He looked from the photo to her, then dipped his head toward his shoulder as he pressed the transmit button on the walkie-talkie anchored there. "Sergeant Bristol we got a photo of Hell's Kitchen in the Priest's apartment. Looks like Eleventh Avenue to me, could be the corner of Dewitt Park."

The radio crackled. "Copy that, Fuchs."

They moved on.

Part of the couple's draw as influencers was their big public relocation from LA to New York. People had been tuning in every day to see how they'd been adjusting to the move, what new restaurants, gyms, and friends were acquired. What amazing parties were they attending this weekend? And the latest excitement – the Priests were going to try for a baby. She'd seen an Instagram photo gallery of the couple shopping for a crib. One image had garnered over two million likes. She'd then read an article that disclosed how the maker of that crib had offered the Priests a hundred thousand dollars to buy it.

So how did they fit in with the other murders? They weren't journalists. Were the parameters broader than they thought? If people who led sensational or profligate lives were targets, most of the modern world was at risk.

The problem was, the FBI's prime suspect for anti-media activity was in a coma. The second suspect was in custody. Anyone else associated with Blackout was under intense scrutiny.

Upstairs, the master suite accessed an expansive terrace. The sliding glass door was open a crack. "Is this how he got in?" Caldoza mused, moving ahead of her. Outside, warm breezes, the scent of fresh bread from a neighboring restaurant, blue and gold views of Lower Manhattan as the sky dimmed and the lights came on. A third level was all outdoors, more of the terrace, complete with a giant grill for cooking beneath a canopy festooned with lights.

"Living the dream," Caldoza said.

Shannon kept watch on the video. They weren't living it now. Faces red, glistening with sweat and tears.

"Goddammit," Shannon said, her own emotion bursting through. "Where are they? We can't just sit here and watch this happen!"

Seventy-five thousand likes.

"How did he manage this? I've just had a look at their Wikipedia page, and James Priest is in good shape. He's thirty-one years old, a hundred and sixty pounds of solid muscle. Works out five days a week. And both at the same time? She's no slouch either. She's done an Ironman competition, for God's sake."

"I don't know," Caldoza said.

Thinking about the black-and-white picture from downstairs, Shannon ran limping back down through the penthouse loft. She went through closets and drawers. She searched the pile of mail in the corner bedroom turned into a home office. Nothing with a Hell's Kitchen address. And anyway, it didn't matter – they were at *his* place, not one of their own. She was sure of it. Somehow he'd captured them. She very much doubted he'd come into the home. Crime scene would dust for prints and go through everything, but that wasn't how it had happened. He'd gotten to them out on the street somewhere.

She searched for phones. For an appointment book. A calendar. Anything with an itinerary. But this was the modern world – everything online and in the cloud. The expensive Google Pixelbook on the desk rejected her few password attempts. No phones in sight. She left the room, frustrated, angry, then tried the kitchen anyway. Just a hunch.

She found it.

On the massive, stainless steel refrigerator, a simple dry-erase board sectioned into the seven days of the week. Today, Tuesday: *Mindy's!! @ PlayerOne.*

"Here!" Shannon called. "Kitchen!"

Agent Morshower arrived first. "What do we got?"

"Need to find out what that means. That's where they were. He got to them between here and there."

More law enforcement gathered around, and people were putting the word out. Less than a minute later, the same NYPD cop, Fuchs, shared the information: "Player One is a club on Houston and Spring. That's right in the neighborhood."

The other FBI agent came into the kitchen with a small three-ring binder with a floral-printed cover. "Address book," the agent said. "Mindy is Melinda Scanlon, looks like a friend of the Priests – just had a quick look at her, and it's her birthday today."

Shannon asked, "Maybe a dinner? Birthday dinner?"

"Player One doesn't even open until nine p.m.," Fuchs answered.

"Maybe they rented it out," Shannon suggested. "Let's go."

MORE RUNNING. Player One was only three blocks away. She didn't know where her cane was. At Prego's? She kept checking the phone.

Ninety thousand likes.

Something changed.

The camera jostled a bit and then stilled, like it had been set down.

Shannon yelled, "Why aren't we getting the source of this video?"

People watched her. People everywhere out in the streets of SoHo as night came on. Cars and trucks rushing past. Music drifting from a third-floor window, a hip-hop song with heavy bass. Shannon looked around. Where was Caldoza?

She couldn't get her bearings. She stumbled into an alley, hoping to shut out some of the noise and commotion as she stared at her phone.

There!

It's him. That's him.

On the video, the killer showed himself: his hand, his arm, the edge of his shoulder. He faced toward the Priests, who were really squirming now, like they knew things were about to get even worse. Evelyn Priest whipped her head back and forth, her hair wet and sticking to her face. James screamed behind the duct tape wrapped around his head. The duct tape was coming apart a little bit, opening at a seam between layers, as if losing adhesion in the heat.

The killer then moved toward James. White, like Olivia Jackson had said. Medium build. He had a hood up over his head. *Dark gray hoodie.* But she'd seen his bare hand and would have to later analyze the video. Maybe a wedding ring? Any scars or tattoos?

The killer blocked the view of James Priest as he attempted to reaffix the loose tape. But James was really kicking, bucking with his whole body. The killer had to keep edging away, then darting back to finish the job. It wasn't working.

"*Aaaahhhhhhh!!!*"

The killer stepped out of frame, out of sight, and James wailed, his tongue poking free.

"Come on ..." Shannon said. Some part of her realized she was on her knees, that she'd been saying "come on, come on," over and over now, rooting for the Priests, rooting for them to somehow get free, because she was here, and she was so helpless, and she couldn't save them ...

"Shannon!"

Caldoza spotted her and came into the alley. Other people

were gathering at the mouth of the alley, unsure, looking in. Some, though, were turning to their own phones. How far had it spread? How many people were watching?

Ninety-one thousand likes. Going faster than ever. Jumping by the hundreds per second.

We *are doing this*, she thought dismally. *People are doing this. People are killing them.*

The Priests continued to thrash and struggle. James howled through the tape covering his mouth. Evelyn, surely terrified to move, to lose her balance, tried to see her husband, tried to look sideways at him.

Ninety-five thousand likes.

"Here we go," a voice said. For a split second, Shannon thought it was Caldoza, or someone on the street, but that was just her mind resisting the reality.

The killer had said it.

The likes approached a hundred thousand, hit it, went past it.

Shannon held a breath. Without thinking, she reached out for Caldoza. He grabbed her at the same time and they locked hands.

"All right!" The killer disappeared from view again, but his voice was loud and clear, like he was just beside the camera. "All right," he repeated. "And there you have it, folks."

Shannon tried to concentrate. Who did he sound like? Definitely middle-aged. That gruff edge to his voice – a smoker?

"There you have it," he said again, and raised his voice some more as he asked, "What do you two think of that? Huh? Your own fans. Your own *people*. Turning on you. Killing you."

James Priest stared with wide eyes. His face was red with fear. But also anger, Shannon thought. His lips pushed through layers of duct tape. "Fuck you," he growled. Beside him, Evelyn shut her eyes tight and sobbed.

"God," Shannon said quietly. She felt utterly helpless.

Trapped here, unable to get to the Priests, unable to stop this. It was happening right in front of her, yet somewhere she couldn't reach.

"Fuck me?" the killer muttered. "I'm not the one. I'm not the one doing this. You have your fans to thank. Your public. Unable to tell what's real or what's fake. Or maybe just not caring either way. Because that's what's going on – it's all entertainment now. No consequences." He paused. "Well, okay then."

On screen, the killer walked to Evelyn Priest and kicked out her stool first. She dropped and immediately started to buck and thrash.

Shannon cried out as Caldoza held her tight. James screamed, too, a blare of guttural pain barely recognizable as human. He tried to strike the killer with his foot when he came close but only succeeded in losing his own balance.

Shannon covered her mouth as James toppled. Hot tears filled her eyes. For an agonizing few seconds, he managed to keep one foot on the stool as he tried to maneuver his way back to standing.

But then the killer flashed through the scene and knocked the stool completely out of the way.

James Priest swung. Eyes bulging in terror, his body spasmed like a fish on the wharf. Beside him, Evelyn Priest's movements were already slowing, her own eyes glassing over as she gradually suffocated.

Shannon set her phone on the filthy ground. Caldoza tried to comfort her, but she gently pushed him away. On all fours, she let her head hang and she closed her eyes.

27

He strangled all of them.

It was roughly true. Baldacci's head had been nearly taken off by an explosion, Spencer's by a deep slashing cut, the Priests hung. The remaining two victims, Diaz and Forbes, were the most technically strangled, but it all nevertheless fit an oblique pattern: he went for the throat. These were brutal kills. As much as she saw the deaths working in concert to serve a greater plan, she saw anger. She saw rage.

Back at the Priests' loft, Shannon had regained her composure and was thinking clearly: if the killer was making a point with the Priests – killed by their own fans, by the very system that had made them – that was in line with an ideologically driven killer. It could be someone from Blackout. And it echoed the indictments within the manifesto, yet broadened the scope to include people outside the news media. But this going for the throat, the manual strangulations and the hangings – something about that felt personal.

And the strap. The nylon straps used to hang the Priests – trace fibers found on Monica Forbes's body – this was significant. Did it fit the MO of a highly exacting, even practical killer? Yes. But could it also have some other significance? She thought so, although why she couldn't say. It itched in a place she couldn't scratch.

She offered her theories and her questions to Tyler, who didn't want to hear it and hung up abruptly with her, and she put away her phone and sat on the edge of the Priests' king-sized bed. Their bedroom smelled of eucalyptus.

After a moment of sitting with her head in her hands, she got up and walked through the house. Crime scene technicians in white jumpsuits were dusting doorknobs and taking samples of toothbrushes for DNA.

She moved through the rooms silently.

There has to be something.

On the phone with Tyler just now, she'd implored him again to get into Todd Spencer's computer. That they needed the personal and work data on all of the victims – what had been provided by their employers wasn't enough. They had Monica Forbes's personal materials through NYPD's 90th, but they needed to look deeper into Diaz's personal life. *Something* connected these six victims beyond the obvious. A reason each was chosen among a world of journalists and influencers.

"Right now," Tyler had said, "the focus is on finding the Priests."

She couldn't argue that. While she roamed their penthouse apartment, forensic specialists continued to hunt the source of the livestream, while others studied the video for details, give-aways of its location in real physical space. She'd already seen it: that moment the killer had moved the camera, widening the shot, she'd seen those same walls in the background. Same as Monica Forbes.

Shannon found herself in the Priests' lavish bathroom, the color of lemony sunshine, staring at the bathtub, thinking about water. About being cleansed. Eva Diaz and Monica Forbes, both scrubbed down.

The *willpower* such an act implied. It was pure methodology, strategy. Someone who understood forensic science, either from books or the internet or experience.

But the emotion, Shannon thought, *that* could be seen in the escalating severity of each crime. From Diaz quietly dumped in garbage bags, to Forbes's death drawing the next victim, Baldacci, nearly decapitated, to the massive panic and bomb scare surrounding Spencer's death, to this – the world participating in the murder of the Priests – each time the Media Killer struck, it was more heinous than the last. Why? Because he needed a bigger fix?

Or was it something else? Another reason why this related to something personal?

In the den, she gazed at the empty spot on the desk where the Priests' laptop had once been, now taken into evidence. She looked through the one photo album she could find. Pictures of their wedding. People they knew. Friends. Family.

Just a tiny fraction of the millions who followed them online.

HER PHONE VIBRATED against her hip.

"Hello?" Shannon was back staring at the refrigerator, the note about the birthday party. The Priests had rented out Player One and had planned to start decorating around seven p.m. They'd never shown.

"Hello?" The voice on the other end was nervous, quiet. Latino accent.

Shannon's attention sharpened. "Hello, this is Special Agent Shannon Ames – who is this?"

"Um, yeah, okay. Um, this is Alfonso Mendoza."

"Alfonso Mendoza ..." She searched her memory. So many names and new faces over the past week. She was usually pretty good matching them up – she was sure she hadn't met an Alfonso. Even if the name was familiar ...

She said, "Okay – you work at Dylan Construction."

"Yeah. Yes, ma'am."

She shifted the phone to her other ear and walked out of the kitchen, back toward the terrace. "Thank you for calling, Alfonso. How can I help you?"

"I, ah ... you talked to Selena Martinez a couple of days ago?"

"Yes, that's right. I came by the office there. I wanted to look at the crime scene. The Eva Diaz crime scene."

"Yeah. You left your card."

"I did ..." Shannon paused in the terrace doorway, the scents and sounds of the city riding the warm breeze. "Is there something you'd like to talk about?"

"I talked to the cops, you know. Because I found her. I found the body."

"Right. Yes."

"And, ah ... so I talked to them and told them everything. Well, I mean I told them almost everything. I don't know why I was not, ah ... Well, I just didn't think about it back then. But I go out every morning, I get the trucks ready. That's my job – get everything ready for the crews."

She was quiet, letting him come to the point.

"And I, ah – you know, before any of that happened, I seen this car sitting there on the street."

"Which street? Fifty-Fifth?"

"Yeah, Fifty-Fifth. Just sitting there. Happened twice. It would sit for a minute, engine running, and then drive away."

"This was before you found the body, Alfonso?"

"Yeah. This was like a week before."

"Did you see the driver?"

"No. I mean, I could tell someone was sitting there behind the wheel, you know. Couldn't see them or anything."

"Okay ... and the make of the car?"

"Um, Dodge Challenger. Really nice."

"Vintage or modern?"

"Oh, definitely one of the new ones. Big and blocky. Metallic blue. But I didn't say anything because, I don't know. I didn't think about it when I found the body. Not really at all. But then, you know, this thing keeps happening. So Selena said you were here, and I thought, maybe you can use all the help you can get."

He fell silent.

"Thank you, Alfonso. That's good thinking."

They talked a little more about it, but that was the gist – a blue Challenger had shown up twice in the week before Diaz was found. On its own, it meant nothing. She thanked him again, ended the call and stood looking out over the night-draped city.

After a moment, she went back through the Priests' home, thinking it all through again, imagining the glamourous lives of a celebrity couple. But the answer to their death wasn't here. She knew it. Not here in the three-dimensional world. Not in their physical lives.

The answer lay in their digital lives.

BACK AT HER OFFICE, the new data points begged inclusion: James and Evelyn Priest, social media influencers. They weren't journalists covering stories, but without a doubt, they disseminated information.

We have never had to apologize for the fear we sell ...

The way we spread fear, generate outrage, and disseminate disinformation ...

Maybe it did fit the anti-media ideology. But that could be a convenient cover for the killer.

With a tall cup of coffee riding the desk beside her, she went through the Priests' Instagram account. Their Twitter and Facebook accounts. Back, back, through their online history.

On Instagram, a picture of Evelyn modeling a new outfit. The both of them posing like *Lady and the Tramp* over a bowl of spaghetti in an Italian restaurant they endorsed. A video of James talking about a new pair of sneakers for running. He held them up and rotated them in the air like a salesman. A very handsome salesman with a boxy chin, two-day stubble, thick, manicured eyebrows hooding big brown eyes. Cut to shots of him running through Central Park. Who was the cameraman? Was it Evelyn? Doubtful. God rest her soul, but she wouldn't have been able to resist a moment turning it around on herself for a wave or a wink. Was the cameraman significant? At the end of the video were brief credits – Shannon took the name down anyway: Saul Bennett.

Back, back, further in time. Instagram was mostly original content, pictures and videos, a plethora of likes. Twitter had much of the same stuff, but then there were copious retweets. Ah, to get retweeted by the Priests! It must have been make-or-break for some people.

She took a break, feeling punchy, getting cynical.

The office was quiet, but a few agents were working. Shannon walked up and down the hallway, passing Tyler's empty office. She focused on her leg, hip, lower back. Tried to imagine knots unravelling. Muscle fibers relaxing their stranglehold, inflammation subsiding.

After midnight now, no one calling with a bead on the Priests. Were they still swinging from their nooses? The account that had streamed the video was gone. There was no more user named CrazyEights88. If anything was for posterity, it would've had to have been screen-recorded by a third party, or maybe somehow by the killer himself. But so far no one had posted their bootleg of the Priests' horrible hanging murder.

Maybe there was a shred of decency left in the world. Or perhaps no one had recorded it.

CrazyEights88. Many brains at the FBI were currently trying to crack that one, too. What did it mean? Someone who liked card games, born in 1988? As good a guess as any.

Shannon stared at the wall. She consulted her database. The four reporters – Diaz, Forbes, Baldacci and Spencer – had exactly nineteen stories in common. At least, ones she'd been able to track thanks to the employment records from their respective TV stations and newspapers and personal records, and thanks to getting access to Spencer's laptop. But she was just scratching the surface with the Priests' online history, let alone their dozens of contracts with businesses and advertisers.

She found something anyway: the first formal exhibition of a famous New York City street artist known as Stellan was an event covered, in one way or another, by all of the Media Killer's victims. The Priests had attended and tweeted. Diaz had reported live for WCBS-TV. Forbes had discussed it with co-hosts the following day on *The Scene*. Baldacci had written a small piece on it in *Newsday*, while Spencer had covered it in much more detail for *The Forward*.

Not exactly the kind of story convergence that stirred up a serial killer, but at least it was something that connected them all.

And there were more. Similar stories to the art exhibition, stories that crossed the entertainment barrier into "serious" news, as writers like Spencer and Baldacci, for instance, could shape philosophical or ethical questions out of certain events.

Shannon searched, she scoured, but found no evidence that the Priests had dipped into the Pelham Bay story. No indication they even knew about the land development or Nikolay Lebedev. And no connection that she could find between the Priests and Blackout. Spencer had written about Blackout once three years ago, but he was the sole victim to connect.

A metallic blue Dodge Challenger had apparently idled outside Dylan Engineering and Construction twice in the week prior to the body of Eva Diaz being dumped there. Who drove a metallic blue Challenger? Was it Lebedev? Was it Raymond Tanzer? He had a different car registered in his name, but it could've been a loaner.

And he sat there in the street, watching – for what? To know when people left for the day, when they returned the next morning? Whether there were cameras watching or guard dogs patrolling? Because he'd gotten fired for slacking off and maybe being a drug addict, and now turned his rage against all media professionals?

One a.m. The coffee was long gone. She was running on pure ambition, her mind going nonstop, like this:

Ray Tanzer was working for Paul Torres. Torres had holdings in a company that paid the Priests to endorse. Blackout was really a much more sprawling underground organization than anyone realized, with growing terror cells and connections to elites all over the city. Perhaps the nation. Perhaps the world.

The name of the two most recent victims was Priest. They could have been selected for that reason alone! For the symbolism of it: social media was the new place of human congregation, the new church, and they were its ordained ministers, offering the sacraments of social inclusion, performing rites against the evils of FOMO – fear of missing out.

Monica Forbes had willingly gotten into the back of an SUV, according to a severely myopic eyewitness. She'd been dumped under a bus.

Thrown under the bus.

To throw under the bus: to betray a friend for selfish reasons.

Monica Forbes, a friend to the killer? An ally?

Nothing could be ruled out. Which meant Shannon was farther than ever from a reasonable hypothesis.

This was bordering on insanity. She was beginning to sound like Heinz.

It was two a.m. and she needed to call it a night. Her day had begun some eighteen hours earlier, a morning heavy with guilt. She'd killed a man. Someone for whom no guilt had been proven. And the day had ended with her inability to save yet two more victims. Her inability to predict where the killer would strike next, because she had yet to learn why he was striking at all.

Without thinking, Shannon gritted her teeth and swiped everything off the side of her desk. The motion sent pens and papers flying, and the empty coffee cup to the floor.

She stood and went to the wall. Her hands hooked into claws, she tore down the faces of Forbes and Diaz. The words of Spencer and Baldacci. Thumbtacks popped from the wall as she ripped away the twine she'd used to connect ideas. Stories to other stories. Names to names. She tore it all down.

BUT SHE DIDN'T LEAVE. There was no one waiting for her at home but Jasper. She'd been here a year, lived in the city a year, and she'd not even dated. She was married to the job. Went to church on Sundays, ran through Prospect Park three times a week, saw the occasional movie, and avoided returning to her family home. Avoided the cloying, almost desperate love of her father, the cool distance of her mother. A mother who never got over the death of her oldest child – and who could blame her?

There was nowhere to be but here. There was nothing to do but this.

So she continued to cross-reference the victims.

She looked while the night cleaner came vacuuming down

the hallway and was gone again. She looked until she'd picked up the coffee cup three different times, only to suck a little air and coffee-flavored moisture from the spout. She searched until she found two more stories covered by all victims that were unlikely candidates for initiating a murdering spree, but then one that ... well, might've been.

It was a story that was covered by Diaz, Baldacci, and Spencer that had also been tweeted about by the Priests. The only problem was, there was no record of Monica Forbes having worked it.

But the more she saw, the more she learned, the more compelling the story became.

As she read Spencer's article for *The Forward*, Baldacci's piece on her own blog, and watched Diaz's report of it on TV, she thought, *Now this – THIS is something that could drive a person to the very edge of sanity.*

She'd been seeing advertisements for the season finale of *American Stars* all over the city. Commercials on TV. They all took on a new significance now.

This one ...

This one she couldn't let go. This one was too good.

This had all the elements.

And it wasn't just one story that involved *American Stars* ...

Really, it was two.

When Shannon finally left the office, she was running.

28

S hannon held her ID to the glass until the concierge let her in. "I need to see Mr. Forbes," she said, coming into the coolness of the lobby.

"Um ..." The concierge, a handsome black man in his late forties or early fifties, looked dubious. "Is Mr., ah, Forbes ..."

"He's not expecting me. But this is a matter of a federal investigation. Please buzz him."

The concierge did, and about thirty seconds later, a sleepy voice came through the intercom: "What is it?"

"Mr. Forbes. I have a federal agent here to see you. She says it's urgent."

There was a pause. "Send her up."

～

THE ELEVATOR DOORS opened onto the penthouse antechamber. Forbes stood in the doorway to his place in sweatpants and a body-hugging tank top. Bare feet. "What's the matter?"

"I'm sorry it's so late."

"It's okay. Please come in." He stepped back and gestured

that she enter his home. The apartment was tranquil, distant lights of Manhattan twinkling in the windows, the hushed rumble of air-conditioning moving through the vents. "I'm picking up the kids today," he said, leading her into the kitchen. He pulled out a barstool for her, then sat down himself.

She stayed standing. "Is there anything Monica was working on that wouldn't be in her records?"

Forbes just looked back at Shannon a moment, then averted his gaze. He rubbed the back of his neck. "Ah, no. I don't know. What do you mean?"

"Anything that, for whatever reason, wouldn't show up in her employment records? Something she might've even scrubbed from her own personal records?"

He glanced up, just a flit of his eyes. "I don't know. Why would someone do that? You think it's relevant? To what happened to her?"

"Mr. Forbes, I know it's a bad time. I know this is a sudden question, and ..."

He patted the air with his hand and bobbed his head. "No, it's okay."

"Did you see what happened earlier tonight?"

He'd gotten up and moved toward the softly humming fridge. Now he stopped and gave her a look. "The influencer couple, there? The Priests?"

"It's the same guy."

Forbes didn't move. He stared off into some middle space between them. She could see him working it out – whether or not to tell her something he knew, making the calculations.

"It's not that bad," Shannon said. "If Monica was involved in what I think she was involved in, it's not that bad. She was just doing her job."

That got Forbes's full attention. He studied her, a mixture of indignation and sorrow on his face, and then turned back to the fridge. "Can I get you something, Agent Ames?"

"No."

His back to her, he said, "Come on. One beer. You drink beer, I bet."

She cleared her throat and found herself sitting up a little bit straighter. "Okay. One beer." Whatever got him talking.

He leaned into the fridge and came out with a bottle in each hand. He rotated around and set them on the corner, then pulled open a drawer beneath. She watched him do all of this, reading his body language, his face. He'd already made his decision; he was just coming to terms with it. That's how people were. She gave him the time.

He opened both beers, pushed hers across the island. When she had it in hand, he raised his own bottle, but said nothing. She raised hers, their eyes connected, and then each of them took a drink. Forbes set his bottle down and stayed standing. He leaned against the countertop with his palms. Let his head lower to his shoulder blades.

"Charlotte Beecher," he said. "That's what you're talking about?"

"It is," Shannon said, feeling a thrill she barely kept out of her voice.

He nodded slowly, his face angled down. "Okay," he said softly. "Okay ..."

Sensing the opportunity, she started, "Mr. Forbes, what I would like to do now is–"

"Monica was mortified by that whole thing," he said. He lifted his face to Shannon, eyes shining with emotion. "She didn't want any part of it. And then when ... when the girl did what she did, Monica was just devastated. I mean, just devastated. She threatened to leave her job. She wanted to." Forbes stood fully upright and took a few steps back as he spoke, until his back was against the fridge, his arms folded in front of his chest. "But they begged her. They *begged* her. We went through it for two weeks. Longer. She was having nightmares. Finally, she said – she was thinking about our kids, okay, about us having enough money for their future, for college – she told the network she'd stay, but she wanted the whole thing expunged from her record. Wanted her name taken off anything to do with that one episode. I think it was episode one-eleven. I don't think you can find it. I think they took it down everywhere it was online. Unless someone filmed it on their TV, or screen-recorded it, whatever that is ..."

Forbes was sputtering out. He gazed down at the floor again and fell silent.

"I understand."

His eyes snapped back. "Yeah. Well, it wasn't good. And so now – you think this is – how does this have to do with that? Who would be ...?" But Forbes trailed off, perhaps finding the answer was right there, right in front of him. He uncrossed his arms and put a hand over his mouth. "Oh my God," he said through the hand.

She was off the barstool a second later and came around the island toward him. "Ben, listen to me."

He was lost in the horror of it, staring into space again.

"Ben."

He focused on her.

She said, "This stays between us right now, do you understand? You can't talk to anybody."

He nodded, but barely.

"Anybody," she repeated. "You need to go get your kids today. You need to tell them whatever you're going to tell them about their mother, but not this. Not this part. And then you need to – I don't know. Go somewhere. Be with them. Get away from here. You hear me?"

Ben Forbes had absently raised his hand to his mouth and was nibbling on a knuckle. He suddenly struck her as childlike, the adult in him broken. "Yes," he said. "I hear you."

"Not because she's guilty of anything," Shannon said. "Your

wife is a victim. This is a sick man. But your kids don't need to see this. What's going to happen."

"It was his daughter," Forbes said, almost whispering.

She started to respond, but Forbes quickly moved away. She let him go. It passed through her mind to have him followed. Maybe even for his own safety, or the safety of his children. But also to ensure that he kept in confidence what had just been discussed.

"Ben?"

He didn't answer or return to the room. He was gone from sight and then a door closed. Probably his bedroom. Now she was torn. There was so much to do. She had him! She had the guy! She knew the identity of the Media Killer.

Don't get ahead of yourself.

She took another quick pull of the beer, then realized she didn't know if it was hers or his. She was in a state. *Don't get ahead of yourself?* This was the break she'd been waiting for, the story she'd been hunting, the piece that tied it all together.

Charlotte Beecher.

"WHO IS CHARLOTTE BEECHER?"

Ready for the question, Shannon booted up the video. She kept thinking about Ben Forbes, but Tyler had signed off on putting someone on him, an agent named Kim Tam.

The YouTube video began to play. Tyler crossed his arms as they waited through a stupid advertisement for car insurance. She'd called as she'd left Forbes's place, then gone right to his house. Four thirty in the morning, dawn just smudging the eastern sky salmon and gold. Tyler was no doubt thinking *this'd better be good.*

The advertisement ended.

The video that followed started with a cut into a program

that was already in progress. A massive audience swelling against a brightly lit stage.

"What is this?"

"This is *American Stars.*"

"It's one of those shows," Tyler said.

"Yes. This is two years ago. Watch."

The host of the show, a supermodel with long legs stemming from a puffy, fur-coat-like outfit, strutted to center stage, microphone in hand, and introduced the next contestant to uproarious cheering. Apparently, this was one of the final rounds of competition for the vocalists. The current contestant rolled out in a wheelchair. One of his arms was bent against his chest. The din rose to distortion-causing levels; the speaker on Tyler's laptop crackled.

"Ames," Tyler said, sounding impatient.

"Hang on ..."

Various sweeping shots covered the audience as they leapt and waved their arms and shrieked for the disabled performer. A few tighter shots selected various overjoyed fans. And then one shot showed a young woman jumping up and down, her arm hooked into a claw, her tongue hanging out. Like she was mocking him.

Then the crowd hushed, the lights dimmed, changed, and the disabled performer began to sing. His voice was astonishingly good.

Shannon hit pause. Her heart was beating hard, both because of what she understood, and her zeal to bring Tyler into that same epiphany. "Now look at this," she said, selecting an accompanying video. It was much shorter, just thirty seconds, and put the mocking young woman's antics on a three-second loop, so that she jumped and flailed and stuck out her lolling tongue and rolled her eyes back in her head again and again.

Shannon risked a glance at Tyler's face. She could see it

sinking in. They were in his home office, a small room with a banker's lamp over the desk. It smelled like he'd recently burned a candle in here. That, and her own sweat – she'd been up for nearly twenty-four hours now, running all over the place, the toasted sourness of coffee lingering in her mouth, a subtle ache in her jaw from all the adrenaline.

"Now this," she said, and typed a phrase into the search field and hit Enter.

Eva Diaz stood in front of Radio City Music Hall with a microphone. She swept a hand in the general direction of the venue. "Right here," she said, "the final rounds of *American Stars* have been playing out. But amid the drama of whose favorite contestant will become America's favorite new pop star, a controversy is sweeping the nation: what to make of the actions of this audience member?"

Shannon's skin stippled with gooseflesh as she watched the same shot of the young woman pulling faces at the end of the performer's song.

The shot came back to Diaz. The attractive young reporter had repositioned herself up a wide set of stairs, and she slowly walked down toward camera for effect, gesturing with her free hand. "It's an image that has stunned millions – an audience member blatantly making fun of a disabled contestant. And it raises the question: even if we have our favorites, is this appropriate behavior? What has happened to common decency? Eva Diaz, Entertainment News for Channel 2."

End video.

Shannon was still moving fast, mindful of Tyler's skepticism. She was aware of him beside her, brushing a finger back and forth over his lips as she navigated to Todd Spencer's piece in *The Forward.* It was called "Cancel Culture: What Happens When It's Not a Celebrity?" Tyler scanned it; she had already read it. In the article, Spencer suggested that celebrities paid a worse penalty for their cultural crimes of indecency or political incorrectness, since they had more to lose. Everyday people, on the other hand, could fly beneath the radar, be indecent, politically incorrect, and come away unscathed. Spencer, who mentioned having a daughter of his own about the same age as the unnamed girl in the video, was disgusted by that girl's behavior.

Shannon's fingers flew over the keyboard to present Tyler a similar article from Jordan Baldacci.

"Baldacci's piece focuses on youth culture, and the idea that the youth are desensitized, isolated in their social media bubbles, and out of touch with reality. Makes a pariah out of the girl."

Tyler thought about it, finger swishing back and forth. "And the girl is Charlotte Beecher."

"Yes. I can get to that now."

He put out a hand. "How are the Priests involved?"

"This was two years ago. They retweeted a video clip that went on to get over a hundred thousand likes."

"Retweeted from whom?"

"I've just got the Twitter handle for that, no user yet."

He leaned over the laptop. "How did the first clip even come into being? I mean, it's a live TV show …"

Shannon felt a little pulse: *he's on board.* She clicked the keys. "Okay, this is the first video I could find. It's from Smiley-Grady004 and it's the whole song. Probably a fan. You can see this is a video camera recording off his TV – see how it's kind of distorted right there? And then someone took a screen recording of this and excerpted the bit with Charlotte Beecher. That's this user here, and this is where the tweet links to."

Finished, she stepped back, letting Tyler think.

After a few seconds staring at the laptop, he asked, "Forbes?"

"I spoke to her husband an hour ago. She discussed it on *The Scene.* He said her network pulled that episode after Charlotte Beecher killed herself. And Monica asked that she be completely disassociated from having anything to do with it."

Tyler looked at her. "Have you seen that episode of *The Scene*?"

"No."

"How did the girl kill herself?"

Shannon had been waiting for it. "She hung herself, Mark." After letting him absorb this, she said, "Her family has a house in Astoria Heights."

His eyes were unfocused. "Astoria ..."

Shannon bent toward the computer again. She hit a few keys. After a moment, Tyler was beside her, looking.

"This is her father," Shannon said quietly. "Henry Beecher."

Tyler didn't say anything at first. He just nodded two times, then shook his head, then grunted. "Ah, fuck," he said.

29

They sat a safe distance from Henry Beecher's house in Astoria Heights, with the sun just breaking over the rooftops. Shannon was in the passenger seat of Tyler's car. He'd ordered her to stay put and was out on the street, talking to local PD and pointing.

Shannon studied the house. Long and skinny and two stories. Beige vinyl siding, black plastic window shutters. The relatively large yard was the major amenity, a coveted element in this working-class neighborhood.

Black-clad SWAT officers in helmets crept in close and surrounded the place.

The excitement of discovery dissolved into the somber reality: two years ago, Henry Beecher's daughter had ostensibly mocked a disabled performer on a massively viewed television show. A short time later, she'd taken her own life. By all accounts, her suicide was the result of a relentless online bullying that followed her unwitting appearance on *American Stars*.

Shannon watched as three SWAT cops prepared to enter the front. Two flanked the door; one knocked. She watched

Tyler, waiting across the street. He'd pulled on some tracksuit pants and a sweatshirt, like he was trying to be Luis Caldoza.

The cops at the door knocked again. One rang the doorbell. Four others had gone around to the back of the house. The cop who'd rung the doorbell spoke into the radio transmitter clipped to his shoulder. Déjà vu washed over her. She had visions of the minivan in Amityville, smoke roiling from the hood, the dead man behind the bullet-punctured windshield. The oozing hole in his neck. Winston Hitchcock. Now, more than ever, looking like someone who had nothing to do with the media killings.

But this wasn't that. If anyone had motive, it was Henry Beecher. Not only that, he had opportunity. Diaz, victim number one, lived only one mile away in Ditmars-Steinway. Forbes was just over in Williamsburg. These were targets he could access, and they had been his first.

Don't let the conclusion lead the evidence: her own frank advisement to a superior.

Which was why finding out that Beecher had been part of the awards dinner security team had been a critical find.

As a security guard for the awards dinner in Manhattan, Beecher had gained yet more opportunity. He'd managed to get into the audio-visual technician area and splice his video into the presentation. Then he'd positioned himself by the front door, so that as everyone ran screaming, he could cut Spencer's throat.

Chilled, she tried to distract herself by looking at the other houses on the street. The color palette was subdued: pale blues, light greens, grays and whites. All the roofs were gray shingles. What a thing, New York City. From skyscrapers to projects to residential homes in a row. Turn a corner, something completely different. Thousands of independent universes, just a block or two in dimension, all coexisting in this one place.

A car came rolling down Seventy-Third. A Mustang –

Caldoza. It stopped, double-parked, and the NYPD detective got out, tucking a button-down shirt into his jeans. He looked at Beecher's house, then saw her in Tyler's car, and came over. She rolled down the window.

"Holy shit," he said when he reached her.

"Yeah."

They both watched the house. The SWAT cop at the front entrance was now picking the lock to the outer door, an out-swinging steel security door.

"How you doing?" Caldoza said.

"I'm okay. You?"

He nodded. "Good. Just can't believe this. The whole department is going crazy. How sure are we?"

"We're never completely sure. But this is looking close."

They watched as Tyler came over. He gave Caldoza a kind of dirty look, and Caldoza backed away from the car. Tyler said to Shannon, "Not home. House is cleared. We're going in."

She opened the door. Both men moved to help her, and Tyler cut Caldoza another one of those looks. She closed the door and ignored them both, walked to the sidewalk and up to the front door of the house without much limping. Caldoza had the cane again, anyway – she'd left it in his car the night before.

The lock-picking cop had gotten through the outer door. Four more guys moved past her up the steps with a small battering ram and busted through the inner door. Shannon noticed some faces in the windows of the surrounding houses. Then Tyler went past her, into the house, and she followed.

THE SWAT COPS who were first through didn't like what they saw inside. "The fuck? Beecher? I know this guy," one said.

Caldoza stepped through the entrance, overhearing. "He's retired," Caldoza said to them.

One guy, beefy, removed his helmet. "So he don't get due process?"

"He got his due process," Tyler answered, from out of sight. "The FBI has evidence to place him as the number one suspect in the media killings." Tyler emerged from deeper in the house, past the stairway. He pulled a piece of paper from the pocket of his navy blue track pants. "Got the warrant right here. Thanks, guys, you can wait outside."

The two SWAT cops gave him the stink eye, then one said to the other, "Fuck this," and they left.

On the wall near where they'd been standing hung Henry Beecher's picture. With the American flag behind him, Beecher smiled big and a bit crookedly, dressed in the navy blue shirt and peaked cap of his NYPD uniform.

Shannon and Caldoza followed Tyler back to the kitchen. Not bad. Recently redone, everything new and shiny and a freshly retiled floor. Shannon lingered over a different picture on the fridge: Henry and Charlotte and another woman. Her name was Teresa, Shannon knew, Henry's wife. Charlotte's mother.

"All right," Tyler said, looking around. He put his hands on his hips. "Let's get everybody. And I mean *everybody*."

THE LACK of sleep was starting to get to her, but she pushed it aside. Henry Beecher stared at her from the blown-up version of his police headshot. Tyler had it up on the main screen at the resident agency. The supervising agent had changed from his tracksuit into a professional three-piece for the small crowd of law enforcement, FBI, and New York City police present in the conference room.

Tyler said, "Okay, here is what we know. Henry Beecher, fifty years old, former New York City Police officer. Beecher retired after twenty-two years of service. Apparently, he'd planned to stay longer, until mandatory retirement at age sixty-two, but for the death of his daughter and the subsequent hospitalization of his wife, Teresa."

Tyler hit a button on the remote he was holding, and the image changed to a woman's face. "This is Teresa Beecher. Forty-nine years old. Currently an inpatient at Kingsboro Psychiatric Center in Brooklyn. She's been in and out of there over the past two years, suffering from chronic depression and acute anxiety."

Another click of the remote. "And this young lady is Charlotte Beecher. Young Miss Beecher completed a suicide after feeling humiliated by a spate of news and social media covering her actions during the live taping of a reality TV competition show – you all have that in your briefings – you can watch on your own time."

Tyler switched back to Henry. A silence followed, heavy and remorseful. "Look," Tyler said, walking toward the group. "We're not happy about this. Nobody is happy to have our prime suspect be a decorated police officer. But let's not focus on that, but instead, what it means." Tyler ticked off the attributes on his fingers as he listed them. "It means he's very capable, very smart. He's had access to things ordinary citizens might not have. He knows people. And people who know *him* said he's a highly motivated person. Always had a project going. He's a bit on the introverted side. He's quiet, a serious guy who stays busy. There's every chance he's been planning this for a long time. Charlotte Beecher hung herself in August. That's two years Henry Beecher could have been putting this together."

Tyler had kept walking into the seated group of them while talking. He stopped next to Shannon. "All right, everybody. Right now, I want to turn this over to Special Agent Ames. Many of you know Agent Ames." He glanced down at her, then swept the group with his gaze. "For those of you who don't,

Shannon was the one who cracked this thing open." He turned to her again. "Agent Ames?"

She got to her feet.

~

THEY'D SPENT hours in Beecher's home, looking for clues to his present location. They had his phone number; calls went straight to voicemail and the phone wasn't showing up on any satellites – it was powered off or destroyed. Somehow, Beecher had known they were close. Either that, or he certainly did now and wasn't going to ever come out of hiding.

Shannon pointed to a map on the screen. "There's two things I want to touch on, then I'll leave you to it. The first thing, we know Beecher's beat as a police officer was, at least for a time, an area that included Long Island City and Hunters Point. That means, not only does he know the area well, but he might have a home base there, a place where he's bathing his victims, or hanging them, in the case of the Priests. But while we're out there canvassing, I want everyone to bear something in mind – we don't know that he's finished. This thing – this event with his daughter, her gestures during the *American Stars* broadcast – this was picked up and distributed as news by all sorts of people. Journalists, reporters, commentators like Monica Forbes, social media influencers like James and Evelyn Priest." She paused, looking over the faces of the men and women in the room listening eagerly. "As Agent Tyler just said, we have to consider that Henry Beecher has been planning this for a long time. And ... I can't be sure of this, but it seems reasonable to think that there are more potential victims."

An agent, dark hair pulled back in a tight ponytail, tilted her head. "So what's the criteria? You just said there are dozens of people involved in this thing. I mean, could be hundreds, if you think about it. Anyone who passes something like this on.

You look at child porn, you're complicit in the crime. He's out there playing judge and jury – why these *specific* people? And it's not just opportunity based on proximity – he got Baldacci, and she lives outside his area."

"It might be the reach," someone said before Shannon could respond. A male agent near the back. "You know, how many newspapers in circulation, how many viewers a show has, how many likes a tweet got ..."

The female agent shook her head in disagreement. "He's somehow calculating all of that? TV viewers? Who is he, Nielsen?"

A few people chuckled.

Shannon listened, feeling exhilarated. At least they were talking along these lines, thinking critically, figuring it out. She said, "You're right – I don't think it's an exact science for him, but by the gut. Imagine that this was you ..."

"No thanks," interrupted the argumentative agent, drawing a few more laughs.

Shannon's gaze connected with Caldoza, who gave her a wink of encouragement. She said, "I'm saying, if you can manage to put yourself in the shoes of a man who lost his daughter. What's your metric for determining the guilt of the people you feel drove her to her death?" Shannon took the remote control for the laptop and flipped back to the slide of Charlotte Beecher. It showed on the huge, connected flat-screen TV in the room. Everyone looked at the fourteen-year-old girl. Auburn hair pulled straight back and frizzed out at the sides. A sprinkling of freckles across her upper cheeks and nose. Brown eyes, despite the fair complexion. Smiling, one tooth in front slightly pushed ahead of the one beside it.

"This is a young woman whose life was cut short," Shannon said softly.

The agent in the back grunted through his nose.

"You have any kids?" Tyler asked. He'd been in the corner, observing. "Agent Rappaport – you have any children?"

"No, sir."

Tyler just left it there and nodded at Shannon.

"My question," she began, "is not one I'm looking for you to answer, but to keep in mind today. As we're out there looking, as this whole city is looking for Henry Beecher, I want to impress this upon you – he may not be done. He may become desperate, act capriciously. But I don't think so. I think this is a very methodical man. I don't think he fears jail or even his death at this point. He wants to complete his list."

Shannon turned and looked at the smiling face of Charlotte Beecher, that touch of melancholy in the girl's eyes. "The question is, *who* is on that list?"

30

WEDNESDAY AFTERNOON

The sky was gunmetal gray through the rain-flecked single window of her office. Shannon's muscles felt stringy, nerves knotty, vision grainy. But she couldn't stop working the question around in her head: who might be next? And really – would he go after someone else *now?*

A few remnants remained of her victim wall – the torn corner of a photograph, a few scraps of newspapers clinging with Scotch tape.

Her own impulsivity – tearing down the wall – had surprised her. But it was over now; they knew the identity of the Media Killer, and they were going to get a net around him, bring him down. It was only a matter of time. What mattered, to her, was making sure he didn't take anyone else down with him. The FBI, along with half the NYPD and the Department of Homeland Security, were out hunting Henry Beecher. They would be watching the hospital that kept his wife. Watching his wife's parents in Flushing. His brother in Connecticut. Talking to every friend from the police force. They would have Beecher eventually, but so far he'd been smart and elusive. Could he be up to something? Could he have expected the events of that morning as an eventuality and planned for it?

The dark-haired agent's question persisted in her mind: what's the criteria? The victims were people who'd publicized or remarked on Charlotte Beecher's gaffe in some inflammatory way. But was there any pattern to the way in which Beecher had killed them? Did such a pattern merely meet with logistical, practical necessities, or was there some judgment rendered?

In other words – had he killed the victims in order of the level of guilt he attributed them? After all, Diaz was just "doing her job" as an entertainment reporter. But the Priests were the ones, by any definition, to truly make the Charlotte Beecher story go viral. It was inarguable that their tweet had been what amplified the thing from a passing curiosity to national social outrage.

Was there someone out there Beecher thought had done even *more* grievous harm to his daughter? It was hard to imagine. Hard to know. And Shannon was utterly exhausted. Her mind buzzed with a kind of background static, bits of conversations looping in her memory, scenes from the past week replaying over and over, everything jumbling together.

She went home. She just needed a couple of hours. It barely seemed possible that the Priests' double homicide had been just last night. She'd been eating dinner, hadn't she? With Caldoza, at an Italian restaurant. It felt like a long time ago.

Too tired for the subway, not trusting herself to drive, she took a cab from the resident agency to her apartment, drizzle coming down. Her role in this was over, according to Tyler. She'd been the one to identify Beecher and his credible motivation. It hardly seemed like the time to be passing out, but that didn't stop her from crawling onto her bed, fully clothed, and collapsing.

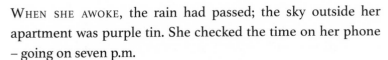

WHEN SHE AWOKE, the rain had passed; the sky outside her apartment was purple tin. She checked the time on her phone – going on seven p.m.

Damn. Four hours down.

She had to pee. She shuffled to the bathroom, blinking at her phone.

A missed call from Caldoza. Two from Tyler. One from her family.

She sat on the toilet, listening to Tyler's first message.

"Beecher's wife, Teresa, is no longer a patient at Kingsboro. Beecher came and got her this morning."

Shannon unspooled the toilet paper and said to Jasper, watching from the doorway, "Oh boy."

They'd just missed him.

Tyler: "We have an eyewitness from outside the hospital saying the SUV, the dark green Chevy Tahoe, was headed west."

They'd run Beecher through DMV, of course, and discovered his vehicle, the Tahoe. Green, like Olivia Jackson had said. Plus, it was a make and model that matched the type of tire rubber found at the crime scene in Hunters Point.

Shannon wondered about the Dodge Challenger seen by Mendoza. Maybe it was nothing, or maybe it was a secondary vehicle Beecher bought for cash and avoided registering. She needed to check for any police reports of unregistered vehicles.

She flushed and rinsed her hands and then leaned against the sink.

Tyler's second message was from an hour later. She'd been so tired she'd slept right through her ringing phone.

"Beecher left the city. Vehicle was on a traffic camera crossing the Whitestone Bridge. And his phone showed up – he made a quick call from New Jersey, and he used his credit card at a gas station. NYPD is at the end of their jurisdiction, but we're on it – we've got our agents on it, and New Jersey has joined up."

She let out a long, slow breath, puffing out her cheeks. Beecher was on the run. Took his wife and hit the road.

She looked at herself in the mirror. Big circles under her eyes. The little bit of mascara she wore had escaped the corner of one eye, like she'd been crying in her sleep. She turned on the tub faucet. As the water pounded the porcelain, she listened to the message from Caldoza. From half an hour ago.

"Hey. Ah, it's just me. Luis Caldoza. The, ah, guy who kind of looks like the new Magnum PI. You ever see that show? Look, I don't care if that dude is Latino. I mean, *I'm* Latino, but so what? I've got every right to want a white guy to play Magnum. That was my childhood. But I don't. I don't care if he's white or brown or green. But I gotta tell you, no mustache? That's just horrible. That's sacrilege."

She felt herself smile and roll her eyes at Caldoza's humor as she ran her fingers under the water. Getting nice and hot. She'd never been big on baths, but since her arm wounds sort of forced her into it, she'd come to like them a bit more.

Caldoza continued, "So, all right, just checking in with you. I heard they're closing in on his ass over in Jersey. Are they gonna let you get a piece of this guy? Talk to him? Anything? Maybe not, huh? You're just the woman behind the scenes. You ride into the town, you save the villagers, and then you just sort of disappear. I like that, you know."

He was quiet a moment. She suddenly felt nervous, like he was about to tell her how much he liked *her*. That he was going to cross that line from vague flirting with plausible deniability into the undeniable realm. Say something he couldn't take back. She didn't know if she wanted him to or not.

"Give me a call," he said finally. "If you can. When you can. All right?"

The message ended.

She stripped out of her clothes and slipped into the hot water, keeping her arms above her head.

AFTER A FEW MINUTES OF SOAKING, she picked up her phone again and listened to the call from her family, expecting to hear her father's voice.

"Hi," her mother said.

Shannon sat up straighter in the bath, luxurious soak forgotten.

"I've, um, I've been following this case on the news, and I just ... I hope everything is okay with you."

She hastily rubbed some water from her face, listening intently.

"And I hope you're ... that you're getting your rest and eating well." There was a murmuring voice in the background. Deep. Her father. "Your dad says he loves you. He says not to be a hero. All right. Goodbye, honey."

Shannon set the phone down on the edge of the tub. Her vision blurred as tears filled in the edges of her eyes.

It had been a long while since her mother had called. Or expressed any sort of emotion around her, let alone concern. Shannon had stopped expecting it altogether and grown accustomed to communicating through her father.

This was progress. This was a start.

But what made her cry, she realized, wasn't the promise of a reconnection. The sad part was, she'd accepted the freeze between them, become inured to it. Ten years was a long time to have your mother treat you like you didn't exist, or when she did acknowledge you, as if you were a disappointment. A mistake.

The dripping water made splatting sounds on the cool,

hard floor. Shannon realized she'd gotten out of the tub and was standing naked. She toweled off and left the bathroom, dressed in loose and lightweight slacks and a simple white blouse. She ground some fresh coffee beans, with Jasper circling her legs, then put some food in his bowl and stroked his spine. With the coffee brewing, she sat down at the antique desk in the living room and opened her laptop.

Charlotte Beecher.

Shannon looked through the online articles and information she'd already bookmarked.

Fourteen-year-old condemned for gestures on American Stars *takes own life.* That was probably the biggest one, carried in *The New York Times.*

Has Outrage Culture Gone Too Far? Baldacci's own *Newsday* had speculated as much.

Hundreds of articles from all over the region, from the northeast, from across the country, covered the sad story of Charlotte Beecher. The consensus was the opposite of what Todd Spencer had opined. Here was a girl essentially stoned to death by a culture that frenzied over wrongdoing. Even the more liberal of outlets seemed sympathetic, claiming that "cancel culture" had taken its first true victim. While senators and celebrities – adults – might have possessed the faculties to help them navigate public rebuke, a teenaged girl had neither the mental maturity yet, nor the house in the Hamptons in which to hide out for a while. She didn't have the spokesperson to shield her from the press, either.

Shannon imagined the girl looking out the window of that narrow, brown home on Seventy-Third. A news van parked in the street. Reporters calling to her as the girl rushed off in the morning to get to school.

Shannon found one picture, of Henry Beecher, holding his hand up to block a photographer's shot. *Father Defends Daughter's Actions.* "'She's just a kid,' Henry Beecher, NYPD, aged 50, had to say. 'And anyway, she says it's not true. It's not what people think it is. And I believe her.'"

The taping of the show, a semifinal round in the vocals performances on the globally popular show *American Stars*, had been in late July, two years before. Charlotte had hung herself just before the start of the new school year.

For one month, she'd endured it. According to an article in the *New York Post*, the Beechers had called the police twenty-eight times in a single week to complain of people outside the home, taunting Charlotte, throwing sticks and rocks, lighting off firecrackers. When Henry Beecher caught two young boys trying to spray-paint *Cunt* on the sidewalk, he chased them off with his gun.

Shannon wanted to find the point that Charlotte's identity became public. When had she gone from "Girl Makes Fun of Disabled Performer" to "Charlotte Beecher, Astoria Heights"? But it seemed impossible to discern. As far as Shannon could tell, no one had explicitly doxed her. And no journalist with integrity would've revealed an exact address, even if they'd learned her identity.

God, Shannon thought, *if only she'd held on a little longer.* The world had a short attention span. Something like this would have surely faded.

But it had just been too much, apparently.

Jasper leapt up onto the desk, purring. She scratched behind his ears. When he sat, his tail swished back and forth over the keyboard. "All right. Go on. I'll be with you in a minute."

She stared at the computer. She had, currently, thirteen open tabs in her browser. It had to be here somewhere, the moment Charlotte went from being anonymous to literally having rocks thrown at her home. Maybe someone recognized her and talked to the press? That didn't mean they'd be named as a source.

Shannon leaned back and bit her thumb for a while.

Maybe she was coming at this thing from the wrong direction.

Maybe, if there was someone with secrets to spill, they'd already spilled them.

She got up from the desk, picked up her holster and gun, and strapped it on. Jasper sat in the middle of the living room floor, white fur almost iridescent in the semidarkness. "Be right back," she said.

THE 90TH PRECINCT WAS BUZZING. Heads turned as she walked along the edge of the bullpen; voices murmured.

She found Caldoza at his desk, nose buried in his computer. Heinz was in place at the opposite desk. He saw her first.

"There she is."

Caldoza looked up. The change in his expression was unmistakable. He stood and briefly touched her shoulder. "Hey. Ah – hi."

"Hi."

"Got my message?"

"I did."

Shannon glanced at Heinz, who snapped a piece of bubble gum and looked away, as if interested in some paperwork on his desk.

Caldoza glanced at Heinz, too, then focused on her. "What can I do for you?"

"Actually," she said, "I was hoping you could help me with something."

Paperwork formed dunes and drifts in the filing room. Shannon wasn't interested in the hard copies of the hotline calls – she wanted the database Whitaker had shown her. And she had access from her office, but this was better ...

"Here we go," Caldoza said. He booted it up and logged in and pulled out the chair for her.

Sensing him watching over her shoulder, she looked up. "I'll probably be a while."

She saw him take offense – a knitting of his brow, hardening of his lip line. He tried to make light of the situation. "Oh, it's like that, huh? Just use me and throw me away?"

She stood up. He seemed caught off guard and took an uncertain step back. She kept going like that, backing him against the wall. The door to the room was still open, and she gave it a hard push with the tips of her fingers. He looked at the door when it slammed, then his eyes slid back to hers as she pushed her body up against his. This time, touching; she got him good and sandwiched between her and the wall behind him.

"Listen," she said, lips an inch from his own, "I think you're all right, Luis."

"I think you're all right, too."

His hands came up her back and she grabbed his forearms, pushing them gently but firmly down. "And after this is over, and Henry Beecher is behind bars, and everyone is safe, maybe you can take me back to that Italian place."

He searched her eyes. "Yeah?"

"Or maybe somewhere else because I'm not super into Italian." She delivered the line flatly, matter-of-fact, and his breath burst against her face as he laughed. He smelled chocolatey, like he'd just sneaked a donut. But his body wasn't soft. He had hard arms and a hard stomach. She reached up between them and laid a hand against his cheek. "Is it a deal?"

"It's a deal."

They kept eye-locked for another few seconds, the heat between them rising. She slowly backed off. He said, "Can I ask what you're looking for?"

"Anything," she said, gradually returning her attention to the database. She sat down at the computer and cracked her knuckles. "Was just going to start with a simple keyword search."

He was behind her, but at a distance. "What's the keyword?"

"Charlotte."

∾

A FEW MINUTES LATER, she had it. Two calls, both originating from Astoria Heights. One from Sunday, one from Tuesday. Same phone number. Same caller.

All calls were recorded and stored digitally. She pulled up the file and listened.

"*New York Police Department tip hotline. Can I have your name, please?*"

"*Josie. Ah, Josephine Tenor.*" She sounded anxious.

Shannon glanced at Caldoza, who nodded and said, "Tenor. Got it."

"*What can I do for you today, Josephine?*"

"*I'm ... I'm gonna ... I'm gonna be killed. I know it. I'm gonna – he's gonna come for me. Because of Charlotte.*"

Another look between Shannon and Caldoza. There it was.

"*Wait – sorry? Are you talking about the suspect in the–*"

"*Yes. All of it. The guy doing all of it. He's going to come for me. He's going to come for me, and he's going to kill me just like all these other people he's going to–*"

"*Ma'am? Josephine? I'm gonna need you to calm down. Josephine – how old are you?*"

Shannon felt cold. "How did this not come through? How did you not get this?"

He was shaking his head. "I don't know. I mean, we got three thousand calls since we opened the lines on this."

"Three *thousand*?" Her incredulity gave way to reason: in a city of eight million, three thousand was less than point-zero-zero-one percent. A tiny fraction given a city connected by the media, all gripped in fear or fascination that a serial killer rampaged among them in the dark.

"There's got to be a better system," she said quietly.

On the call, Josephine gave her age: "*Sixteen.*"

Same age as Charlotte. Well, same age as Charlotte *would* have been.

"*Okay. I'm going to put you through to talk to an investigator, okay, Josephine? We're overloaded with calls, so it might take a minute. Stay on the line.*"

"*Okay.*"

But then the call ended.

"What happened?"

"Looks like she was on hold for about twenty seconds."

"She just hung up," Shannon said. More memories of the past week flooded her, instances of her own hedging and doubt. And she was a professional. Considering the typical insecurities of a teenaged girl, it was surprising that Josephine had even called in the first place.

"Let's check the second call," Caldoza said.

But she waited a moment, letting something work its way through in her thoughts. "Sunday. Sunday morning was after the awards dinner."

"Yeah."

Some people surely called just to comfort themselves, to feel some sense of control. Others were more narcissistic, wanting a part to play. And some, certainly, had to be thinking that they had genuinely helpful information.

She pictured this Josephine watching TV, or learning about the bomb scare some other way – maybe social media. And it activating her interest – even spooking her. She sounded legitimately afraid. Why? What did she know?

"Where does she go to school?"

"Hang on," Caldoza said, working on the next computer.

Shannon clicked the keyboard. "Gonna play it while you look for the school."

"Okay."

The recording began, "*New York Police Department tip hotline.*"

The girl sounded more confident this time: "*My name is Josephine Tenor. I'm at 22-28 Seventy-Second Street in Astoria Heights.*"

Shannon froze. A second later she was fighting the urge to get up and run out. "That's the next street over from Henry Beecher ..."

Caldoza was looking at Shannon, still listening to the call.

"*I know who he is,*" Josephine said.

"*Who who is?*"

"*The Media Killer ...*"

"*Okay. Let me put you through to an – oh. I see you here on the screen, Miss Tenor. Yes, we have your call, it's on file, and someone will get back to you as soon as possible ...*"

"Got it," Caldoza said, having gone back to his search. "She goes to school at Long Island City High." He added, "Same as Beecher."

"*He's not going to stop,*" Josephine said on the call. "*He's going to get everyone.*"

31

WEDNESDAY EVENING

Shannon had Caldoza send a patrol car over to the Tenor residence. She'd called twice now and gotten no answer. Two minutes later, Caldoza picked up his desk phone, said, "Okay ... okay, good. Thank you. Yeah. Yeah. No, I understand. Listen, tell her ... All right, listen – no, I get it – tell her that someone is going to come by and talk to her. All right? Be nice and assure her everything is going to be all right."

He hung up and looked at Shannon.

She opened her hands, palms up. "So?"

"Officer Rosen says the girl is there at the house."

"Okay. Okay, good."

"She's a bit jumpy, he said. Parents are divorced, she lives with the mom, the mom is somewhere with her new boyfriend. The girl has her music blasting, didn't hear the phone."

Shannon was ready to go. Caldoza seemed hesitant. He added, "And I guess she's been drinking."

"Okay ... so?"

"Rosen asked her how much, and she said none of his business. Then she said, 'All week long, motherfucker.'"

"She doesn't sound drunk to me on that call. And if she was?"

Heinz came walking up to the desks with a fresh paper cup of coffee. He blew on it and looked up through his eyebrows at them. "Hey, so what's the latest on the guy? Beecher?"

"They're right on top of him," Caldoza said. "Any minute now."

Heinz nodded. At his desk, he checked the magazine of his Glock and slipped the firearm back into his hip holster.

"We're just talking about one of the hotline calls. Teenaged girl says she knows the killer. Or thinks she does."

"Uh-huh." Heinz pulled some Tic Tacs from a desk drawer, popped one in his mouth. He looked between them, then shook the package at her.

"No thanks." She turned to Caldoza, who was looking at his watch. She got the sense they were leaving. "You two on your way somewhere?"

Caldoza just looked back at her, then averted his eyes, as if ashamed.

"We gotta go knock on somebody's door," Heinz said. "We got a lead on a guy who fits a suspect description on a hit-and-run."

"A hit-and-run?"

Heinz said, "Hey, I got fifteen open cases. Monica Forbes landed in our lap because of jurisdiction. It's time to get back to work."

Heinz walked away and Caldoza lingered a moment. "I'm sorry. He's right. It's why we're even here on the night shift – we're backed up, bad. Forbes sucked up a lot of investigative oxygen."

She fought through the immediate sense of betrayal. Ridiculous – Caldoza and Heinz weren't hers to control. They had their own jobs to do. She could call Tyler, but for what? The whole city was closing around Henry Beecher. No one wanted to devote resources to some hyperbolic teenaged girl when this thing seemed to be over.

"It's all good," she said to Caldoza.

He looked like he didn't believe her.

"I understand," she said. "Now go. Get to work."

He hung his badge around his neck. "Listen. Rosen will be there at the house. If you're going to swing by, he'll wait until you get there. And if you need anything, just call me."

"I can handle it," Shannon said. "This girl is freaked out. I'm going to talk to her – if she's legit, maybe it'll help me put my official profile together."

He nodded, then lowered his gaze. After a moment, he lifted his eyes to her. "Hey. Mexican food, Thai food, whatever. I'll eat fucking chicken liver if I can see you again."

She laughed. Jerked her head. "Get outta here." She added, "I'll be seeing you. All right?"

His eyes held on her for just another moment, then he was gone, walking through the soft chaos of the 90th and out into the night.

After a few seconds, she followed.

SHE DROVE with the radio on, listened to a little '90s rock music – Nirvana's "Come As You Are" followed by "Been Caught Stealin'" by Jane's Addiction, and she felt pretty good. Maybe she could use a few more hours' sleep, but that would be soon enough. Things might have even turned a corner. Tyler's relationship to her had changed. Technically, she was still on probation, but it didn't register in his eyes the same way.

She took the interstate, 278, the Brooklyn-Queens Expressway, and traveled northeast. The night traffic was thick, but at least moving. It was midweek, and the heat had finally lifted some. She drove with the window down, risking glances at the

Manhattan skyline in the distance. All those lights. The wet rush of traffic all around. Distant ambulances racing off towards some other tragedy.

It was possible she was starting to love this place.

After crossing Newtown Creek into Maspeth, going over Queens Boulevard, through Woodside, she exited on Astoria Boulevard and made a right onto Seventy-Third. She remained impressed by the quaint homes on the street – something about them almost storybook-like – then she slowed as she passed the Beecher residence. The windows were lighted squares, shadows flickering past as forensics continued moving through the place, gathering further evidence for prosecutors. Two NYPD cars sat parked out front. A cloud of cigarette smoke drifted toward the street, and the uniformed cop who had exhaled it gave her a long hard look as she rolled past.

She rubbernecked until the house was out of sight, then turned left and got over onto the next block, watching the house numbers until she was at the Tenor place. Rosen was sitting in the car out front. As soon as she slowed, he got out and put a flashlight on her. She still had the window rolled down and announced herself.

"Ah, all right, yeah. Sorry. Caldoza said you was comin' by. Just park anywhere."

She found a spot three houses up and had to parallel park to make the tight fit. She brought her ID and phone with her and locked up the car. Rosen had relocated to the front entrance. A chain fence, painted white, surrounded a postage-stamp yard with a little patch of grass and a birdbath in it. "She's in there," Rosen said, nodding at the brown storm door. "Saw her stick her face in the window a couple of times. She flipped me the bird, too. Real nice."

"Thanks," Shannon said. He opened the gate for her. Three strides and she was there, the front door atop four brick steps. She took one step, swung open the storm door, and knocked.

Music vibrated inside; the windows were rattling. Shannon located the doorbell and pressed it.

"I just talked to her," Rosen said from behind Shannon.

"No problem."

She waited.

"So, pretty crazy," Rosen said. "You really think Beecher did it?"

"We'll see." The last she'd heard from Tyler, he was in a helicopter looking at a 2018 Chevy Tahoe registered to Beecher, sitting outside a Jersey motel.

Rosen said, "You must wish you were out there right now, right? I mean, this whole thing is kinda you. That's what I heard. You found Beecher out. Man, I'd want to be out there right now."

Shannon heard footfalls approaching. The inner door lock made a clicking sound and the door swung open. The girl just inside was pretty, on the round side, wearing heavy eye makeup and big fake lashes.

"Josephine Tenor?"

"Yeah?"

Shannon put her ID up against the transparent part of the storm door. "I'm with the FBI. My name is Shannon. Can I come in?"

Josephine's eyes lit up. "It's *you*," she said. Her face bloomed red. "I saw you on TV ..."

"Oh yeah? Listen, can we talk? I know about your calls to the police ..."

Josephine blinked the big lashes, then glanced past Shannon at Rosen. Her lip curled in a snarl of distaste. "Yeah – a lot *they* did." Then her gaze came back and she pushed open the storm door.

Shannon stepped through into a foyer. A row of hangers on the right for jackets. A skinny table with a bowl for keys. Straight ahead, carpeted stairs going up. It smelled predominantly girly, lots of shampoo and perfume and makeup. Intertwined with those scents, the fermented odor of cheap wine. "Nice place," Shannon said.

Josephine only stood there a moment, looking at Shannon in a way that suggested she was trying not to stare. Then she said, "Thank you."

"So your parents aren't around? Your mom?"

Josephine shook her head. "Uh-uh. No. My mom's in Atlantic City."

Shannon nodded. "You want to go sit down and talk?"

"Yeah. Um, yeah, sure. Let's go in the kitchen." She started past the stairs and Shannon followed, checking out the hanging pictures in the short hallway – two women, ages roughly seventy and forty, sat beside a twelve- or thirteen-year-old Josephine in the kind of studio portrait you got at a department store. Did they still do those?

Next were other framed photos of Josephine and then several of a boy who looked a little like her. In one, he was taking a knee, hand resting on his football helmet, his jersey white with blue letters.

Shannon stepped through to the kitchen. "You have a brother?"

"Yeah." Josephine stopped at a tile-topped kitchen island. Something about the décor was very 1980s. Maybe it was the buttery yellow colors, the curvy handles on the cabinets and drawers.

"He's older?"

"Yeah. He goes to Stonybrook? Out on Long Island?"

"Oh yeah? What year is he?"

"It's, ah ... he's, um ... it's his third year."

"Cool," Shannon said.

Josephine pointed at the refrigerator. Brown, the kind with the freezer on the side. "Can I get you something to drink or anything?" There was an empty wineglass beside the sink.

"No thanks." Shannon turned her attention to the table and chairs in the corner. "Mind if I sit down?"

"Oh yeah, go ahead."

Shannon sat, but Josephine remained standing at the island. Then she moved around between it and the kitchen sink behind her. A window above the sink overlooked the backyard. The way she kept looking at Shannon made her feel like some kind of celebrity. Or that, maybe – the way Josephine's eyes glinted – the girl had a crush.

"So," Shannon said, "have you lived here your whole life?"

Josephine bobbed her head. "Yeah. Yeah, but when Robbie was little – my brother – my parents lived in Flushing. My dad is back there now. My parents, um, they got a divorce a few years ago, and my dad moved back there. He lived with his brother for a little while, and then he got his own place. He's always saying how crazy divorce is because you have to pay double for everything."

Shannon's phone buzzed against her hip. She glanced at the number – it was the resident agency – but left it for now. She asked Josephine, "You spend a lot of time here alone?"

The girl only looked back at Shannon for a moment. Then she hung her head, as if in shame. "Yeah, I mean, I thought about that a lot. That I was just … you know … too much in my head. You can get that way and, like, overthink things. Make more out of something."

Shannon held out a hand. "I didn't mean you should doubt yourself. I'm glad you called. I think you did the right thing. So, did you know Charlotte Beecher? Go to school together?"

Josephine's forehead creased in a frown – the exaggerated concentration of the alcohol-buzzed. "We've been best friends since the first grade." When her skin smoothed, she stared off into space. "I mean, we *were*. Best friends."

"So you were close, yeah. And you think … well, why don't

you tell me, in your own words, why you were worried. Why you called the hotline."

Josephine's eyes remained unfocused, her finger rubbing absently at the corner of her mouth. "Because I was watching TV. Seeing everything that was happening. The people. You know, the reporters, the woman from TV, and I thought ..." Josephine seemed to sort of coalesce back into the present moment, and she looked at Shannon with a mixture of fear and determination. "So they're going to get him?"

"They might be putting the cuffs on him right now."

Josephine stared off, as if picturing it. Then she said, "I thought I was part of that group because of what I did."

Shannon's phone buzzed again. Tyler this time.

"I'm sorry, Josephine. I have to take this."

"It's okay. You can call me Josie."

"Josie. Great. This will take one second." She put the phone to her ear as she walked out of the kitchen through a second doorway and into a living area. "Hello?"

"Ames, where are you?" It sounded like Tyler was near traffic. Plus voices, radios going off around him.

"I'm with Josephine Tenor. She was a hotline caller, went to school with Charlotte Beecher." Shannon looked at a clock with a cat's eyes going back and forth, tail swishing with the seconds.

"Ames ... Beecher is not with the vehicle."

It took a second to register. "Not with the vehicle?"

"The 2018 Tahoe. It's his wife, Ames. Teresa Beecher. We've got her in custody. She had the phone – *his* phone we've been tracking. He's not with her. Ames, you hearing me? We don't have Henry Beecher."

There was a knock at the front door.

～

THE FACE of Officer Rosen floated in the high, small window of the interior door. Shannon approached with Josephine behind her. Rosen saw them and shouted something.

Cautiously, slowly, Shannon opened up. Rosen blurted, "I got called back to the Beecher place. Something going on."

"Yeah," Shannon said, not wanting to elaborate in front of the girl. "I just got that message, too. We're doing all right here. Just going to finish up and we'll be on our way. In fact we'll head over to you right after."

Rosen opened his mouth, then looked past her at Josie. When his gaze came back to Shannon there was understanding in his eyes. "Got it. Yeah. Hurry up, we'll see you over there. We'll take care of you."

He gave a quick nod and turned, bounded down the steps and hurried to his vehicle.

From behind her, Josie said, "What's going on?"

Shannon let the storm door close. She backed inside, shut the interior door, and faced the girl. "Listen, everything is all right. But I'd like you to do something for me. I'd like you to come with me over to Charlotte's house. The Beecher house. Can you do that?"

Josie's eyes were wide with alarm. "What happened? They didn't get him, did they?"

Shannon reached for her, but she recoiled. "Everything's all right," Shannon said. "Listen, you can come stay with me if you want. You want to grab a couple of things? Go ahead."

She seemed frozen in panic. "I've known him my whole life."

"Okay. I understand. But, Josie, you haven't told me – why would he want to hurt you? You're his daughter's best friend. Okay? You're not in the media. You're not an influencer ..."

Josie's eyes instantly filled with tears. "Because of what I did."

"What did you do?"

Shannon's heart jumped at a sound behind her – the storm door squawked as it reopened. Rosen must've forgotten something.

She turned into the interior door just as it opened – too fast, too hard – and it slammed into her.

She was shoved back as the door was forced all the way open. Her hands went up to protect herself, but the intruder was quick. He hit her in the head with something and she dropped to the floor.

Josie screamed, but the scream was cut off abruptly when the intruder hit her, too. Then he jumped on top of Shannon before she could pull her weapon. He pressed a damp rag against her face. An acrid, chemical odor filled her nose and throat and she kicked at him and clawed at his hands. She held her breath, but it was too late – the intruder's breathing and grunting sounded like it was coming through an elongating tunnel – she was passing out.

Her body forced her to breathe automatically. Her vision went fuzzy. Sights and sounds faded, tattering, spiraling off into a dark emptiness.

32

A headache grew and pulsed in time with her heartbeat, like the worst hangover. At first, Shannon thought it was her graduation, the last time she'd let friends convince her to go out and get really ploughed. A country western bar in Stafford – she could even hear Waylon Jennings singing about Bobby McGee in the background.

But as soon as she sensed that her wrists and ankles were tied, the phantom music died and she shed the false memory. Images of the attack flooded her mind, bringing her back to reality. With her vision still blurry and her mind sluggish, she stared into the blank, black eye looking back at her. It took a moment before she realized what it was.

Camera.

She went for her gun, but her hands were caught. Her holster was empty anyway.

This was a basement. Felt small, cluttered. To her immediate right, a washer and dryer, wafting the scents of detergent and fruity-smelling dryer sheets. To her left, the girl, Josie, tied up in another chair, her head bent forward, upper vertebrae of her neck shining in the harsh overhead light.

"Josie," Shannon said, the word slurring. "Josephine ..."

Her head ached. The more she grew in consciousness, the more the pain took specific shape, from the front left side of her skull, radiating across her forehead and down her neck, around her ear on that side. He'd pistol-whipped her? Struck her with something very solid anyway. She could feel the slow ooze of blood. And then he'd forced her to inhale sevoflurane.

Straight ahead of her were messy shelves of household items ranging from cans of pureed tomatoes to rolls of toilet paper, a clear bin of plastic knives and forks, and, on the lowest shelf, some sporting items like figure skates and basketballs.

Shannon couldn't turn around. The back of the chair was too high, her arms wrapped back around it at a painful angle, a ligature binding her wrists. But she got the distinct sense that he was back there behind them.

"I'm a federal agent," she said.

A foot scuffed the concrete floor, something clicked, as if plastic being fitted together, nothing more. Quiet breathing.

"The whole city is looking for you," Shannon said.

Beside her, Josephine moaned. The girl's eyelids fluttered, but her head stayed down. A long strand of drool hung from her mouth and connected with her thigh. The anesthesia he'd used on her, too, was slower to wear off.

Beecher continued to move around behind them.

Where was Rosen? It'd been a minute, maybe less, after the NYPD officer had left that Beecher came crashing in. He'd been hiding somewhere, waiting. A dozen or more law enforcement personnel attended his house a block away while he just ran around the neighborhood. He'd sent cops on a wild-goose chase after his depressive wife.

How long until Tyler wondered why she wasn't responding and sent someone around? Fifteen minutes? Half an hour? He would be scrambling to locate Beecher after botching the big moment. Police all over the city would remain focused on the manhunt.

Yet here was the killer.

Here he was in Josephine Tenor's basement. Why here and not the place he'd used with the others? The more she thought it through, the more sense it made that, with law enforcement so close on his heels, Beecher was improvising.

The camera was dark, no discernible red light. Unless he'd somehow hidden or disabled the indicator, it wasn't yet recording. What was he planning now?

The victims are in order of guilt.

It was a persistent theory that made sense – from the entertainment reporter already covering *American Stars* to the rich social media influencer couple who could make or break people with a single retweet ...

And the way in which Beecher killed them had a certain ring of poetic justice to it. Imperfect, yes, but nevertheless a kind of turn-the-sin-against-the-sinner MO. For the Priests, Beecher had created a scenario in which their own mindless fans were their murderers, bringing the couple closer to death with every pressing of the 'like' button. For narcissist Spencer, his colleagues ran past and trampled over his bleeding body in order to save themselves ...

So – what had Josie Tenor done to make her so important on the list?

And what was he going to do to punish her?

Shannon was starting to form an idea when Beecher, of all things, suddenly sneezed. The unexpectedness and force of it sent her heart into her throat.

"Fuckin' dusty down here," Beecher said.

It was the first time she'd heard his voice. Good God, he sounded like anyone else. A normal man. If profane.

Her mind racing, she said, "It's a basement. Better dusty than mildew and mold ..."

"That's because of the vintage," he said without missing a

beat. "These old houses have imperfections. Cracks and gaps where the air gets in."

He was talking to her like this was any other day. Like they were a couple of acquaintances.

"Cracks and imperfections are a good thing for a house – lets it breathe, keeps the mold from forming. The places that get mold are these newfangled places. Energy-efficient green homes."

Ben Forbes flashed through her mind, if for no other reason than his work in construction.

Knowing every moment that passed was one closer to police coming to her aid, she said, "Mold is mentioned in the Bible. Deuteronomy. Or maybe it's Leviticus."

"Uh-huh," he said. Something made a clicking sound, like plastic.

"It's part of punishment for disobedience," she said, heart rate gaining speed as she came out of the anesthesia fully. "The Israelites were worshipping idols, not obeying God's commands ..." She trailed off and fell silent. Her whole body was shaking.

Calm. Stay calm and steady.

No response from Beecher. Another flash: sitting in church with her family. Mother in the pew in front of her with John. Shannon behind them with her three other brothers, who were always squirming and arguing, and their father, placed there to keep them in check. The back of her mother's head, her dark hair, the sweater she liked to wear with the frilly collar ...

Shannon took a shuddering breath. "You know what? Wait. Leviticus is where God gives Aaron and Moses instructions for removing mold. Right? I remember, he said if a homeowner found mold or mildew, they had to contact a priest. And the priest would come and remove all the items and close the house for seven days ..."

She fell silent again, waiting.

Josie moaned and her head came up, then dropped again. Shannon felt a tear slip down the side of her face. Or maybe it was blood. *Don't. Don't lose it. Not now.*

Beecher squeezed past her on the right, moving between her and the washer and dryer. He was wearing a dirty pair of tan work pants with cargo pockets. A gray, long-sleeve shirt with some writing and decals too faded to read. Black boots on his feet. Blue plastic gloves on his hands. He kept his back to her as he manipulated the camera. Shannon watched, feeling the heat draining from her body as panic took over.

Beecher then moved between the camera and Josie with something in his hand. He lifted her head and attached it to her shirt – a small microphone which connected to the camera with a thin black cord. "The batteries were dead in the wireless," he said to Shannon. "This will have to do."

A stubble of grayish, reddish beard peppered his square jaw. His hair was buzzed short but just starting to grow over his ears. He was in shape, a man of average height, with a compact sort of physique, barely an ounce of fat on him.

He looked strong. Wiry.

He had yet to make eye contact.

Finished clipping the microphone to Josie, he stepped back. He put his gloved hand on her forehead and pushed her head back. Her eyelids fluttered, opened a little, and she said, "Erguff ..." and he slapped her once, hard.

"Keep your hands off her!" Shannon tried to get up, pure instinct, but her ankles were held fast. They were tied beneath her and secured to the chair. Both chairs were the metal folding kind, a stabilizing crossbar between the two back legs.

Josie's head had bent to the side with the slap; now she righted her head with her face contorted in pain, eyes shut tightly. She opened them, blinking through the tears.

She looked at Beecher, pure terror in her gaze.

"Oh no ..." she whimpered. Her voice was high, light, and

tearful. Like a small child's. "Oh no. No, no, no ..."

This was her nightmare. Her worst fear made manifest.

"Touch her again and I'll kill you," Shannon snapped. She hadn't planned to say anything.

Beecher's head slowly turned as he looked at her at last. His eyes were a kind of chameleon gray, the color of the room, the emptiness of an alleyway. He bent forward and moved toward her. He made a fist.

Pain exploded in her nose and upper lip and teeth. Something snapped in her neck as the force of his punch rocked her head back. She couldn't see, couldn't hardly think through the pain shooting through her face and head.

"Shut up," Beecher said.

She watched him, his shape distorted by her tears, fixing Josie's hair and clothes. Then he walked back to the camera and clicked on the camera light. Josie flinched and blinked her eyes some more. She was still whimpering the word, very softly, "No ..."

"Josie? I need you to tell me your Wi-Fi password."

"My Wi-Fi ..."

"Tell me your password."

"It's f ... It's freesocks199."

"All lowercase or what?"

"Yeah."

He was quiet as he poked at the back of the camera. A panel there, Shannon guessed, with menu options. His camera was able to connect to the internet. He was going to livestream this.

A moment later, the red recording light came on.

"Okay," Beecher said. "We're live. First thing, I want you to tell everybody your name."

Josie dropped her chin to her upper chest and sobbed.

"Lift your head up. That's it. Look right here. Tell the world who you are."

"Josie. Tenor."

Shannon whispered, "Stop." Her head was a scrambled network of shooting pains.

Beecher ignored her. "Good. Now tell everybody what you did. Get it off your chest."

Josie's expression was slack a moment, as if, suddenly, she'd forgotten everything – where she was and the horror of the situation. Like she was simply listening to an adult giving her instruction.

Then she crumbled again. She lowered her face and cried.

"Come on, Josie," Beecher said. He glanced up the stairs, which were directly on his right side.

He doesn't have much time and he knows it.

As Beecher continued to prod Josie – in an eerily patient and gentle way – Shannon got a hold of herself. Put some thoughts in order. Beecher knew he was busted – had to. He was calm because he'd planned everything out. That was one thing – when you planned everything ahead of time and weren't acting emotionally and impulsively, it helped you keep a cool distance. Almost like you were working for someone else, carrying out a job.

But how many more people did Beecher think he could get with the entire city closing around him? This had to be the endgame.

Or maybe that was naïve. After all, he was here now, right under the noses of the NYPD, with a federal agent abductee in the basement of a potential victim's house. And he was a cop; he knew how cops thought. Familiar with all police frequencies and codes, he'd surely known the precise moment Rosen was called back to the Beecher home because he'd been listening. And if that was true, he would've known that Rosen had been posted at the Tenor home in the first place, that FBI – Shannon – had been en route. Yet he'd come anyway.

Because he was going to see this through to the end.

"Josie," he said, a note of impatience in his voice at last, "come on now. Tell the world about Charlotte."

Josie's chest jumped with a sob. She nodded – two big exaggerated bobs of her head. Then: "Charlotte was my fr – fr – my friend ..."

"That's right. Your best friend. For many years. For many years, right? Until what happened? Josie? What were you supposed to do together?"

Josie breathed in rapid bursts, like she'd been crying a long time. She was watching him, looking to him for some sign of hope, some possibility of forgiveness: seeing it made Shannon sick. This man was someone Josie had known her whole life, she'd said. How many dinners had she spent at his table? How many nights sleeping over in Charlotte's room, under his roof?

"We were ..." Josie managed.

"Go ahead."

"We were supposed to go to the ... to the *American Stars* show together."

"That's right. You both had tickets. Tickets that I bought."

She slurped back snot and tears and nodded. It looked like she was marshaling strength. Then she sobbed again.

"That's enough of that," Beecher said. "Stop that. You don't get to cry. Okay? My baby girl ... my daughter hung herself because of what you did. You understand?"

Josie sobbed harder.

Shannon said, "This won't bring your daughter back."

He stabbed a finger at her. "You shut the fuck up. This isn't your show. You're not even supposed to be here. Shut up and let her talk." He drilled into Josie with his eyes. "Come on. Come on, you little dyke. Pretending to be her friend. Pretending to care."

"I *was* her friend!" Josie shrieked with sudden ferocity. Her face was red and wet with tears, but with anger in her eyes now, deep defensiveness. "I was her friend," she repeated.

A moment later: "But we fought sometimes. And a couple

of days before we were going to go to the *American Stars* show, we had a big one. Like, a really bad one. The kind where you called each other *bitch* and say you never want to see each other again."

Profound surrealism washed over Shannon: here was a middle-aged man interviewing a beaten teenaged girl in her basement. Like the most bizarre, sadistic reality TV show.

"I hated her," Josie said about Charlotte. "And then she went to *American Stars*, and I watched it. I was so angry. And then it came to the part where she made that face, where she sort of wiggled around like that when the boy in the wheelchair was about to sing. I knew she was just being stupid. She was the nicest person. She was probably messed up because of how bad we were fighting. I know she would've told that boy she was sorry–"

"She did," Beecher said from behind the camera. "She did apologize. But the media didn't care about that story. They didn't cover that. This is your turn, Josie. Your turn to tell the world."

She was crying again. "I'm sorry."

"For what? Come on! For what?"

Shannon could smell him – a kind of acrid stink, like anger and adrenaline. He reached behind himself for something and turned back around with a photograph. He held it up for Josie to see. Then he showed it to the camera.

"My daughter went into hiding," Beecher growled. "She didn't leave home. We had rocks thrown at the house. She got death threats. People said she was a horrible person. Not just in the news – random people. They wrote her and said she was the worst person. That she should rot." He was getting teared up. "Charlotte couldn't go outside, Josie. She couldn't go online. She sat in her room and she cried. She was mortified. Do you understand? You understand what you did? What you started when you put that video online?"

Josie cried and nodded. "Yes. Yes, I know ..."

Shannon's mind raced. It was clear now: Beecher blamed Josie for starting the campaign against his daughter. "It's not her fault," Shannon said abruptly. "If it hadn't been her, someone else would've shared that video. And how do you know she was first? The Priests retweeted someone else's post. I never even *saw* Josie's stuff online. You gonna go after all of them?"

His face darkened with blood. "She was her best friend! She knew the truth! That Charlotte wasn't like that!" He looked from Shannon to Josie. "She should've spoken up. She should've said something. But she didn't and my daughter hung herself."

"You want someone to blame. I can understand th–"

Beecher was quick. He came for her and this time gripped her neck. His knuckle and thumb sank into her flesh, incredibly painful, cutting off her air. The world started to dim. She made gagging sounds as she stared up into his eyes. His skin seemed to ripple as he choked her.

Then he let go, and she gasped for air. Bright spots danced around in her vision.

"That's what she felt," he said, pointing to the picture he still held. "That's what my daughter felt when she took her own life."

He stepped back and stared down at Shannon as she took ragged, burning breaths, her vision starring with fresh tears. Beecher said, "You've been in my house, I'm sure. You know how steep the stairs are. Charlotte went out to the shed, got one of my winch straps, tied it off to the banister on the second floor. When you push off that top step, and you swing down, the strap cinches tight. She hung there, feet dangling. Didn't break her neck, but stretched it. Suffocated. All while she was probably looking out the front door. Out to the street. Out to

the world that had written her off as a terrible human being."
He turned to Josie and said, "Just like you."

Josie, who'd managed to pull it together for a few seconds,
was on the verge of a fresh breakdown. Beecher squeezed
between the two of them and disappeared into the back of the
basement.

Shannon was finally able to breathe normally again, but
her throat burned and her neck throbbed.

When Beecher reappeared, he was holding a length of
Scotch tape. He loomed above Josie. "You feel bad for what you
did?"

"Yes ..."

"You think you understand what she went through? What
Charlotte went through?"

Shannon said, "Don't ..."

Beecher slapped her across the side of her head and kept
going with Josie. "Do you think you understand the pain she
felt? The humiliation?"

Josie's lip trembled. "Yes ..."

Beecher just stood there. "You don't have a fucking clue," he
said finally.

He showed the camera the four-by-six of Charlotte one
more time, then taped it at the bottom of the lens, so both Josie
and Shannon could see it.

Josie was fully bawling. She'd gone over into a place of total
resignation and regret.

Beecher said, "You don't understand, but you will. The
whole world will see you come to understand."

Beecher walked between them again, out of sight.

Josie sobbed and moaned.

"Josie," Shannon whispered. "Hey, it's gonna be okay."

"No, it's not." Beecher was back. He stood behind Josie and
he slipped a nylon strap under her chin and tightened it against
her neck.

33

Josie's eyes went wide. She writhed in the chair, arched her back, and twisted against her restraints. Her tongue flailed, and gagging sounds issued from her open mouth.

"Stop it!" Shannon leaned toward Josie, tried to reach her. Her feet tied, she couldn't kick off against the dryer and knock the chairs together. But she could rock that way, throw all of her body weight to the left, grunting, breathing explosively as Josie was strangled beside her and Beecher bore down with intense, sustained pressure, his face reddening, teeth clenched, eyes rolling over white ...

Shannon toppled her chair into Josie's chair. Beecher let go and the strap slackened. "God *dammit*," he said. Shannon was lying across Josie's lap, but starting to rotate forward. If she crashed onto her front side, the chair would be on top of her and she'd be uselessly hog-tied on the floor. But Beecher intervened anyway, grabbed her by the hair and one shoulder, and righted the chair. She tipped too far, but inertia brought the chair back down on all four legs with a bang.

Beecher returned to Josie. She was screaming now, high-pitched siren sounds, but distorted by a raw throat. She stopped and coughed and gagged as he searched for the strap on the ground. Sweat beaded along his forehead and ran down the sides of his face.

For Shannon, everything seemed to slow down. Tied to the folding chair, staring at Josie and Henry Beecher, she suddenly existed bestride two worlds – she was here, now, and she was looking into the icy water at her brother's floating body.

Floating in all that black.

There, in the frigid water, because of her.

"John? It's me."

The memory played in her head of its own accord.

"Can you come get me?"

Calling on her brother for a ride because she'd been too drunk to get herself home. He'd done it because he would've done anything for her. It was easy to romanticize people in hindsight, but John had always been a giver. He'd become a local sheriff's deputy for no other reason than to help people. She knew it was pure truth. And she'd taken advantage, and he'd come for her, and his car had hit the ice on the bridge ...

Shannon pulled a breath through her damaged nose, feeling sharp nettles of pain. But the pain there and on the side of her head was fading. Everything was slowing, getting quiet, sharpening.

Beecher found the strap. He stood up and positioned himself behind Josie.

For years, Shannon had lived with the worst guilt of her life. Endless nightmares of John in the water. Sometimes, she'd jump in after him. Sometimes, she could only watch from afar.

All that guilt. Until one day, she'd known it had to stop.

Josie's head hung, and blood and drool and snot oozed from her face onto her thighs. Beecher grabbed the girl's head, lifted her face. If there was anything human left in him, it had almost left completely.

Shannon said, "Have mercy."

Beecher either didn't hear or ignored her. He twisted his right fist around one end of the strap, then his left fist around the other, and pulled it taut.

"Have mercy," Shannon repeated.

A nerve fired just outside the corner of his eye. He slipped the strap down over her face, up against her neck. Josie continued to cough and whimper.

"Show the world," Shannon said quietly. "Show the world what's right."

"Shut up," he breathed.

"Everything that happened to Charlotte was wrong. People threw her away when she needed forgiveness. Show the world what it looks like to forgive."

A tear carved a track through the sweat and dust on his face. His lower lip wobbled like he was about to fall into the emotion, but then he gritted his teeth. He brought his fists together at the back of Josie's neck, once more strangling her.

"Show the world ..." Shannon said. She felt disconnected from her body. She repeated the phrase, like a mantra, until there came a banging sound above them.

Beecher instantly loosened his grip on the belt and looked up at the basement ceiling.

The noise came again. *Knock knock knock.*

Someone else was at the front door.

BEECHER HAD DISAPPEARED BEHIND HER. When he was back between her and the camera, he had a gun. He looked up the stairs.

A muffled voice, possibly familiar: "NYPD! Open up! Agent Ames? Miss Tenor?"

Beecher made no comment, only bent his body slightly

toward the stairs, as if he were about to mount them and head up, but then tilted back and regarded his two hostages. Josie was slumped forward, having passed out from shock and fear. A ragged wheeze indicated her breathing. Her head moved in barely perceptible measure with her shallow breaths.

Then Beecher's eyes locked on Shannon's.

She had no idea what this exacting killer was going to do next. Because, she thought, he didn't either. This was a coin toss. A moment of fate. Or perhaps saintly intervention. He tore his gaze from her and ran up the stairs.

Shannon let out an explosive exhalation. She worked furiously to free herself, first leaning forward, coming to the edge of falling over and holding there. From such a position, the chair folded incrementally. It was enough to get her arms up over the back of it. Now her bound wrists were directly behind her back. She strained to lift her buttocks, both legs twisting in pain, kneecaps grating against cartilage and bone. She gnashed her teeth, wriggled and shook and struggled until she had her bound wrists now at the back of her knees. Bent forward like this, she was able to touch her ankles, which were lashed to the crossbar of the chair.

Two feelings washed through her almost simultaneously: relief that her ankles were connected to the chair with a rope she could potentially untie. But despair that they were fixed together, like her wrists, by plastic zip ties.

A floorboard creaked above her head. Beecher had gone up and was in the kitchen. Remembering the layout of the main floor, she knew there were two ways to come upon the entrance. Down the hallway with the pictures of Josie and her brother, or through the living room. Another floorboard gave way, confirming Beecher's use of the latter route.

"Beecher is here!" Shannon screamed. "Beecher is in the house!"

Knock knock knock. "NYPD! Ames, you in there?" Then the

doorbell rang. Whoever it was hadn't heard her or understood what she'd said. "All right, I'm coming in!"

Slam.

Nail-filled mason jars rattled on the shelves with the impact. The cop had rammed himself, or something, against the front door.

She shouted again, "Beecher is armed!" Then she felt for the knot. Once she had it, she worked feverishly with her fingertips, her muscles straining, ligaments stretched to their limits. Force to bend forward, she stared at the concrete floor, saw every granule of dirt, every puff of dust.

Josie wheezed beside her.

"Hang on, girl," Shannon said. "Josie, you hang on. Hear me? Listen to me – you keep listening to me. Keep hearing my voice."

Something gave way in the knot. Her heart soared and her excitement tried to gallop ahead of her. She tried to yank her feet free, but there was still more untangling to do. A drop of bloody sweat fell from her face and splatted in the dirt and dust.

Slam.

The house shook a second time. "Down here! I'm down he–"

Two gunshots boomed upstairs in quick succession. Something hit the floor. It was followed by thudding footfalls. A second later, three more gunshots, rapid fire – these had a different pitch, from a different caliber.

Beecher was shooting it out with the cop.

Shannon lifted her face to the camera. Red recording light still on. The killer wouldn't give up without completing his masterpiece, would he? He was going to come back down here. At this point, forget the poetry, he'd just shoot Josephine and follow it up with a bullet in Shannon's brain.

The rope! The last bunch of the knot came loose, and her

feet, though still bound, were released from the chair. She was able to touch down on the floor and straighten her upper body.

When she stood at last, shaky on her still-tied feet, the chair, which had been staying open by clamping itself against her body, folded the rest of the way and clattered on the hard floor.

Someone ran across the living room above her.

She dared to turn from the stairs and look back. There in the corner, what she was hoping for: a workbench on which a few random tools were scattered. First, she lowered her wrists down behind her. The tie bit flesh as she worked around her buttocks. Once she got her wrists to the backs of her ankles, she was able to step through the loop of her arms. Now her wrists were in front of her. She hopped to the bench, picked up a bright orange box cutter and went to work sawing away the tie clasping her ankles together.

A new noise upstairs, like a door thrown open. Back of the house. Like Beecher had escaped.

Freeing her wrists was much harder. She was shaking too much and unable to leverage the box cutter at the right angle. It wasn't working. Of all the things they taught you at Quantico ...

Instead of working the blade, she twisted her hands back and forth, the hard plastic digging even deeper into her flesh and drawing blood. No good. Cops used these every day on criminal suspects, and they were virtually unbreakable. She scrambled in front of Josie and patted the girl's cheeks. Josie's eyes fluttered and showed only white crescents. She'd been partly strangled and had lost critical oxygen. That, or shock, or both. Shannon started to work at Josie's bonds.

"Help!" It was a hoarse cry, a croak, from upstairs.

Shannon sat bolt still. She looked into Josie Tenor's face, the mass of sweat and tears and matted hair. She brushed aside some of that hair with her bound hands and kissed the girl's forehead suddenly, without thinking. "I'll be right back."

She returned to the bench, found a ballpeen hammer. Then she ran to the stairs, and up them, and stopped before she stepped through the open doorway. It could be a trap. It hadn't sounded like Beecher, but he could be right there, waiting. She'd only thought she'd heard the back door open and close.

She held her breath, stepped through the doorway and into the back of the kitchen.

Sprawled on the floor was Luis Caldoza.

THE BULLET WOUND in his abdomen leaked blood that looked like cherry syrup in the darkened kitchen. At some point, Beecher had turned off the lights.

"Luis," Shannon said. "Luis, hang on."

"In back," he grunted.

"He went out the back?"

Caldoza could barely talk – the words seemed to ride the ragged breaths coming through his nose.

She laid the hammer beside him and took his gun. She was able to hold the grip in one of her bound hands and just get her finger through the trigger loop. "I'm going to go look," she said.

She moved through the dark to the rear entrance. The door was still ajar. If Beecher was still on the premises, he might've gone around to the front, so she jogged quietly that way, avoiding the windows. She eased down the hallway, past the pictures of Josie and her family, aiming Caldoza's gun at the front door. She breathed and waited as long as she could bear. Beecher was gone.

Returning to the kitchen, Shannon managed to stick the handgun in her pocket. She felt along the wall above the countertop for a light switch. Her hands left bloody streaks. She found the switch and snapped it on. Harsh white light frosted the room. Now everything was bright and too real – Caldoza's blood crimson, his usually handsome complexion blanched and sickly. He looked up at her. "I'm sorry ..."

She searched the drawers for a clean towel.

"I felt bad," he said. "So I pulled out of the job with Heinz."

"Shh. Don't talk."

"Heard over the radio they didn't ... have the guy. Came to see ... if I could help." He was on the linoleum, his legs bent beneath him. He groaned and straightened out and laid his head back.

"Stay with me, Luis!" She found a dishtowel and knelt beside him, pressed it against his wound. The way the blood was pouring, Beecher's bullet had gone through Caldoza's body. She felt beneath him, her fingers encountering blood-soaked clothing. Another towel for the exit wound, more pressure. "It passed through," she said. "That's good."

Car tires screeched outside. Maybe a few houses down.

"Go," Caldoza said.

"No." She glanced at the basement door. "The girl is downstairs. Josie Tenor."

Caldoza suddenly gnashed his teeth and pushed himself up.

"What are you doing?"

He continued to push himself, sliding on the floor, back against the cabinets, closer to the basement door. "Give me back my gun. I'll protect her."

Could she do anything to help Luis or Josie? No, but abandoning them as they lay injured – it wasn't part of who she was. And Beecher had fooled them one time too many.

The front door flew open. "NYPD! Coming in!"

Shannon got to her feet awkwardly, using her tied-up hands to grab a drawer handle and pull herself up. She limped to the hallway and got a visual. Two uniformed cops were aiming their weapons at her. When they saw her hands, the cops relaxed. "Officer down," she said.

"That Caldoza back there?" One cop started down the hallway while the other checked the rooms.

"He's been shot," she said.

The other one said, "Ma'am? You alone here?"

"Girl downstairs. She lives here. Josephine Tenor. She needs an ambulance."

The first cop moved past her into the kitchen. The second tucked his head to his shoulder and pressed the talk button on his radio. He relayed the information to a dispatcher.

Shannon stepped back into the kitchen.

"Shannon," Caldoza said. His eyes were clear, even as his face seemed lined with worry and pain. He stared at her, into her. "Go get him."

She went back to the cop who was clearing the house. He looked at her. "Shit. You okay?"

"What do you know?" she asked.

They stood in the dark living room as he used a tool to detach her wrist tie.

"Beecher was seen on foot, headed southeast, couple of streets over. Exchanged fire with our officers."

"He's got a secondary vehicle," she said, massaging her abraded wrists. "Might be a Dodge Challenger. Metallic blue."

The cop just looked at her. His name tag read Gray.

She said, "Officer Gray, I've got an eyewitness – Alfonso Mendoza – who saw that car outside Dylan Construction, probably as the killer cased the site as a potential dump spot. Twice. I need you to get everybody on the radio."

34

WEDNESDAY NIGHT

J osie Tenor and Luis Caldoza were taken to different hospitals. Shannon argued to stay at the scene, but allowed an EMT to treat her superficial wounds. In the Tenors' bathroom, she studied her reflection and took inventory: Beecher's punch had bloodied her nose and darkened both of her eyes. Her wrists were bandaged. Mostly, it was her pride that hurt.

Josephine Tenor had almost died. Law enforcement had failed her. Shannon had failed her.

When she went back downstairs, she recognized the blonde agent in the basement as the scene was processed and Beecher's equipment got bagged by technicians. Shannon remembered her name – Agent Amy Dodd, from digital forensics.

They talked for a few minutes about Beecher's methods. As far as Dodd was concerned, this particular video might not have successfully streamed. "We haven't seen it," Dodd said. "We're not getting any reports of it."

Shannon thought back. "The girl gave him the wrong Wi-Fi password?"

"He's got a device called Black Magic – quick rendering for

livestreaming. It looks like he was connected. But it might've been weak down here in the basement. The family doesn't have a very powerful router, so not enough bandwidth to stream effectively."

Shannon's phone buzzed. Tyler. The supervising agent sounded concerned. "You didn't let them take you in?"

"I'm all right."

A pause. "Beecher took your weapon?"

"I think so, sir."

"Might be another way we can track him. If he uses it."

"Sir ..."

"The wife is completely uncooperative," Tyler said. "Literally hasn't said one single word since we picked her up." He let out a long breath that rattled over the connection. "Ames, where is he?"

"Sir, I don't know. But his beat as a cop was Hunters Point. He's had some place he's based his operations. I think it's likely he'll retreat there. Or he might run. I don't know."

"We haven't seen the vehicle so far. How solid are you on it?"

"He might've stashed a murder kit somewhere on the property here, sir, but we haven't seen any evidence of that. And I don't think he was carrying the tripod and camera and gear, plus a chemical inhalant around with him on the subway or in cabs – we haven't found a bag or backpack. And he got out of here quick. Local NYPD has been doing the door-to-doors, and we've had one visual confirmation."

A witness two streets over had looked outside during the firefight between Beecher and the cops, seen a man running, then jumping into a car described as a blue "race-car-looking thing." But Tyler made one last protestation: "We checked DMV as soon as we had Beecher as a suspect. No Dodge Challenger was registered in his name."

Shannon said, "So he has a friend at the DMV. This guy has

been able to stay one step ahead because of his experience and connection as a former police officer. It's his car."

Tyler, clearly gun-shy after the last manhunt debacle, was nevertheless compelled. "All right."

TEN MINUTES LATER, the alarm: an officer searching in Hunters Point had seen a car matching the description parked in the garage of a disused factory.

They roared through the night, lights going, sirens wailing. Shannon rode with Officer Gray. When they got close to Hunters Point, she advised everyone to kill the sirens. A dozen NYPD cruised the streets with their deck lights off but the occasional searchlight sweeping the blank-face buildings of abandoned factories and warehouses. Long Island City's extra-wide roadways lent the city a sprawling, disconnected feel. A fat moon hung low and yellow-tinged over the Manhattan skyline.

"This place," Gray said again. "The yuppies love it."

He turned down a side street. A busted chain-link fence glinted in the moonlight as they neared a green four-story warehouse.

Three NYPD vehicles parked in the road at odd angles to each other. The cops stood around arming themselves for war.

Shannon sucked in a breath and held it. She searched the black windows of the building. Gray stopped the vehicle and hopped out. A van rolled slowly down the street toward them, the letters S.W.A.T. painted on the sides.

Gray popped the trunk and handed her a bulletproof vest. She grabbed it and put it on. Third time in one week. He took off his standard utility belt and replaced it with another, loaded with ammunition. She looked up at the building.

"Do we know what this place was?"

"Swingline Stapler, maybe? Pepsi? Who knows. There's

been every kind of company and manufacturer around here at one time or another."

As he talked, three more vehicles arrived. Bomb squad. Another unmarked pulled in after them. Shannon glanced at the building. If Beecher was in there, he had to know he had company.

Tyler stepped out of the unmarked car behind the bomb squad and spotted her. They approached each other in the middle of the street. He put a hand on her shoulder and looked into her eyes. "Caldoza is going to make it. So's the girl."

She felt the emotion welling up and fought against it. Later.

He studied her. "You sure you're okay? You're up for this?"

She nodded.

Tyler looked past her at the building. "I'm sorry," he said. "We thought we had him ... *I* thought we had him ..."

Shannon took a cleansing breath. "It's okay. Let's do this."

SHE FOLLOWED behind Gray and Tyler and a SWAT team holding their high-powered rifles. Then they split up, with half the guys running down the street to get around behind the building. The rest gathered in front of a large retractable door. Tangles of power cables hung looped and disconnected; phone lines sagged from the corner of the building across the street to a pole. According to Ben Forbes, banks often owned buildings like this – reclaimed after city taxes went unpaid. No one really policed them, and they sometimes became home to squatters and drug users. But mainly they sat, ignored, waiting for a rich buyer to breathe new life into them.

After the bomb squad team examined the entry for any triggers or switches, two SWAT members used bolt cutters on a rusted padlock and raised the door.

Dark inside. A pungent smell immediately fumed in her

nose – gasoline. As her eyes adjusted, she saw the Dodge Challenger. The sound of an engine was louder, but still a ways off.
It wasn't the car engine; it was likely a generator. Beecher had
power.

The SWAT team moved in, folded together in a tight pack,
and Shannon went in behind them with Tyler now flanking.
Headlamps probed the darkness – a cavernous room, three
stories high, concrete floors and walls, suspended ductwork
overhead.

Then a light beam fell across the strangest thing, the most
out-of-place thing, sitting in the middle of the giant space.

A bathtub.

The old kind, claw-footed, ivory white.

It had a single word painted on it in dripping red paint:
SMILE.

"Nobody move," someone said.

Another voice: "Don't touch anything!"

Tyler: "We need to get the bomb squad in here, now."

Shannon had her light shining. Without proceeding any
farther into the room, she swept the beam through the darkness. She saw the red, blinking light in the far corner before the
light illuminated the device.

"Camera," she said. "Right there."

"Got another one over here," Gray said.

"He's filming us."

"Yeah, but where the hell is he?"

The voices were near-whispers, just audible over the
grumble of the generator somewhere in proximity.

"Check that out," someone said.

Their flashlight beams clustered on two artist's easels, each
propping up an enlarged photograph.

"Jesus ..."

The photo on the left was the familiar school picture of Charlotte Beecher. Smiling bright, full of life and hope for the future. The one on the left was a morgue shot. Beecher must have obtained it through police channels, using his retired cop status, his grief as the father. A striking contrast, those two images. The warmth of life and the cool touch of death.

Bomb squad arrived – four guys. SWAT formed a protective shell around them. They moved forward in their tight formation, zeroing in on the bathtub. In seconds, SWAT were pointing their rifles into it. "Ah, guys? Feds?"

Tyler and Shannon moved forward. Coming upon the tub, a kind of preternatural memory flooded her mind – nothing she had herself gone through, but as if she was able to know what the victims had. Awakening here, perhaps, in this dark and dripping place, being washed by a stranger. A man who had abducted them. Someone they'd initially trusted, because he'd appeared as a cop.

Two bodies were laid out in the tub – James and Evelyn Priest. They'd been positioned to just fit inside, arms and legs folded over one another, evoking children. Their flesh had discolored to blue, their necks showed the mottled bruises of their hangings.

One of the cops coughed, like he was dry-heaving.

"This is a tell-all," Shannon said quietly.

"What?" Tyler looked at her, and so did all the other faces gathered around the white tub in the dark room.

She said, "It's a confessional moment. He's left everything here for us to find."

She shined her beam up at the ducts crisscrossing beneath the ceiling. She moved the light along the walls, the chipped paint, the streaks of rust. Beneath the ubiquitous muffled growl of the generator, a rat squeaked somewhere in the shadowed distance.

The SWAT commander, a graying guy in his late forties built like a linebacker, waved his arm forward. "Spread out, eyes up. Go two by two. Let's find this son of a bitch."

Shannon went with Tyler and two SWAT guys into the dripping black. Radios burst with static and voices, light beams slid over the rotting walls. Tyler breathed loudly beside her as they searched. "Is he here or what?"

SWAT located the generator. Shannon and Tyler found the soundproofed room where Beecher had likely recorded Monica Forbes. His police uniform was located in a third room, laid out with all its decorations, along with three white jumpsuits – the head-to-toe zip-in kind worn by crime scene technicians – plus a box of blue latex gloves, booties that covered shoes to reduce contamination, and several hair nets.

A moment later, SWAT were talking to each other about the second floor. Shannon and Tyler ascended to what was probably once the administrative center of the factory, including several offices. In one were elements for explosives, including a thyristor, model rocket fuses, and a pile of stripped USB cables, copper laid bare. Near these, a box of dynamite and two bags of fertilizer. The high-in-nitrogen kind. Tyler alerted the bomb squad, who handled it.

In another office, two long folding tables sat end to end. Scattered over their surfaces were half a dozen pay-as-you-go phones. One file box was brimming with receipts. Three more boxes contained photographs and paperwork. It was a glut of information that mirrored the wall she'd torn down in her own office.

Tyler said to the SWAT commander who'd joined them, "Keep looking. We'll be here."

As law enforcement continued to search the structure for Beecher and more evidence of his crimes, Shannon pored through the boxes with Tyler. Encountering pictures of Baldacci and Diaz, and sifting through more pictures of people she'd yet to recognize, she shared her theory with Tyler that there was a hierarchical order to Beecher's killings.

She added her own caveat: "But he risks something with that structure. He risks getting caught before he can reach the ones he considers most culpable."

Tyler grunted. "I don't think anyone is going to argue that Beecher's mind is organized like a normal person's." He pushed around some paperwork – printed articles and even the CVs of some victims and potential victims. "Or maybe it's hubris, and he just thought he'd never be caught."

The lights of Hunters Point glimmered in the bank of office windows, but it was mostly dark in the room. She looked across the table at Tyler's shape, then illuminated him with her flashlight. "Who do you think was next on the list? After the Priests, who was next?"

He shielded himself from the light with a hand. She moved it off him.

"Let me talk to Special Agent Dodd. She's been the one going through his computer." He keyed his phone and put it to his ear, walking toward the windows.

Shannon continued to look over the information. More reporters, most of them. But someone else she thought she might recognize as affiliated with the *American Stars* show. Where would Beecher stop? With cameramen? Producers? Shareholders of the network that aired the damn program?

Tyler hung up. "Dodd says it's not clear. Going by your theory, there are some people who should've already been killed. Low-level types, spot news reporters. Maybe his list isn't perfect. Maybe he had to ignore some because they were too logistically inconvenient."

That didn't gel with what she felt about Beecher. These killings weren't driven by something abstract. These people writhed under his skin. The idea of them walking around, breathing air, when they'd so callously and thoughtlessly set

the wolves on his daughter, that wasn't something Beecher
could stand.

The night sharpened. She and Tyler continued searching
the evidence. Papers rattled with a crisp urgency. The faces in
Beecher's stash of photos seemed to stare at Shannon as she
hunted for just the right pattern.

Tyler was on and off the phone, calling for police and FBI to
locate the people potentially on Beecher's list and protect them.
At one point, he held up an image of a gray-haired man. "Here,"
he said. "Frank Percy. According to this little dossier, not only
was Percy the director of the *American Stars* episode, but he's
quoted by Todd Spencer saying that Charlotte Beecher had no
soul." Tyler shook the photo with certainty.

Shannon felt a sour twist in her stomach. She'd seen the
name Percy while reading Spencer's article and could even
remember the quote. If she'd been more on top of things, she
would have been thinking laterally like this – considering not
only the reporters and TV people who covered the story as
culpable in Beecher's eyes, but those people who gave interviews and shook their heads woefully, who called Charlotte
soulless and evil.

Someone came running up the stairs and into the room.
Officer Gray was slightly out of breath. "We got into the car."
His eyes widened as he saw what Tyler was holding. Gray
pointed at the photo of Percy. "That guy, right there. That same
photo is in the Challenger."

Tyler glanced at Shannon. He returned his attention to
Gray. "Then that's where he's going next."

The two men hurried out of the room.

35

S hannon didn't move. Tyler and Gray's sudden departure left a kind of stultifying vacuum around her. Her head throbbed with a developing migraine; her bones ached with fatigue. But a single, clear thought cut through all the chaos and exhaustion:

This is what he does.

And then came an onrush of further understanding.

Tuned in from the beginning, Beecher had anticipated their every move. He'd set up an elaborate plan, each crime serving the next, each victim a stepping-stone. There was no proof that he had a kill order beyond that which worked to his opportunity and convenience, but it made sense that he did when you considered the role each victim had played in the Charlotte Beecher story, the exposition of her poor behavior which led to her humiliation and her eventual death.

This is what he does ...

Along the way, Beecher had set up misdirection. Red herrings for the cops to follow. *Dissemination of disinformation.* Maybe Frank Percy made some sense as a high-value target in

Beecher's eyes, but it also made sense Percy was more misdirection. And that someone else, ultimately, was the one Henry Beecher considered guiltiest of all.

In Beecher's twisted mind, that was probably sixteen-year-old Josie Tenor, his daughter's best friend – the girl who'd betrayed her. The one who'd been one of the first to circulate the video online and hadn't risen to Charlotte's defense when the attacks got underway. Perhaps worst of all, the girl who had simply survived to serve as a living reminder of what had been taken from Charlotte: her light, her future, her life. And too, a reminder of what had been taken from Beecher himself – his only child. His wife's mental health. His world.

And yet, not only had he been unsuccessful in killing Josie Tenor, he'd also failed to complete turning her sin against her – the Wi-Fi in the Tenor home had been too weak to livestream her confession.

So?

Would Beecher just give up his pursuit? Write her off as the one who got away?

This question in mind, Shannon finally made her way out of the factory. Men and women rushed past her as they processed the mother lode of evidence inside the massive crime scene. Outside, in the swirling lights and chaos, a few onlookers had gathered. It was late, approaching midnight. The area was neither residential nor commercial, but that mix of old and new – though it still drew a few night owls who watched as forensics crews in their ghostly white jumpsuits carried bags upon bags of evidence from Henry Beecher's lair.

The onlookers continued watching – and word was probably already spreading – as two bodies came out, zipped into black bags.

The Priests.

A mortuary service waited to take them away to the morgue in a specialized van. An ambulance also waited, and Shannon limped to it. Its back doors were open. A paramedic regarded Shannon with concern, his eyebrows raised in question. "Like me to have a look at you, ma'am?"

She gazed back at him, then her attention floated to the Priests again, now being loaded into the dark van. She then watched as a couple of uniformed cops stood around, one talking into his radio. Thinking more about Beecher's motives and tactics, Shannon held up a finger to the paramedic and took out her phone. She called Tyler.

"What is it? We're getting close to Percy – he's way uptown. Might be at some party tonight, is the word."

"Percy's not the target. It's still Josie."

"Why? How do you know?"

"We chase what he wants us to chase. But he wants her. I don't think there's anyone in Beecher's mind who's as guilty as she is. Maybe there were more that were supposed to be before her. But her death – her *confession* – it justifies everything for him."

There was some static and background commotion on Tyler's end. He sounded frustrated. "So what are you saying? He's going to come back for her?"

Shannon glanced at the ambulance as she spoke. "Yes. I believe so."

Another pause from Tyler. "Then we send NYPD over there. I mean, there's already units there keeping an eye on her, but we'll reinforce."

"He'll still get her."

"How?"

"I don't know. Maybe he's got people who will sympathize. Cops who don't think he's guilty. But more than anything, he's got ears on everything we do." She took a breath, steeling herself. "It's got to be me. It's got to be me, alone. And it's got to be quiet. Everybody stays back, radio silence."

"Ames, absolutely not. You stand down. I'll make some calls to–"

"It has to be now. Or he'll run and hide and wait us out. He's waited this long. He'll never rest until he's finished."

"Ames! Stand down. You hear me? That's a direct–"

She hung up and put her phone in her pocket. Having drifted out of earshot of the paramedic, she now returned to him and said, "I think I need to go in."

He snapped into action, seeming relieved she was going to get the medical attention he clearly felt she required.

As the paramedic helped her up into the back of the ambulance and laid her down on the gurney, she asked him if he knew which hospital Josie Tenor had been taken to, reminding him who she meant.

He nodded. "Yeah, I know where she went."

"That's where I want to go."

He watched her a moment. "All right, we can make that happen."

FROM THE AMBULANCE, she called one other person on her cell.

And that was it. No turning back now. She could almost feel it, the squeeze of being between a rock and a hard place. If Henry Beecher didn't show up, she'd be screwed with Tyler. Maybe with the FBI.

If he did, she could be killed.

But she knew Mark Tyler a little bit. Angry as he was with her, he would follow her lead. Probably he would have the place surrounded, but with everybody back and staying off-radio.

She was going to be on her own.

ONCE IN AN ER room at the hospital, she pulled the IV from her arm and unclipped the pulse monitor. The machine made an angry buzzing sound, and she shut it off. When a young-looking nurse came in, Shannon showed her ID and assured her everything was all right.

"Can you tell me which room for Josephine Tenor? Has she been moved to the main hospital yet?"

The nurse shook her head. "No, she's still here in the ER. The attending doctor hasn't seen her yet. It's been a busy night." She gave Shannon a head-to-toe look. "You sure you don't want to get back in bed?"

Shannon offered a warm smile. "In a minute."

She left the room and walked through the busy ER, catching glimpses of people in rooms like hers, a few doors open or ajar. A twentysomething guy with a big beard holding a bloodied arm. An elderly woman with ginger-colored hair frayed out like the puffy panicle bloom of a smoke tree. A man sitting on the side of the bed, coughing and gagging into a trash can.

Josie's room was last on the left. A uniformed NYPD cop stood outside her door. He saw Shannon shuffling along and tensed until she brought out her ID again. "How's she doing?"

"She's had like eight medical people in to see her, all asking the same questions," the cop said, sounding frustrated. "What is it with hospitals? The people who work here don't talk to each other?"

"I'd like to see her."

The cop gave her another wary look. "Yeah. Okay."

He opened the door, but Shannon stayed put a moment, sizing him up. Mid-twenties. A brush cut that seemed to continue from the back of his head down his neck and beneath his collar. The way his jaw clenched, she sensed it, like she'd been sensing from all the local cops – they hated that this was one of their own. They dreaded the media spin, the public outcry, and any damage to their credibility. Being a cop wasn't easy. It was dangerous. But the people held law enforcement to account. Their reactions weren't always right, weren't always wrong.

"Keep your eyes open," Shannon said to the cop before going in. As she crossed the room, she willed herself calm. She sought the place within herself that had always been natural to her, a place of easy confidence where her faith in herself and God buffered against life's meanness and uncertainty. It was challenging to get there.

Josie Tenor slept, a state that turned the clock back on her a few years, like she was twelve. Or younger. Ten.

Shannon felt her heart break a little. The way this girl had suffered. The guilt she'd been carrying. And then the horrible trauma Henry Beecher had inflicted on her. She'd never be the same. She'd carry the scars the rest of her life. And for what? Beecher's action wasn't righteous. He'd taken an overreaction in the media and doubled down on it. Or worse, really. There wasn't any multiple that could quantify the pain and anguish he'd caused in his efforts to get even.

The calm she was seeking turned to an anger instead.

Shannon reached out carefully and knuckled away a lock of dark hair across Josie's forehead. The girl didn't stir.

Shannon watched Josie sleep a moment, then walked to the window, filled with the night sky above, a vast parking lot below. Flooding her thoughts, suddenly, a recap of the horrors: Eva Diaz dumped over the fence into a construction company backlot. Monica Forbes stuffed beneath a bus. Eyes open. Jordan Baldacci, obliterated by an IED. Todd Spencer, his neck cut raggedly, so that he lay there bleeding out as his colleagues ran past and trampled him. And then Josie Tenor, tied to the chair, head lolling, moaning, then crying as Beecher berated her like an angry parent for what he had hoped would be a live audience.

Shannon took slow, steadying breaths through her nose. She tried to find a place to put these feelings and these images from the past week. She got the sense that this type of compartmentalizing was going to be as much a part of the job as anything else. If she still had a job after this.

Maybe Beecher would get scared off and not come. Maybe he'd realize he'd been discovered and go into hiding. They'd smoke him out eventually.

But she didn't think so. Like she'd told Tyler, Beecher needed to humiliate Josie in order to validate everything else he'd done. In his eyes, she was the start of all the trouble. If she'd gone with Charlotte to the show, this might've never happened. If she hadn't posted the video, if she'd defended her friend when the outrage market started cranking up ...

Shannon's phone buzzed against her hip. It was Bufort, whom she'd called from the ambulance.

His voice came in breathy bursts, like he was walking fast. "Ames – he's here."

She felt her heart rate quicken, but stayed focused, ready.

Bufort explained, "The local cop watching the east entrance has been knocked unconscious. He's going to make it, but, Ames – it's got to be Beecher. He got in and he's coming to you."

She pulled a few more deep breaths through her nose, and she closed her eyes.

This is it.

John flashed in her imagination. Her older brother's pale face beneath the clear, tannic water.

His beautiful, serene face.

And then it faded as he sank into darkness.

She opened her eyes and went to the door. She explained to the officer there that Beecher was in the hospital and that he was on his way, but if they used the radio, Beecher would hear them. He'd run and might hurt more people.

The cop looked terrified. "So what I want you to do," Shannon said, "is step away."

He started to argue, but she shut him down. "There's no time. Beecher is armed. He'll shoot at you; there are innocent people here." Her voice was an urgent whisper.

The cop refused to do as she instructed. "He's not going to do anything to me. He's never hurt another cop."

"He might've just taken out one of your fellow officers downstairs."

She saw it register in the young man's face as she held out her hand. "I need your weapon and I need you to get yourself somewhere safe. *Right now.*"

At last, he gave over. She took his service weapon and retreated into the room, closing the door as she went. She pulled the chair at the side of Josie's bed over into the corner, then slid the enclosure curtain halfway around the bed, leaving the door side exposed. She found the light switch on the wall and killed the lights.

In the darkness, the heart monitor beeped, and Josie breathed deeply. Shannon sat in the corner chair and checked the weapon, her heart thumping.

Help me.

Guide me.

She watched the space beneath the door. When she saw the shadow of feet, she quickly left the chair and hid behind the curtain.

The door opened. Someone entered the room and the door swung shut.

Her skin tingling, pulse singing in her ears, Shannon breathed as shallowly as possible while the person approached. A light shone against the curtain between Shannon and the bed. Probably the light of his phone. He'd want to record this, of course.

Beecher spoke.

"Josie ... wake up ..."

Shannon threw open the curtain and aimed the gun at Beecher's chest. His eyes flared wide, then narrowed a split second later. Phone in one hand, belt in the other. He was in a moderate disguise, a ball cap pulled low, a white short-sleeve button-down and plain slacks.

She waited for him to go for the gun he was surely carrying. Waited for him to twitch.

Her phone buzzed. Bufort again, probably. There was commotion outside the room. Loud voices and footfalls fast approaching. Beecher made a slight turn of his head, as if to get a glimpse behind him. He knew what was happening. His upper lip peeled back as his mouth formed a snarling type of smile. Between them, Josie Tenor lay unconscious, just breathing.

"They killed my daughter," Beecher said.

"I know."

Beecher only breathed. Looked at Shannon.

She said, "But it's over. You've done it all. You've shown everyone. You've held them to account. And now it's done. There are police all over this hospital, right outside that door."

The same way Beecher's had, the feet of cops outside darkened the gap beneath the door.

Her phone continued to buzz.

Beecher's eyes were empty.

Shannon said, "Let it go."

He slowly set his phone down on Josie's bed, and the nylon belt beside it. Then he gazed down at the girl, hate filling his face.

"Let it go," Shannon repeated.

Beecher made a move for his gun and she pulled the trigger.

The blast was deafening. Josie Tenor's eyes flew open just as Henry Beecher crumpled to the ground.

A moment later, the door burst open, flooding the room with people. Flooding the room with light.

36

THURSDAY MORNING

And after all that, she wasn't free of the blessed hospital.

"You're not going anywhere until a doctor says so," Tyler instructed.

And anyway, it was a good place for her to be while she weathered a fresh bout of officer-involved-shooting questions from the FBI's internal agency. She also spent a great deal of time on the phone, fending off reporters who'd managed to get her number, and texting with Caldoza, who'd come through his gunshot wound endowed with even more romantic confidence.

What are you wearing?

Cute, Caldoza.

She played along and also brought him up to speed, conveying the amount of evidentiary material found at Beecher's base of operations. *The guy was meticulous,* she texted. *He even kept receipts.*

She explained how Beecher had expected them to consider Frank Percy as the next target and pile all of their resources on that bet. Which was exactly what had transpired, save for her insubordination. And after a moment's hesitation, she shared her concern that the FBI might send her packing. Confronting Beecher with no coordinated backup had worked, but it had also courted unprofessionalism. It had been dangerous.

You crazy, Caldoza said.

Maybe.

Maybe Beecher would've been brought down eventually. But Tyler had already read her the riot act and admonished her severely for her actions. She didn't need to do it to herself.

There'd been enough of that in her life already.

Done texting with Caldoza, she wondered if this hospital had any of the nuclear-green Jell-O. It remained to be seen. But her mouth was dry, cottony. She searched beside her for some water, ice chips, anything. Finding none, she got up out of the bed. An IV slowed her up. Some things never changed. She grabbed the apparatus and wheeled it along beside her as she limped to the bathroom. She turned on the light and filled a plastic cup from the tap.

When she looked in the mirror, the woman looking back seemed different, somehow. Older, maybe. Like she had a secret.

An hour later, she was finally able to get out of the hospital gown and put on her own clothes, courtesy of Mark Tyler, who showed up with a bag of her personal items, including a toothbrush, which was heaven sent.

They went downstairs in silence, riding the elevator, both of them watching the numbers. Tyler had a driver, so they could sit in the back and talk.

"Where we going?" Shannon asked, when it was clear they were headed west, away from Rego Park and Kew Gardens.

"To see Moray."

Twenty minutes later, she was seated across from him. His corner office viewed the Hudson River, New Jersey beyond. The Statue of Liberty was in the scene, and it brought her back to being in Todd Spencer's apartment.

She focused on the here and now: Two chairs, a short couch and a mahogany table formed an informal seating area away from his desk. Moray crossed his long, knobby legs. "Get you anything, Special Agent Ames?"

"No, sir. Thank you."

He leaned forward and picked up a file. Her file – she saw *S. Ames* written on the tab. He thumbed through it. Then he said, "How do you feel about things? About how everything ended up?"

She glanced at Tyler seated in the second chair. She was in the middle of the couch. It was the moment of truth. Tyler hadn't fired her, but Moray just might.

The best way forward was complete honesty.

"I feel sad."

Moray instantly lowered the file and looked at her. "Why?"

"The loss of life. The victims. Agent Stratford. And the man I shot in Amityville."

After a moment, Moray said, "Winston Hitchcock."

"Yes, sir." She was sure she'd be seeing Hitchcock's face in her dreams for the rest of her life. She kept this idea to herself. Honesty didn't necessarily mean hyperbole.

Moray nodded, like he understood what she was feeling. Or what she was thinking, anyway. He cocked an eyebrow as he tossed her file onto the table with a slap. "Would it help if I told you we've just seized ten kilograms of crystal methamphetamine in Tanzer's home? Along with two thousand in cash, rifles, a handgun, a crossbow, thirteen mobile phones, and various drug paraphernalia?"

She thought about it. She'd strongly suspected that Tanzer and the others were not operating as, or on behalf of, the anti-media group Blackout, but that they'd reacted forcibly to the presence of law enforcement for what must've been, for them, a very good reason. She said to Moray, "I understand these were not innocent men, but they were innocent of the crime we were investigating, sir, and I consider them casualties."

Moray sat back. His expression seemed to suggest he was surprised by her, but not upset. Tyler looked slightly uncomfortable, though. It was his usual state, she decided.

Moray said, "Tanzer is going to make a full recovery."

"Good."

"And Henry Beecher ... how do you feel about him? I know you've spent all morning answering to our internal department. But for my own ears ..."

She drew a breath. "Henry Beecher felt he had good cause. He wasn't ... the killers we usually encounter in these cases get some sexual gratification. There's no evidence Beecher did. There was no mutilation. He cleaned the victims before he killed them because he would be too sickened to wash a dead body, I think. He was doing this for his daughter. For revenge. Which might make him one of the coldest killers we've seen yet. I'm convinced there was no other way to stop him. That I had to protect Josie Tenor and protect the public." She added, "I don't regret what I did."

Moray watched her a moment. Then, "You're religious, Special Agent Ames?" Before she could answer, he held up a hand. "You don't have to answer that." He turned his face away, gazed out the window, and then he stood and walked toward the view.

Shannon glanced at Tyler, who remained seated, so she remained seated, too.

Moray turned around. He seemed to be waiting for Tyler to speak. Tyler cleared his throat. His gaze slipped away from her and then gradually returned. "Agent Ames, you were right. About Beecher's list. About the order. He actually had three other people between the Priests and Josephine Tenor. Thanks to your actions, he rushed to his end, and we stopped him. And we saved those people."

Shannon looked back across the space at Mark Tyler. "Thank you, sir."

He smiled, just a flicker, but his eyes were soft. "You're welcome."

"Special Agent Ames," Moray said from the windows, "it's my opinion, and it's the opinion of the executive assistant director in Washington, that you've done your country a service and you've done the FBI proud." He was silhouetted by the bright sky, his face harder to read.

She almost couldn't get the words out. "Thank you. Very much, sir."

He slowly paced to his desk and picked up a different file, this one blue, and returned to the sitting area. He placed the blue file in front of her – *Confidential* stamped on its front – and then retook his chair. He crossed his legs again, tented his fingers, and looked at her.

She took it as an invitation to open the file. The first page was an overview of a new case.

"We'd like you to help us with this," he said.

She took a stabilizing breath. "Absolutely, sir."

"But first," Moray said, glancing at Tyler, "we want you to take a couple of days – tomorrow and the weekend. This will be here when you get back."

"And," Tyler said, "it's not a suggestion. It's an order."

"Yes, sir."

37

FRIDAY AFTERNOON

The address was hard to find because not all of the houses showed their numbers. She could have plugged Hitchcock's information into the GPS, but sometimes it was nice just to use your eyes and brain. Still, when she couldn't find it, she used the damn satellites.

The trailer home was white with black window shutters. Surrounding it were similar trailers. An orange-and-blue, battered-looking Hot Wheels lay in the yard. The grass was on the brown side, scorched – the whole area needed some more rain.

Shannon sat in the car, parked on the side of the street, and watched the house. She'd already visited Caldoza. She'd been to see Josie Tenor too, once she'd been moved out of the ER to a secure room, but only after talking to the girl's parents and confirming it was something Josie wanted.

The girl had a hard road ahead. Already shouldering the guilt for what had happened to her best friend, she now felt responsible for Henry Beecher's victims. At least, though, Beecher's video had stayed in his camera.

"None of this is your fault, Josie," Shannon had said to her. "None of it."

Maybe someday it would sink in, but not today.

The family planned on moving. "Too many memories for her in this house," Josie's mother had confided privately, outside the room. "But it's going to be tough to sell after what happened here."

She'd had a point.

Shannon had left after a long hug, and after assuring Josie and her mother that she'd be in touch again very soon.

Now a school bus was coming up the street. It stopped at the street corner and dumped out a dozen kids. Among them, walking toward Shannon, were two teenagers, a boy and a girl, and a smaller girl they had by the hand. Winston Hitchcock's kids.

They didn't notice Shannon as they went into the trailer home.

But they looked okay. The little girl was smiling. And that was something.

ON THE WAY NORTH, she stopped at a mailbox and dropped in an envelope with the Hitchcock address on it, no return address given. Just a little something to help them along.

She crossed the Cuomo Bridge – once called the Tappan Zee, which was a much cooler name, regardless of your politics – and stayed on Interstate 87 all the way to the Adirondack Mountains.

This time of year, the long grasses were cut and drying in huge rolls. As kids, Shannon and her brothers would say the bales resembled giant toasted marshmallows. Her family's land was looking good. The barn had been repaired and was sharp, with the white trim – an X over the front door against the fire engine red. The house was white and sprawling. The two outbuildings – the foaling shed and the tractor shed – brown. The corn silo threw a long shadow in the evening light. The corn, just about ready for harvest, was a sea of green stretching on for acres into the setting sun.

She pulled into the driveway and shut off the engine. Her window was down, the air coming in fresh. Cooler than the city. A man came walking up from the back field, cutting between the barn and tractor shed. Her brother Luke.

He walked up to the car with a curious expression. He wore thick brown overalls and a grubby white T-shirt underneath. His dark, curly hair was heavy with sweat. She smiled up at him. "You look like the last time I saw you."

"And you look like you got into it pretty good." Then: "What's going on? What's with the bruises and the scars? What are you doing here?"

"I'm all right. Good, in fact. Where's Dad?"

"He's out, you know, in the corn. Gabe and Toby went into town." Luke had searing blue eyes that stared into her soul. "Mom's inside," he said. Then he opened the door. "Welcome home, sis."

Shannon got out of the car. They put their arms around each other and walked toward the house, where the figure of a woman waited in the kitchen window.

WE HOPE YOU ENJOYED THIS BOOK

If you could spend a moment to write an honest review on Amazon, no matter how short, we would be extremely grateful. They really do help readers discover new authors.

And feel free to connect with TJ - he'd love to hear from you!

www.tjbrearton.net

ACKNOWLEDGMENTS

This book wouldn't exist without Brian Lynch and Garret Ryan at Inkubator books, so I need to thank them straightaway. I'd also like to thank Stephen Buzzell for answering my legal questions, and New York state troopers Kristy Wilson and Sean Kane for helping me stay sharp on police procedures. Thanks so much to my amazing early readers — David Taylor, Ed.D; John Ramirez; Linda Godfrey; Fritz Aldinger; Linda Rudd; Isaac Kirzner — you are all amazing and deeply appreciated. And to any readers who just haven't had a chance to chime in yet — thank you as well!

As always, thanks to my wife and kids. Having a writer for a spouse / parent might be a little unusual, but they tolerate it with aplomb. Thanks to my parents, my friends, and all the readers out there for buying my books or borrowing them on Kindle or reading them over someone else's shoulder — whatever you're doing, please keep it up. Love to you all.

ALSO BY TJ BREARTON

INKUBATOR TITLES

THE KILLING TIME

(Book 1 in the Special Agent Shannon Ames series)

HIDE AND SEEK

(Book 2 in the Special Agent Shannon Ames series)

IN TOO DEEP

(Book 3 in the Special Agent Shannon Ames series)

NOWHERE TO HIDE

(Book 4 in the Special Agent Shannon Ames series)

NO WAY BACK

(Book 5 in the Special Agent Shannon Ames series)

ROUGH COUNTRY

T.J.'S OTHER TITLES

HABIT

SURVIVORS

DARK WEB

HIGH WATER

DARK KILLS

DAYBREAK

GONE

DEAD GONE

BURIED SECRETS

BLACK SOUL

GONE MISSING

NEXT TO DIE

TRUTH OR DEAD

THE HUSBANDS

WHEN HE VANISHED

DEAD OR ALIVE

Published by Inkubator Books
www.inkubatorbooks.com